The mist swallowed the raft in gulps of sinuous gray damp

Ryan noticed an unnatural flurry of movement among the rancid weeds that crowded down to the brink of the water, now only fifty paces from the raft.

"Push it away," he called urgently, taking one of the branches himself and poling off.

"What d'you see?" Krysty panted, throwing all her weight against the steering oar.

"Nothing. Something. I don't know."

"I heard something. Like someone laughing. But someone who didn't have a proper mouth. Does that seem stupid?"

"No. Not down here it doesn't."

A hand erupted from the water, gripping Ryan's wrist with grotesquely long fingers. The skin was creased, hanging at the wrist in folds, and the face that emerged from behind the hand was worse than anything from the depths of a jolt-spawned nightmare. The fearsome jaw protruded eighteen inches beyond the gaping holes of the nostrils, and the clashing teeth! Row upon row of overlapping, sharp fangs.

With his left hand pinioned, and lying on his right side, Ryan couldn't get at either his blaster or his panga.

Life was a bare handful of heartbeats.

JAMES AXLER

DEATH LANDS

Homeward Bound

A GOLD EAGLE BOOK FROM
WORLDWIDE.

TORONTO • NEW YORK • LONDON • PARIS
AMSTERDAM • STOCKHOLM • HAMBURG
ATHENS • MILAN • TOKYO • SYDNEY

A hand in the darkness and a smile in the noonday sun.
As so often before and for always, this is for Liz with
all of my love.

First edition January 1988

ISBN 0-373-62505-7

The earth is all the home I have.

—W. E. Aytoun

Chapter One

"IT'S DEAD."

Ryan Cawdor took the high-image intensifier away from his good eye, tucking it back into one of the pockets of his long, fur-trimmed coat.

"Nothing?" asked J. B. Dix, the Armorer.

"Nothing. From this high you can see for miles. Not a sign of life. When it's cold like this there should be smoke. Folks got to keep warm. There's wood enough around for 'em."

Across the steep valley the sun was sinking into a nest of tangled violet chem clouds. Ryan figured the temperature had to be already close to freezing. His breath plumed out ahead of him, and the skin on his stubbled cheeks felt tight. The slopes of the hills opposite from the cavern entrance were streaked with snow, and the small pools around the snaking lead-gray river were dulled with ice.

Running alongside the slow-moving water, Ryan had been able to make out the shattered remains of a two-lane blacktop, its edge eroded by a century of neglect.

Krysty Wroth's hand rested on his arm. He glanced at the girl, smiling at her startling beauty, his eye almost dazzled by the bright crimson of her tumbling hair. "It's Doc," she said quietly.

"What?"

"When we came out of the gateway he was throwing up. Face like parchment. Lori took him back into the main redoubt entrance to sit him down."

Ryan sucked on a tooth, looking to his left, where the original road to the concealed fortress had been destroyed—either by a landslip or the nuking that had devastated the entire length and breadth of the United States. Nearly a hundred years back.

In 2001.

A young boy stood on the rim of the sheer drop, head to one side as though he were listening to something. The bleak wind tugged at his long hair, blowing it across his face. His hair was whiter than the driven snow, his eyes red as polished rubies, set in sockets of honed ivory.

"You hear something, Jak?" Ryan asked.

"Thought I heard something howling, like a banshee back in the swamps."

Jak Lauren hadn't been with Ryan and his party for very long. They'd picked him up in the dank vastness of the Atchafalaya Swamp, in what had once been the state of Louisiana. His slight frame concealed a powerful, wiry strength. Ryan Cawdor, who was a good judge of such things, figured Jak as one of the most lethal hand-to-hand killers he'd ever seen.

Jak was fourteen years old.

J. B. Dix stepped to the edge of the cliff and joined the young albino. Squinting into the distance, concentrating, he said, "Could be a wolf."

Krysty Wroth's keen hearing enabled her to confirm J.B.'s guess. "Yeah. It's a wolf. And there's more of 'em, a pack of around a dozen. Four, mebbe five miles northeast of here."

"Where in fireblast are we, J.B.?" Ryan asked, hunching his shoulders.

The Armorer had a tiny folding comp-sextant in one of the capacious pockets of his dark gray leather coat, with its smart silky collar of black fur. He pulled it out and looked around, easing back the brim of his beloved fedora, and took the necessary sighting. He picked a crumpled chart and consulted it.

"Near as I can figure it, we look to have landed north of what they used to call New York State. And that river has to be the Mohawk."

Ryan glanced both ways along what remained of the roadway. Each end had been sliced clean off. "That's why the redoubt hasn't been entered," he guessed.

"Uncle Tyas McCann told me how the east and the northeast were hard-nuked," Krysty said. "All the big cities and most power places. There's lots of hot spots."

"Check the rad count," J.B. suggested. "Broke mine getting off Wizard Island."

Ryan flicked back the lapel of his coat, moving the end of the weighted silk scarf out of the way. He pressed the On button of the rad counter and listened to the faint cheeping of the machine. The glowing scarlet arrow veered erratically across the scale, wavering uncomfortably into the orange sector.

"Warm," he said.

"Closing in on hot," Krysty observed.

"Too late to leave 'fore dark," Jak said, moving back from the rim. "Be night in less than an hour. Better wait and find a way down in the morning."

Ryan wasn't sure that it was going to be that easy to get off the sheer plateau. When you found a redoubt that hadn't been entered since the long chill had begun, it meant it was hard to get at. Which generally meant it was also damned hard to get out of.

"Sure," he agreed. "Krysty says Doc's sick. We'll all go back in and scout for some food. I saw a shelf of self-heats. Reckon its soy meat." He grinned at the look of revulsion on J.B.'s face. "Know what you mean, friend," he said. "Can't say I like that tepid sludge myself. Let's get in and close off the rad doors. We'll make a clean start in the morning at first light."

THE JUMP HAD NEARLY KILLED them all.

All over the Deathlands, which had once been the United States of America, there were a number of hidden fortresses. These redoubts had been known to Ryan Cawdor from his earliest days with the traveling guerrilla leader they called the Trader. But only in the past few weeks had Ryan learned of the other, secret uses of these redoubts.

Many of them concealed a small security fortress within the main complex, which was called a gateway.

The key to these installations had been Dr. Theophilus Tanner—Doc, a scrawny old man in tattered clothes who seemed to have come from the prenuke era. Doc's brains had been scrambled by some horrific experiences, but every now and again he came out with pearls of arcane wisdom that puzzled and fascinated Ryan Cawdor. And the most bewildering concerned something called Project Cerberus.

Eventually Ryan and Krysty had stumbled upon the secret of Doc Tanner. Back in the late 1990s, only a few years before the civilized world vanished in the war that ended all wars, American and Russian scientists were working on ways of moving human beings through space and through time. In the United States this was Project Cerberus. In max-sec labs attempts were made to trawl a living person from the past. Many attempts were made, and some of the results were ghastly. But one succeeded.

Doctor Tanner was born in South Strafford, Vermont, on February 14, 1868. He married in 1891 and had been successfully time-trawled and brought forward, alive, to the fading end of the twentieth century. Doc proved so unstable and difficult that he was eventually sent forward on a chron-jump, this time ending up in the heart of the Deathlands. His mind constantly tottered on the brink of madness, with only the occasional shard of crystal-clear memory remaining.

But slowly things had improved. His memory had grown stronger, and he had been able to give Ryan information about Cerberus, about the gateways and how they could be set for mat-trans jumps.

But the secret of time travel was still locked somewhere in the back of Doc's ravaged mind.

With his help the group had been able to make a number of mat-trans leaps, going from Alaska to Louisiana in the blink of an eye. But not all of the gateways remained undamaged. Doc had warned that their operation was completely unpredictable and that there remained the possibility they might jump to a gateway that was under a thousand feet of rock, or be drowned at the bottom of a California lagoon.

This last leap had brought that prediction frighteningly close.

The glass walls of the mat-trans chamber had been a deep red. The six friends had all entered the small room, sitting down on the floor of polished metal disks, readying themselves for the jump. All the references for controlling where the destination was had long been lost. All any of them knew was that the act of closing the gateway's inner door triggered the mechanism and sent them hurtling on a trip into the unknown.

RYAN HAD BEEN THE FIRST to recover consciousness, awakening with the familiar feeling that his brains had been splintered and put through a mixer, then hastily reassembled. His stomach churned and his eye pained him. For an instant everything felt like all the other mat-trans jumps.

He couldn't breathe.

The air was agonizingly thin, and his lungs sucked frantically for oxygen that wasn't there.

"Fireblast!" he tried to yell, but all that came out of his throat was a faint mewing, like that of a drowning kitten. None of the others showed any signs of coming around from the jump, but in the dim light Ryan could see that all of them were breathing fast and shallow.

The pattern of disks was different on the floor and on the ceiling, and the chamber seemed smaller than the others. The walls were dark blue glass, and only the dimmest light penetrated.

The moment Ryan Cawdor began his struggle to stand up, he knew this gateway was frighteningly different than the others. His body felt oddly light, and he stayed on hands and knees, gagging, a thin worm of yellow bile dangling from his open mouth.

"Got to..." he panted. "Got to fucking move from..."

He crawled over the outstretched legs of Lori Quint, snagging his pants on the tinkling silver spurs on her crimson boots. The effort of moving from one side of the chamber to the other made him pant as if he'd just sprinted a mile over a furrowed field. Ryan found himself swaying, almost floating, as if the gravity in the gateway had been reduced to near zero.

He fumbled for the handle of the door, his fingers clumsy. It seemed as if all sensation had gone from his body, and he staggered sideways, banging his shoulder hard on the wall. Ryan heard someone moaning and coughing behind him. His guess was Jak Lauren, but there wasn't time to check.

The Heckler & Koch G-12 caseless automatic rifle dropped with a clatter, but he didn't notice that it had fallen. After an infinity of effort, he managed to wrench the door open, revealing the familiar small room beyond it. The farther door was also open, and Ryan glimpsed flickering lights and comp-consoles turning and chattering to one another.

The gateways were triggered by the closing of the door, operating on a random principle. With the last of his fading power, he succeeded in slamming it shut once more. Gasping, his eyesight dimming, Ryan dropped to his knees, conscious even at that moment of the peculiar slowness of his fall. The chamber lights began to dance and glow again, and the blackness clawed its way across the front of his brain like a tendriled web.

When he'd come around, the sickness had been far worse than ever before. All of them—except Jak Lauren—had thrown up, and the chamber floor was awash with vomit. Oddly Ryan was the only one with any recollection of their stopover. And he hadn't any idea of where they'd gone.

He tried to ask Doc. "Did Cerberus ever have any way-weird gateways?"

"I fear that my present intestinal incapacity renders that question difficult to respond to, my dear Ryan. Perhaps at some other time?"

"It was like I was floating, Doc. The air tasted thinned down like double repure water. Couldn't breathe, and only just made it to mat-trans us. At least the air's safe here.''

Doc looked puzzled. He shook his head, eyes squeezed tightly shut. ''Floating, my dear Ryan? How can one float? And air that is thin! It's truly the most arrant tar-adiddle I ever did hear.'' For a moment Doc's eyes opened, and Ryan saw the fierce intellect that still blazed. ''Unless of course, they... There was some talk of a gateway that was to be built upon...''

He was interrupted by Lori rolling her head on his lap, tiny bubbles of yellow froth hanging on her lips. She moaned and reached for Doc's hand, breaking the brief run of his concentration.

Ryan leaned down over the old man's shoulders. ''Come on, Doc.''

''What?''

''You were saying about what you thought the bastard gateway might have been.''

''I was?''

''You were.''

''By the three Kennedys, but my head feels as though some knave's been dancing a polka inside it. I fear I can recall nothing of what I was saying. Do forgive me, Ryan.''

''Sure, Doc.''

It was something else to keep on the mental back burner. There'd been something about that dark blue gateway that had been like nothing on Earth.

''Like nothing on Earth,'' Ryan muttered to himself.

THE MAIN POWER PLANT for the redoubt was only running at about half supply. From the cracks in the concrete walls it was obvious there'd been a lot of seismic movements from the nuking, and well over half of the lights in the fortress had malfunctioned. The heating was barely enough to hold off the chill outside.

Unlike some of the other redoubts that Ryan and his party had encountered, this one in upper New York State was in excellent condition, well preserved and swept clean. Most of the main storage areas were empty, as though there'd been sufficient warning to evacuate them.

While the others stayed together, recovering from the double mat-trans jump, Jak Lauren went off on his own, scavenging for food, weapons and anything that might be useful.

In the whole set of linked caverns, there were only a half-dozen sections that hadn't been emptied. Some held self-heats, some clothes. Only one of them had been used for armaments.

Between them the six companions had a varied range of weapons.

Ryan Cawdor was delighted to come across an opened case of ammunition for his G-12. Since they all traveled light, he was beginning to worry whether he might actually run out of the unusual caseless ammo for the lightweight, fifty-shot gray blaster. He also found magazines of fifteen rounds of 9 mm bullets for the SIG-Sauer P-226 handgun that he'd carried for years on his hip. It was complemented by an eighteen-inch steel panga, honed to razor sharpness.

J. B. Dix picked up some ammunition for his mini-Uzi but couldn't find anything for his handblaster, his trusty Steyr AUG 5.6 mm. Apart from his firearms, the Armorer was a walking arsenal. He still had some pieces of high-ex plas left, sewn into his clothes and hidden in his high-laced combat boots. There were a couple of thin-bladed flensing knives as well as the beautiful Tekna knife he'd found back in West Lowellton.

Krysty Wroth, in her knee-length fur coat, so deep black that it was almost blue, stocked up on bullets for her silvered Heckler & Koch P7A-13 handgun, slipping a couple of the 13-round mags into her pockets.

Lori scarcely ever used her blaster, a delicate little pearl-handled Walther PPK. Despite Ryan's warnings that it was only a toy gun and that you needed more than a .22 to stop a man, the tall teenager clung stubbornly to her pretty pistol.

Jak Lauren went to the opposite extreme, hefting a massive satin finish .357 Magnum that looked absurdly huge in his small fist. But that didn't stop him from making lethal use of the big blaster.

It wasn't very surprising that Doc Tanner wasn't able to find any ammunition for his own blaster, a gun that was almost as eccentric in appearance as the old man himself, and only a couple of years older. It was a twin-barreled Le Mat. The large barrel was bored out to take a single scattergun round, while the other barrel fired one of nine .36 caliber rounds. The Le Mat, providing it didn't burst, could be utterly devastating. Doc also carried an ebony walking stick with a silver lion's head on its top, which could be pulled apart to reveal a slim rapier blade.

In the depleted armory none of the six found themselves any new weapons.

The last guards who'd been on duty in the redoubt had left their blankets and bedding behind. The sheets had long rotted into dry flakes of powdery material, but the blankets remained, thick and dark brown, with the faded letters USFNY in one corner.

All of the group had finally recovered from the ordeal of the double jump. Doc was sleeping like a baby on a tattered mattress, one arm draped across Lori's slender body. Jak was curled up under a pile of blankets, his mane of silky white hair drifting across the coarse material like windblown spume. J.B. slept on his side, fedora perched over his eyes, one hand gripping the butt of his blaster.

Ryan had dragged a couple of mattresses together, covering them with blankets. It was undoubtedly safe to sleep without posting a guard in the redoubt. They were almost certainly the first living creatures in the place for a hundred years.

"Warm enough, lover?"

Krysty nodded. She'd peeled off her khaki coveralls, folding them neatly at the bottom of their makeshift bed. Her cowboy boots stood alongside them. The overhead neon strips that still worked threw pallid light, glinting off the silver chiseled toes and silver leather falcons that ornamented the designer boots. The only thing that marred their elegance were the splashes of gray mud and the dappled, darker patches of dried blood around the heels and the sides of the soles.

Ryan took a chance on undressing, breaking one of his own cardinal rules. He'd slit the bottoms of his pants so that he could pull them off over his combat boots. Carefully he ranged his weapons alongside the makeshift bed.

Krysty lay on her left side, facing away from him, and he cuddled against her, spoon-fashion, feeling his swelling erection as it pressed snugly into the strong curve of her buttocks. For a moment she responded to the pressure, then half turned toward him.

"Sorry, lover," she whispered. "I know it's not the most original excuse, but I really do have a bastard of a headache from the jump."

"Yeah. I guess I don't feel at my steel-breaking best. The jumps get worse. I wish I knew where the fireblast we ended up on that one today. One of these days we're going to end up reconstituted under a million tons of mountain."

"Quick way to go," she said. The idea made her start to giggle, making her body press harder against him, with the inevitable result.

Afterward, Krysty cradled him in her arms. "Ace cure for a headache, lover," she whispered.

Chapter Two

IN ONE of the stone-walled rooms near the main entrance of the redoubt, they found a shelf filled with backpacks. At J.B.'s suggestion, everyone in the party took one, filling it with spare ammo and self-heats. Each of them also carried a couple of clear-plas cans of springwater, the kind that had a ring-pull opener. At some time a round button had been kicked under a metal cabinet. Jak Lauren picked it up and pinned it to the lapel of his ragged leather and canvas camouflage jacket. It was bright red and carried a picture of a helmet. The gold-lettered words said simply: Forty-Niners Go.

The 352 code opened the outer door, revealing a morning of bright sun bursting from a sky tinted purple. The chem cloud storm of the previous evening had vanished. The temperature was a few degrees above freezing. Far on the other side of the wooded valley, Krysty spotted a hunting bird, circling on a thermal, its great wings spread wide. Its wingspan looked to be about fifteen feet.

The bird was the first sign of life they'd seen since the jump.

The first problem to overcome was to find a way down from the redoubt. Inside the main door Lori had found a plan of the entire fortress, with its corridors lined in blue, the exit marked in orange. There was only the one exit shown.

Ryan checked both ends of the broken roadway. The drop was sheer for about forty feet, then he could make out the remains of tracks beaten through the scrub.

"That's what's kept the place clean," he said. "Unless you had a rope launcher, you'd never get up that face. It's smoother than...than Jak's chin."

"For an old man with only one eye, Ryan, you got a fucking big mouth."

"Just a joke, son, just a joke."

"See me laughing, Ryan?"

"When friends fall out, then their enemies make merry," Doc said, pouring a little oil on the troubled waters.

There was an uneasy moment of stillness within the party, which was broken by the Armorer. "Need some fixed lines up here. Then we have to find a way of making sure nothing an' nobody gets in while we're away."

Ryan stood a moment, looking out across the wilderness. "Anyone had any thoughts about where we're going?"

"Let's have a look around," Krysty suggested. The wind was still strong, tugging at them as they stood on the broad ledge. She'd tied back her long crimson hair to keep it out of her eyes.

"You know anything 'bout this place, Doc? Where we landed?"

"Upper New York, I believe you said, my dear fellow. Then that must be the Hudson. Or, perchance, the Mohawk River. Yes. I believe I have been here before. Hunting in the Adirondacks for deer. Ah, so delicate and pretty until the ball struck them. Then the eyes glazed o'er and the spirit fled."

"We head west for a few days, we could meet up with what's left of the Trader's party," J.B. said, scratching at the stubble that darkened his chin. "Cohn an' Ches, Kathy, Loz an' all the rest of 'em in War Wag One. If'n they're all still living."

The idea attracted Ryan Cawdor. It seemed several lifetimes since he and the others had split off from the remnants of the Trader's small army. Since then they'd suffered losses: Abe, Hunaker, Okie, Finnegan and Henn. Already there were so many dead and near forgotten. So many.

"How far from the ville where your brother rules as baron?" Krysty asked.

"Forget it," Ryan snapped.

"Why?"

"Because that's past. Then was then, but this is now."

"Virginia is not too far from here, my dear Ryan," Doc said. "A few days traveling if we could only lay our hands upon some suitable transport."

"I don't give a—" Ryan began, stopping as Krysty's fingers tightened on his arm. "Why d'you . . . ?"

"Because I *know* what you want, Ryan. I can feel it. Trust me. You have to go back to find your roots. To claim what is yours. You have to try."

"Which direction is Virginia from here? The Shens were south of Newyork city. Must be south. Must be a good ways off."

"Why don't we just go look?" J.B. suggested. "I'd kind of like to meet your brother. Heard plenty 'bout him the last few weeks."

"And none of it good," Jak added, grinning.

"Let us journey on," Doc said. "Truly, like brothers in arms."

JAK AND J.B. MANAGED to find a rope inside the redoubt, dark blue plaited plaslon that was strong enough

to lower a war wag over the cliff. They secured it at the
top, and each member of the group rappeled down, landing safely among the scattered conifers dotted with stately
hemlocks. Once everyone was down, J.B. hooked the
bottom of the rope on a jagged overhang of splintered
granite.

"Be there for when we come back from where we're
going." He looked intently at Ryan. "Into the Shens, I
guess."

Ryan didn't answer him. He led the way down the narrow path, toward the river. The wind was not as forceful
as they walked among the trees, and they could make out
the sullen sound of the water as it rolled over great platters of gray stone.

As he picked out the trail among the loose scree, Ryan
thought back to the boy he'd once been. He thought
about the great sprawling mansion that lay at the core of
the ville of Front Royal, down in the blue-muffled Shen-
andoahs, the endless waves of the Shens. And he thought
of the man that he'd become.

Behind him, he heard Lori trip and stumble, cursing in
her odd, flat little-girl voice. Doc soothed her. If only
she'd throw away the ridiculous bright red thigh boots
with the stiletto heels. He'd tried to persuade her to settle
for combat boots, but the blond teenager had refused.
And Doc hadn't been any help. He'd merely grinned and
commented how much he liked them.

"Upon my soul, Mr. Cawdor," he'd said. "Surely a
man must be permitted a little harmless deviancy, every
now and again?"

The river grew closer, the sound of its rushing waters
louder. The trees thinned out and the trail widened. Ryan
stooped and examined the ground, seeing tracks that he
recognized as elk, and the round pad marks of wolves. He

knew from old books that in the olden times, before the long winters, wild animals had been limited to what had been called national parks. Bears and wolves lived only in the desolate high country, rarely seen by man. But since the nuking had decimated the population and destroyed every city, the creatures of the night had come back, growing bolder and often mutated into even more ferocious beasts than before.

The wolves were among the worst.

Something moved in the bushes to his right, and he leveled the G-12, finger tightening on the trigger. The gun was set on triple-burst, ready to cough out three rounds in a fraction of a second. His eye caught a slithery, gleaming animal, larger than an otter, scurrying across the damp boulders, making for the foaming edge of the Mohawk. It paused and stared directly at him, seemingly fearless. Its eyes were deep-set, glittering like bright emeralds, and its jaw hung open in a snarl of manic ferocity. Ryan held the rifle steady, ready to smear the creature into rags of bone and blood. But it turned its head contemptuously away and slipped silently into the water.

Only in the second it disappeared from sight did Ryan notice that the animal had six legs, tipped with claws like ivory daggers.

"If we could find a boat of some type, we could sail down to where the Mohawk meets the Hudson, just above Troy, and thence we could navigate clear to New York itself," Doc said, joining Ryan on the shore of the river.

"If we could find a copter and get some gas for it, we could fly to Front Royal and never get our damned feet wet," Ryan retorted.

They followed the water, heading south, picking their way along indistinct paths. Around noon Ryan called a halt for them to take a drink from the widening river and to open up a self-heat each. During the afternoon there was a rain shower that persisted, becoming a steady, dull drizzle that quickly soaked them all to the skin.

"Take us a year to reach Newyork if'n we don't find us some transport," J.B. said, looking up through the ceaseless rain to the west, where the sky was darkening. "Be night in an hour."

"Wait!"

They all stopped to look at Krysty, who stood with an expression of concentration on her face. Her saturated hair clung to her shoulders like a fiery, frightened animal.

"What?" Ryan asked.

"By Gaia, it's smoke! I can smell woodsmoke."

Ryan held his head up, ignoring the teeming rain that dripped over his face and ran behind the black patch that covered his ruined left eye. He sniffed at the air.

"Yeah, I can smell it, too. Wet weather keeps it low down. Can't be more'n a mile off."

"I will be liking getting warm," Lori said, wiping a strand of sodden yellow hair from her face.

"Not just warm," Jak said. "Fire means people. And in a place like this, people means boats."

"People also means guards and mebbe some chilling to be done. So, step cautious." Ryan led them on again, ever watchful.

IT WAS A RAGTAG COMMUNITY of double-poor muties. Mud huts, covered in rough branches, had been built around a hewn clearing at the edge of the Mohawk. A large fire of green wood smoldered in the middle of the huts, and a rusty iron caldron was suspended over it. From the smell that bubbled up from the pot, it was some kind of fish stew.

The villagers were all small, not one of them topping five feet. Most were heavily muscled and had shaggy hair that hung over low foreheads. Their jaws jutted out, and they seemed to communicate in a language that consisted mainly of grunts.

They wore jerkins and breeches of a sackcloth, dyed dark green and russet yellow. It was difficult to tell the sexes apart. While Ryan and the others watched from the shadows at the edge of the forest, one of them came to pass water only a few yards from them. Krysty, with her sensitive nose, could easily catch the rancid stench of sweat and grease from the mutie's body. The sickle moon that swooped over the hills behind them also revealed to the watching six that the mutie was grotesquely sexually endowed.

J.B. caught Ryan's hand, pointing urgently beyond the farthest of the tumbledown houses. Hauled up above the level of the river was a crude raft. It was from hewn logs, bound with creepers and was about eight feet square. A stump of mast at its center and a steering oak, hacked from a single long branch, were the only signs that it might be maneuverable.

Ryan leaned closer so that his mouth touched the Armorer's ear. With muties, you never knew what kind of skill they might have. These primitives might be deaf, or they might hear as well as cave-born bats.

"Soon as they sleep," he whispered.

J.B. nodded his agreement, then passed the message quietly to Krysty, to Jak, on to Lori and finally to Doc.

THE MOON HAD DISAPPEARED behind a bank of cloud so dense it seemed like a floating mountain. A storm was brewing, and the air crackled with ozone. Ryan could feel his hair standing on end with static electricity. The stew had been eaten by the muties, and the fire was dying to glowing embers. The valley was less cold than the upper slopes, outside the hidden redoubt, but there was a biting dampness that seemed to creep through the layers of fur and leather, seeping into the marrow of the bones.

Ryan hooked the G-12 to a loop on his belt and drew the pistol, feeling its familiar weight. 25.52 ounces, precisely. Back when they'd been with War Wag One, J.B. had shown him the crumpled, brittle field manual for the SIG-Sauer P-226, and he remembered all of the details about it.

"Let's go, my friends," he said quietly.

There'd been no sign of anyone out on patrol around the filthy little hamlet. Apart from the rafts, there wasn't likely to be anything there worth stealing. With a wave of his hand, Ryan motioned for Jak Lauren to take the lead. Out of the six of them, the albino boy was probably the best at creepy-crawling. His bleached hair blazed like an incandescent beacon, making Jak easy to follow.

Ryan came second, with Krysty at his heels. Doc and Lori were together and J.B. brought up the rear, several safe paces behind to cover them in case of a sneak attack.

Against the rumbling backdrop of the fast-flowing river, it was hard to make out any other sounds. As they passed between the stinking hovels, Ryan heard a woman's voice. She was singing a mournful dirge, soft and low, with no recognizable tune to it and no words at all. It was fortunate for them that the villagers didn't seem to keep any dogs to warn of strangers. But their hamlet was so isolated that it was doubtful they even knew what human enemies were.

The raft had no sail, but there were a number of smoothed branches, each about ten feet long, that looked as if they were used to propel and guide the clumsy craft.

Jak turned, asking, "We go on this?"

"Yeah. Get ready to cut the rope. We'll have to push her out into the flow, or we'll beach on those rocks a few yards downstream."

In fact, the raft was so firmly grounded that it took all six of them to heave it off the sloping beach of shingle. It sat so low that the Mohawk bubbled over its logs. With six of them on board, Ryan knew they were in for a wet journey. Only the rope held it, knotted around a frost-riven boulder, high up on the bank.

"Get on, and move slow an' easy!" Ryan ordered, eyes raking the sleeping village for any threat.

"Keep to the center," Doc urged, folding Lori Quint in his long arms.

"Right?" Jak called, crouching with one of his leaf-bladed throwing knives in his fist, waiting to slice the knotted creeper apart.

Ryan took up the mooring line, hung on to it with both hands and braced himself against the pull of the current. He kept the raft steady for the boy to run down and board it.

"Now," he said, staring intently into the gloom, able to see only the splash of whiteness that was the boy's hair.

There was the blur of movement as the knife whispered through the rope, and Ryan felt it go slack, so that all the weight was on him. But, as he watched, he saw a chunk of the night rise from behind the boulder and grapple with Jak.

"Fireblast!" Ryan yelled, helpless to assist the boy.

But Jak could look after himself. The mutie had grabbed at him, pulling him to the earth. It uttered ferocious grunting noises, its foul breath nearly choking him. Its stubby fingers ripped at his coat, groped for his eyes, trying to squeeze them from their soft sockets.

The albino still held the knife, its taped hilt snug in his fingers. Using his superior agility and strength, he was able to wriggle out from under the attacker, turning the creature on its back, digging his knee into the soft flesh of its groin. In pain and shock the air burst from the mutie's lungs, a thin scream breaking the silence of the night.

The flesh of the mutie was coarse, almost reptilian, the skin like flaking scales to Jak's touch. His first cut was deflected, the edge of the blade skittering off the side of the stump of a neck. Jak fended off a flailing fist with the side of his forearm, thrusting once more with the knife. As a weapon, it wasn't ideally suited to hand-to-hand fighting, but against the weak and clumsy mutie it was more than enough.

He felt the blood gush out from the deep, narrow wound, steaming in the pallid light of the moon as it appeared from behind the clouds. Jak turned his wrist, like the experienced knife fighter he was, and drove the steel deeper into the mutie's flesh so that the flow warmed his hand.

The body went limp under him, and he started to rise, pulling the throwing knife from the creature's throat. But the mutie wasn't done yet. In a convulsive spasm of dying rage, it reached up for him, fingers locking around the boy's skinny neck, holding him there, the two locked together in a ghastly tableau.

"Chill him, Ryan!" Jak choked out, hacking at the scaly forearms of the mutie.

But Ryan was too busy struggling to hang on to the frayed end of the creeper that held the raft steady against the driving current. J.B. was in the center of the tossing, waterlogged craft, his pistol drawn, sighting along the barrel. But the movement of the tumbling waves threw off his aim, and he didn't dare squeeze the trigger in case he shot Jak, unable to distinguish between the tangled bodies in the murky light.

The mutie was screeching, its blood spouting black and spattering on the damp stones all around.

"Help me!" Jak shouted hoarsely, trying and failing to break the mutie's death grip.

"Cut the fingers," Ryan yelled, head twisted as he tried to make out what was happening behind him.

"Can't!" The screaming had stopped, but enough noise had been made to rouse a regiment of sleeping sec men.

Krysty saved the moment. Jumping surefooted, like a great panther, she landed on the loose stones, her hair breaking free from its binding and whirling around her head like a torrent of fire. She held her Heckler & Koch blaster in her right hand, the moonlight dancing off the mirrored finish of the barrel. In the blinking of an eye, the girl was alongside Jak and the dying mutie, stooping and placing the muzzle against its sagging mouth.

The crack of the 9 mm round was oddly muffled, almost inaudible against the pounding of the Mohawk. The back of the mutie's skull burst apart as though someone had struck it from inside with a sixteen-pound sledge, the contents of the brainpan slopping in the dirt. The fingers convulsed and then relaxed their grip, allowing Jak to break away.

"Come on!" Ryan called, feeling his boots sliding in the wet pebbles that lined the cold waters of the river.

Krysty led the way, running toward the bobbing raft, holstering her pistol as she sprinted. Planting a kiss on Ryan's cheek as she jumped across the gap, she landed on all fours on the moss-slick timbers, grabbing at the mast to steady herself.

"Double-hard bastard to chill," Jak said as he came down the slope, panting like he'd run a desperate race. "Thanks, Krysty. Owe you one."

"Let her go, Ryan," J.B. said. "Be getting us company soon."

The gap between the shore and the raft had been gradually widening, despite all of Ryan's efforts. He dropped the rope and jumped for it, landing awkwardly on the edge, legs trailing in the icy water.

The raft began to move away from the shore ever so slowly, just as fifty or more muties came bursting over the top of the slope toward them.

Chapter Three

IF ANY OF THE STUPES had owned a blaster, then Ryan's group would have taken some chillings. Even a couple of long-barreled Kentucky muskets would have picked them off like hogs on ice. Even bows and arrows, or straight spears would have been lethal at such close range, against helpless targets. Hanging on the slimy logs of the bobbing raft for their very lives, none of the six could even hold a blaster, let alone hope to hit anyone with one.

The muties hadn't come prepared, and the only weapons they had were the stones from the narrow expanse of the beach.

At less than twenty paces, the jagged missiles were potentially lethal, but the rocking of the raft that prevented Ryan and his friends from wiping away the muties also made *them* difficult targets. Krysty caught a painful blow on the left elbow, and Doc was cut on the forehead, but most of the stones bounced harmlessly off the raft.

A whirling current made the cumbersome vessel pitch and spin, then it broke free and began to move faster down the Mohawk, away from the murderous muties. As the raft steadied, J.B. stood up with his mini-Uzi, balancing himself against Ryan.

"Want me to take some of the bastards out?" he asked.

"Be easy."

"No. Leave 'em," Ryan replied, peering behind them into the darkness. "Best take care when we come back to the gateway."

"That's too damned right," Krysty agreed, rubbing at her damaged elbow.

The river gradually became wider, the raft floating sluggishly in its center. As it widened it also became calmer, with no hint of rapids. The banks were each a hundred paces away, leaving them safe from attack. The night wore on, and most of them managed to snatch a few hours' sleep, though Ryan took the precaution of keeping one of them awake and on watch.

"Keep careful—keep alive," had been one of the Trader's rules of living.

Just before dawn they passed another of the squalid little riverside communities. From a distance it was hard to see, but Krysty, with her sharp eyesight, was certain that it wasn't a nest of muties. Just double-poor folk dredging up an existence on the razor edge of poverty.

An arrow was fired from a screen of dull green pine trees, but it fell woefully short of the raft. On a narrow headland, daubed pink by the florid orange sunrise, the six were watched by a pack of hunting dogs, with slavering jaws and a crust of yellow froth around their long incisors.

Gradually the sky lightened. Around eight in the morning one of the limitless thousands of chunks of space debris, dating from the ill-founded Star Wars defense system, finally reentered the atmosphere of the Earth. It burned up in a dazzling display of green-and-red pyrotechnics, breaking up and melting as it ripped through the clouds in a fearsome explosion.

Doc Tanner took off his beloved stovepipe hat and wiped sweat from his forehead with his handkerchief, which was decorated with a swallow's-eye design. His eyes dimmed as he rubbed absently at the dent in the crown of the hat. "There will always be that sort of memory. Millenia will come and go and still that damnable filth will boil in the spatial maelstrom, falling now and again to remind us of the futility of it all. Oh, if only..." The sentence, unfinished, trailed behind him like a maiden's hand in the rolling water.

"Look," Lori said, shading her eyes with one hand and pointing ahead of them with the other. "Road across water."

"It's called bridge," Jak told her, balancing easily against the pitching of the raft. The vessel seemed even ＿wer in the river now, the clear waves seeping over the ＿t of the logs.

＿it was a place where the river narrowed, the banks closing in on either side, rising steeply to wooded bluffs. The bridge seemed to be made out of cables or ropes, strung like some dizzy spiderweb, dangling low in its center, barely thirty feet above the level of the surging Mohawk.

"And we got us company," J.B. said, unslinging the mini-Uzi from his shoulder.

They could see small, dark figures silhouetted against the light violet of the sky, scurrying toward the middle of the bridge, swinging hand over hand like tiny malevolent insects. Unlike the muties from farther upstream, these wore long cowled robes that concealed their faces and most of their bodies.

"They got no blasters," Jak said.

"Some got stones. And those two on the left have hunting bows," Krysty exclaimed, pointing with the muzzle of her P7A-13 handgun.

The raft was swooping fast toward the bridge, pitchin
and rolling. Ryan squinted ahead, clutching his G-1:
caseless, trying to estimate how severe the threat was.
Getting involved in a firefight in these circumstances was
highly hazardous. The enemy, if proved hostile, held all
of the jack. To try to blow them off their vantage point
would be difficult at best, and extremely costly in ammo
at worst. Even an ace shot like Ryan Cawdor couldn't
guarantee wreaking much havoc from the unsteady platform of the waterlogged and rotating raft.

"Hold fire!" he yelled, hoping everyone could hear him
above the pounding of the white-topped waves surrounding them.

"Be hard to chill 'em," Jak shouted from the front
the raft, where he crouched with his beloved Magnum
spray washing over him.

"Doc! You an' Lori take that steering oar and try to
keep the bastard steady. Keep her going forward and hold
her from circling."

The girl and the old man staggered to the stern, Doc
slipping and coming within an inch of toppling into the
swollen waters. But they clawed a hold on the misshapen
branch that trailed in the river, throwing their combined
weight against it, gradually controlling the swinging of the
clumsy craft. It was some improvement, but the chances
of pulling off any accurate shooting were still dozens to
one.

There were about thirty people on the fragile bridge,
making it pitch and dip even lower.

Oddly none of them was showing any obvious signs of
aggression toward Ryan and his group, no waving of fists
or throwing of stones. The couple with bows simply held
them, unstrung, in their hands.

J.B. glanced toward Ryan, the unspoken question clear on his face. He reached up and wiped spots of water off his wire-rimmed glasses, shaking his head in puzzlement.

"Why don't they...?"

Ryan readied himself. "Mebbe they aren't against us."

Doc heard him above the sound of the river. "Wrong, my dear Ryan. Anyone who is not for us, *must* be against us."

They were less than two hundred yards from the bridge.

One hundred yards.

"They're going t'let us through," Jak yelped, staring up at the hooded strangers.

"Mebbe," Ryan muttered. It was true what Doc had shouted. In the ravaged world of Deathlands you had few friends. And a mess of enemies.

Twenty yards.

A fish leaped in the air off to the left, bursting in rainbow spray, taking everyone's eyes for a crucial moment.

"We making..." began Lori, eyes wide with the tension of the second.

Dangling monkeylike from the center span of twisted cords, one of the silent watchers reached out as the raft floated directly beneath him—or her—and opened a hand, allowing something to drop. The object landed with a metallic thud on the logs, hitting the mast and wedging itself between two of the knotted creepers.

It was oval in shape, about the size of a man's fist. The top was dull, steel glinting through a number of gouged scratches. There were scarlet and blue bands painted around it.

"Implo-gren!" J.B. shouted in a thin, cracking voice, shaken into dropping his normal laconic mask at the sight of the bomb.

It had been a similar implosion grenade that had broken through the creeping fog when Ryan had entered the first mat-trans gateway. Using some very basic experimental anti-grav material, the hand bombs created a sudden and extremely violent vacuum so that everything around the edge of the detonation was sucked into it. The displacement was more ferocious than with a conventional explosion. Very few of the implo-grens had been made, and it flashed through Ryan's mind, even at that moment of maximum danger, to wonder how these isolated villagers had gotten hold of one.

The other thought that flooded into his brain was to try to recall what kind of fuses the grens had. Twelve seconds? Ten?

Five?

Doc and Lori were helpless, hanging onto the steering oar at the stern. J.B. was nearest, but the bulk of the mast obstructed him. Jak was the one with the fastest reflexes, but he was kneeling at the front of the raft, gun drawn, looking up at the monklike figures who hung on the bridge above them.

Krysty Wroth began to move. Despite having part-mutie sight and hearing, her reflexes were no faster than any normal person's.

Which left it in Ryan Cawdor's court.

As he started to dive for the implo-gren, he remembered about the fuse.

They were generally eight seconds.

Chapter Four

THE METAL WAS COLD, slippery with the waters of the Mohawk.

Ryan's fingers closed on the gren, and he hefted it from the sodden logs, cocking his arm to throw it over the side of the raft. The rope bridge above them replaced a four-lane highway bridge that had crumbled in the first minutes of the nuking of 2001. Even now, a century later, some of the original stone and girders still lay in the river, just below the surface. At that moment the laden craft struck some relic of the ruined bridge, jarring into it with a sickening crunch.

The raft swung into a sullen half circle, throwing Ryan completely off guard. He stumbled, fighting for balance. He tried to dump the grenade over the side, but his fingers had locked over it as he fell. At the last moment he struggled to roll on his shoulder, but the slick cold wood betrayed his footing and he tumbled sideways. His shoulder thumped against the stump of the mast, and he half rolled on top of Krysty, who snatched at his coat to check him from falling over the side into the Mohawk. The implo-gren slipped from his hand, clattering under both their bodies.

The crowd on the spiderwork bridge gave a ragged cheer, waving their fists at the clumsy craft beneath them.

Ryan groped for the fallen grenade, feeling the raft hit again, with a jagged, splintering sound, holding it in the same place. Even as he touched the icy metal, his brain screamed to him that he was way too slow, that the eight seconds were up and gone. The metal would disintegrate and he would be sucked into the hissing vacuum and destroyed, along with everyone on the doomed raft.

He dropped the gren twice more, until he was finally able to grip it securely, sitting up and holding it in his right hand. Ryan was almost unable to believe their good fortune. Above him the cheers turned to screeching anger.

"It's a fucking malfunk!" Jak yelled. "Lemme chill the monsters."

"No. Let's get out," Ryan called. "Doc? Push us off with that steering oar."

"Consider it done," the old man replied.

"Throw it, lover," Krysty said, face white with shock at their narrow escape.

"Sure." He looked up at the horde of cowled figures hanging from the network of creepers and shouted, "Here, have the bastard back!"

Once, about eight years ago, Ryan had been with the Trader when they'd broken into a small redoubt, a long way west, in a valley of the Rockies. They'd found some old vids stashed away and a sealed battery player. Most of the tapes had rotted and crumbled, but they'd watched a few minutes of one of them. It had been a film of a football game. Ryan couldn't recall the names of the teams or the players, but he still remembered the grace and power of the man who'd thrown the football, flexing his arm and letting it go, soaring upward and on.

He hefted the implo-gren and heaved it toward the watchers on the bridge, hoping to hit one of them and maybe even pitch him into the river. The raft was already starting to roll uncontrollably down the Mohawk, and it wasn't worth wasting any ammo.

He watched the scarlet and blue bands revolving in the cool, damp air.

The sound of the grenade detonating was unmistakable: a muffled, inward, whooshing sort of noise, as the implosion sucked everything into itself. The gren had been at its highest point, hanging in the air only a few yards from the bridge, when the fuse finally worked.

The frail structure of knotted creepers disintegrated instantly, its strands spinning toward the whirling circle of air that had been the implo-gren. And the hooded figures were tugged with it, tumbling into screaming space, into the waiting river, which received them gratefully.

Ryan and his friends watched the destruction of their enemies with disbelief. The small bodies splashed into the fast-flowing water, most of them not even resurfacing, dragged down by their heavy robes.

Doc and Lori abandoned the steering, allowing the heavy raft to find its own direction and speed. All six of them stared behind at the spectacular results of the malfunctioned gren. On either side of the river they could see the dangling cords, snapped off short, that had held the bridge. But the whole center section had disappeared, floating past them in torn and fragmented sections.

Only one of the muties made it to the surface and tried to swim toward the raft. Its clothes were gone, and it resembled the muties they'd seen higher up the Mohawk— short arms and legs, and skin like a reptile. This one had no hair at all on its wrinkled skull, and they were shocked to see a vestigial third eye, staring wildly at them, in the center of its brutish, low forehead.

As it floundered along, closing in on the slow-moving raft, its lipless mouth stretched open and it screamed to them in a feeble voice.

"Elp, elp, elp, elp!"

Its fingers groped for the rough-hewn edge of the logs, near where Lori stood.

"I'm helped you," the girl shouted, still trembling from the shock of their brush with death.

Before anyone else on the raft could move, the slender girl hefted one of the ten-foot-long branches that served as paddles, lifted it and brought it down on the bobbing face. The stump of wood pulped the man's nose, splitting his lips, breaking off several of his teeth. Blood jetted, flooding his throat, making him choke. His hands slipped off the side of the raft and he bobbed away, a tendril of crimson trailing from his smashed face.

The last they saw of him was a hand clutching at the cold air.

BEFORE EVENING the Mohawk was joined by another, wider river, coming in from the north. Doc Tanner pronounced that it was the Hudson. Even Jak Lauren had heard of that name.

"Runs by Newyork?"

The old man sighed. "Time was it did, my snow-headed young colleague. But what remains of that great metropolis now I wonder?"

"When I was a kid, folks talked of it as a hot spot, full o'weeds," Ryan said. "Only ghouls lived there, eating each other."

Doc smiled. "Sounds much as it was back in my day, Ryan."

The light was fading and an evening storm threatened. Ryan pointed toward a low spit of land, jutting out, with the shattered remnants of a building just visible at its end. Because of its length and narrowness it would be easy to defend against a sneak attack from the land side.

"Bring us in there if you can," he called to Jak, who was manning the steering oar with Krysty.

The farther south they drifted, the slower and wider the river became, with none of the gushing rapids they'd encountered higher up, near the abandoned redoubt. The water was amazingly clear, with the rocks on its bottom looking close enough to reach down and touch, though a quick measurement with a length of cord and J.B.'s Tekna knife showed them a depth of about fifteen feet. Doc kept wondering at how unpolluted the Hudson appeared.

"Back when I knew it nobody would place a hand in the water, for fear the acids and chem filth would scorch it to the bone."

The raft grounded with a soft crunch on the shingle, and they all leaped gratefully off it, stretching their legs. Jak tied the remnants of the mooring rope around a rusted girder that stuck vertically out of some crumbling concrete. The boy stooped and lapped at water from his cupped hands, wrinkling his nose.

"Tastes of salt," he said.

"Salt?" Ryan queried. "Must be close to the sea. I haven't seen the sea for...for too many long years. Is that right, Doc?"

"We must go down to the sea again, and do business in great waters," the old man chanted. "The wonders of the Lord, my dear Ryan, is what we might all share, one day hence."

"But are we close to the sea?" J.B. pressed.

Doc shook his head, the light wind disturbing his gray locks. He smiled and showed his peculiarly fine, strong set of teeth. "What is close, John Barrymore Dix? How when is up? How meretricious is now? Riddle me that, my friend."

They dropped the question of how close they were to the sea. In fact, it was approximately one hundred and fifty miles from their stopping place to the open ocean beyond Manhattan.

Ryan set guards, giving everyone a two-hour duty during the time of darkness, and left the last watch for himself. The rest of the group huddled together in the open, eating from their self-heats, using the water from the Hudson for drinking despite the faint hint of salt it held.

"Be better in the trees for shelter?" J.B. suggested.

"We haven't seen any sign of life for hours. Not since the crazies on that bridge."

It was true what Krysty said. The banks of the Hudson seemed deserted. Ryan had been taking regular readings with his rad meter, but it hadn't gone seriously across the orange and into the red. The land was warm, but no longer hot.

"Because we don't see 'em, it don't mean they aren't there," he replied.

"Yeah," the laconic Armorer said.

They stayed where they were.

It was a beautiful night, warmer than it had been farther north. The moon was untroubled by clouds, sailing above them, sharpening the edges of all the shadows.

Lori was on watch a little after three in the morning. When the stickies came, they beat the girl to the ground before she could give any warning.

Chapter Five

NOBODY KNEW a whole lot about stickies. They were found in small, vicious colonies, generally in parts of the Deathlands that had been particularly heavily nuked. Some said that the missiles that spawned the genetic horrors that were stickies also held some secret chromosomic deviator that accounted for the peculiar nightmare that they had become.

Some blamed grossly contaminated water supplies in a mysterious process that involved nitrates leached from the soil.

All that was truly known about stickies was that they were triple-crazy. They loved killing and ripping things apart. They liked the sight of blood. They also relished fires and explosions, taking some bizarre and perverse pleasure from staring into dancing flames.

Oddly stickies had only been known in the past twenty or so years. A three-hundred-and-fifty-pound showman named Gert Wolfram was credited with discovering stickies and putting a pair into his traveling freak show. Word was that Gert hadn't lived too long after that.

Stickies had vulpine teeth and staring eyes, eyes that were utterly dead and devoid of emotion, like a basking shark. The main thing about stickies was that they had developed peculiar sucking pads on their webbed fingers, which enabled them to cling easily to smooth surfaces like flies. It was rumored that stickies could come at you across the ceiling, but that was generally discounted. But they could surely climb walls and hang on to windows.

In the entire Deathlands stickies were the only breed of muties that everyone would automatically kill on sight. It was possible to speak to them, but you had to shout and talk very slowly, as though they heard you through a strange kind of lip-reading. They had no ears.

Lori never heard them. Never saw them. She was sitting down, coat wrapped around her, slipping from an uneasy wakefulness into a half sleep. She was recalling the crazed days with her father. Her husband. Lover. Keeper. Quint. White beard to his stomach, stained amber with nicotine. Jacket spotted with sequins. The hooked nose and narrow, cruel mouth. And the violence.

In her dream, the girl was tied, naked and spread, to the metal frame of a bed, while Quint moved toward her, leering and dribbling, a polished chrome phallus in his hand, its tip studded with shards of broken glass smeared with blood. As Lori tried to scream, a hand clamped itself across her mouth.

She woke and tried to scream, but a hand *had been* clamped across her mouth.

Lori was held down, and the last thing she heard before a crashing blow delivered to the side of her head plunged her into darkness was a soft, bubbling laughter.

Ryan had agreed they could build a small fire to hold the night's chill at bay, and it had been its ruby glow that had attracted the stickies, bringing nearly a dozen of them slinking from the darkness under the looming pine trees. They moved with a sinuous quiet, their bare, suckered feet making only the faintest slithering sound on the old stones.

It was Krysty Wroth's special part-mutie senses that saved the friends from a swift and evil ending. Krysty didn't have the true power of doom-seeing, but she had highly developed sight and hearing. In her sleep she caught the noise, like tiny lips kissing, of the advancing stickies.

Her green eyes flickered open, glancing beyond the glowing remains of their fire. She saw the skulking figures of the stickies, their eyes blinking, reflecting the flat color of the fire.

"Stickies! Wake up!" she yelled, reaching for her blaster and ripping off a couple of shots at the nearest of the muties, who were barely twenty paces from where she'd been sleeping.

Ryan, J.B. and Jak all came awake, guns magically in their hands. Doc Tanner took a while longer to reach the surface.

Like many such firefights, it lasted less than fifteen seconds.

Many muties had different body structures from norms, more primitive and brutish. They were, consequently, more difficult to put down—and keep down. Stickies were among the hardest of all to chill.

Krysty took out the first two, her 9 mm bullets punching holes clean through flesh and muscle at such close range. The stickies kicked over in a scrabbling, screaming tangle, their fall obstructing their following companions. Her next two rounds missed, then she hit a third mutie with two bullets, both in the belly, folding him over, vomiting blood.

Jak took out two more stickies with his Magnum, the huge handblaster coughing in the darkness, spitting fire and death. One of the two was up immediately, even though its left arm had been nearly severed at the shoulder by the big .357 round. The creature lurched on, screeching, eyes wide, its blood crimsoning its chest and legs. Jak took careful aim and put another bullet in the middle of its face, the skull disintegrating like a peach beneath a war wag.

J.B. held the mini-Uzi, chattering death, smearing the five stickies on the left of the attacking bunch, raking the barrel of the mean little gun backward and forward, using up the whole mag to make double-sure they were well chilled.

Ryan Cawdor was left with three of the stickies for himself.

Awakened by Krysty's yell of warning, his hands went by automatic reflex to the rectangular shape of the Heckler & Koch G-12. He rolled on one side, kicking away the single blanket that had been his only protection against the night.

Because of the high cross-sectional density of the round, there was very little transverse drift. At such close range, set on triple burst, there was no sideways drift at all. Ryan squeezed the trigger, not needing the laser-enhanced night sight, able to pick his target with ease. The G-12 fired triple bursts at better than thirty rounds per second, the recoil feeling like a single round, barely registering.

The bullets from the blaster didn't tumble at all, reducing their effect on human flesh, but the extreme velocity caused massive trauma in the area of the body surrounding the actual point of impact. Ryan gave each of his targets a single burst of three shots.

The tallest of them, suckered hands stretched out to grasp at the human prey, was hit in the groin, the three 4.7 mil rounds ripping the mutie apart, slicing into its pelvis, exploding the bones, angling upward and destroying the lower stomach. The stickie toppled sideways, fingers reaching for the wound, fumbling among the loops of greasy intestines that cascaded out of its body.

The next mutie had its hands in front of it, and the bullets pulped the fingers, chunks of flesh and bone flying into the homicidal creature's face, blinding it. As it stumbled, the bullets stitched across its chest, driving splinters of torn ribs tumbling through the body, slicing the pumping heart into ribbons. Blood gouted and the stickie fell, dying, stumps of fingers opening and closing convulsively in its murderous death throes.

The last stickie seemed oblivious to the massacre of its fellows and still came on, mouth open in a silent scream. Ryan switched the aim of the G-12, pumping out a triple burst. Unfortunately Doc Tanner, who was just waking to the awareness of the attack, staggered to his knees and called out to Lori, distracting the mutie at the crucial millisecond that Ryan squeezed the trigger. The creature turned in midstride, launching itself at the old man, suckered fingers reaching greedily for his throat. The strength of a stickie's grip was notorious. Ryan had personally seen a man pull a stickie's hand off a friend's face, bringing half the cheek and one eye with it.

The trio of bullets missed the stickie's body, barely clipping the top of its legs, punching the creature off-balance. The snarling mutie fell, only a hand's span from Doc Tanner. Though not normally a great fighting man, Doc calmly drew the rapier blade from his swordstick and thrust it into the stickie's open mouth. The angle was perfect, the steel penetrating a foot and a half down its throat. Doc twisted his wrist like a master of the duel, opening the inside of his enemy's neck. Blood spurted between the bared teeth, splattering across the pebbles. The stickie reached convulsively for Doc, its fingers failing to find a grip on the blood-slick steel.

"Move," Jak ordered, leveling his pistol, waiting until the old man had withdrawn his sword and scrabbled out of the way. Then he put a booming bullet through the back of the dying mutie's skull, kicking it into a jerking tangle of twitching limbs.

"All done?" Ryan asked, his voice sharpened by the sudden explosion of violence.

"I counted twelve in, and I counted twelve down," J.B. replied, calmly holstering his mini-Uzi.

"Where's Lori?" Doc asked, wiping the blade of his swordstick on the rags of the nearest of the stickies, then sheathing it once more. Stooping, he picked up his faded hat and jammed it on his head.

"There," Krysty called, pointing along the narrow peninsula toward the looming forest.

Showing an unsuspected burst of speed, the old man darted like a disjointed crab to where they could now see the motionless figure of the young girl.

The others followed, Ryan and the Armorer taking a few moments to check that all of the dozen attackers were truly dead. With stickies you never could be too careful.

They were all chilled.

"Oh, my sweetest little darling," Doc sobbed, bending and cradling the girl in his arms. His knee joints cracked as he knelt on the stones, pressing her head against his chest. "My sweet dove of innocence," he moaned.

Having seen the way Lori Quint had ruthlessly butchered the drowning mutie after the incident with the implo-gren, Ryan Cawdor wasn't too sure he agreed with the description of her as an innocent dove.

"She is slain," Doc Tanner cried, his grief unrestrained. His head was thrown back, and he was howling like a tormented animal.

"She's alive, Doc," Krysty said, kneeling at his side.

"What?"

"Alive, Doc."

"No."

"Yes," Jak said. "Tits move. Breathing. She's alive."

"Oh, thanks be to the Almighty! By the three Kennedys but it seems barely possible. After those vile monsters had . . ."

"Best let me take a look at her," Krysty suggested.

"Look at? Oh, of course, my dear girl. Do look after the child."

Krysty stared down at Lori. "Light's no good. Ryan, carry her to the fire. Jak, get some wood from the trees there."

"I know where to get wood," he sniffed, insulted at the suggestion.

"Then do it," she snapped. "She's taken a hard knock on the temple. I can feel the lump. Move, Jak!"

It took several minutes before Lori began to show signs of recovering consciousness. The fire by then was blazing brightly, with the pine branches spitting and crackling. Jak and J.B. had gone to the end of the finger of land, watching carefully in case any more of the stickies were lurking there and waiting for a chance to attack. While Krysty worked with Lori, Ryan and Doc managed to shift the bloodied corpses of the muties, dragging them by the heels and allowing the force of the Hudson to roll them away into the night.

"Be in Newyork 'fore us," Ryan said.

But the old man was far more interested in getting back to the fire to see how Lori was progressing. His delight when she started to come around was touching. He knelt at her side, tears coursing down his wrinkled cheeks and through the gray stubble on his chin.

"What happens?" the girl mumbled, eyes blinking against the brightness of the blazing fire. "I dream and then..."

She shuddered, clutching at Krysty with white-knuckled hands.

"What was the dream?" Doc asked, holding one of her pale hands in both of his. "Tell me, my dearest child."

"I dream of Keeper. And he is fucked with me. And hand on mouth...and..." She began to cry. Krysty nodded at Doc, who took her place, holding the girl half on his lap.

"It's all done, lily of my heart. My dear deer. Your heart, dear hart, that pounds within your breast has..." He stopped rambling. "Some mutants came calling upon us, Lori. We exchanged a few words with them, and now they've gone away."

"Where, Doc?" Lori asked.

"Away down river. I think it unlikely they will return to bother us again."

"I think that's right, Lori," Ryan added. "Night swimming always was dangerous."

THERE WAS A LIGHT MIST hanging on the face of the wide river, obscuring the dank forests on the farther, western shore, when they woke the next morning. A watery sun hung among citron clouds, giving a little heat in the shivering dawn.

They pushed the raft off and floated southward, none of them even glancing back at the desolate scene of the previous night's slaughter.

Chapter Six

LORI QUINT RECOVERED WELL from the horror of the attack by the stickies. There was some scabbing and peeling of skin around her mouth from the pressure of the suckered fingers, but it was already healing. She and Doc were happy to be together at the rear of the ungainly craft, handling the long steering oar that kept them moving roughly in the center of the current.

It was a beautiful day. The early morning mist had faded away like the dew on a summer meadow.

Ryan had ridden rivers before, but most of them had been fast-flowing, broken with turbulent rapids, places where a moment's relaxation could mean an instant chilling. The Hudson was different. Most of the time it was several hundred yards wide, rolling steadily toward the sea between wooded banks that showed little evidence of man.

For the first time in a long while, Ryan Cawdor actually felt he could lie back on the timbers and take it easy. The wood seemed to be drying out in the warm sun, and the craft was riding higher in the water.

"Those hills on the right used to be called the Catskills," Doc shouted, lifting his voice against the sound of the river bubbling around the raft. "Folk took vacations there."

"What were vacations, Doc?" Jak asked. The albino boy was sprawled on his back, shading his vulnerable eyes against the golden sunlight. He had peeled off both his camouflage canvas jerkin and the ragged fur vest that he wore beneath it. His skin was as white as paper, stretched tight over prominent ribs. Ryan, looking at Jak, thought at that moment that he barely looked his fourteen years, seeming more like an undernourished and skinny boy, on the threshold of his teens.

"Vacation, son?" the old man mused. "Time was folks would have laughed at you and thought you was joshing 'em."

"It's a time out from killing," J.B. said quietly, wiping spray off his spectacles.

"It's when you can be with the person you want, and go where you want and do what you want," Krysty suggested, smiling at Ryan.

"Can't do better'n that," Ryan agreed, venturing a rare smile at the girl.

"I know," Lori called. "Doc tells me. It's good time out of bad. Like a day Keeper doesn't fucking up rectum." She looked proudly at Doc, who shuffled his feet.

"Took me all this time t'stop the chit from saying something a deal worse than rectum."

Jak wasn't satisfied. "Tell us what vacation was, Doc."

"Saltwater taffy, balloons, laughter, hot dogs, ribbons and bows, gingham and lace at collar and cuffs. Smell of frying and best scent and a lot of sweat. Did I mention laughter? Believe I did. Key ingredient in any vacation, laughter. Ice cream on a stick. Fiddler in the park. Fresh-baked apple pie with a spoon of cream on top. Kids, everywhere. Taxi-dancers. Jazz bands. Linked arms along the boardwalk. Hot lips together under the boardwalk. Talking of hopes for better days. Dreams. Laughter and dreams, Jak."

The raft was silent at the litany from the long-dead, long-gone past, words that Ryan had only ever read. Doc's head dropped on his chest, and he continued to speak, softer, his voice matching the stillness of the river.

"Emily and I had but one true vacation together. My work...I couldn't... Had I but known what the future held. Ah, the future. We talked much of the future that summer's day in 'ninety-six. Rachel toddling bravely beside us, and young Jolyon on his blanket."

A flock of what looked like pigeons flew from some sycamores on the eastern bank, the sun striking the bars of vermilion on their fluttering wings. The river was in a wide sweep to the right, flowing slowly and calmly. Doc's voice became even quieter.

"I had friends among the Apaches of New Mexico Territory, and we visited them. They made us welcome. It was ten years to the very day that the old fox, Geronimo, surrendered to General Nelson Miles. Wonder what happened to...? Never looked after I'd been trawled on the chron-jump. Never thought to. The sun shone every day. The Apaches loved Rachel and Jolyon. Happiest time...laughter... Harriet Beecher Stowe died that summer, as I recall, and there was some news of prizes for scientists by the man who...dynamite...name's gone. Emily joked I would win one of them, one day. Oh, God, but I was never so happy as on that vacation. That's what it was, Jak," he said, turning his face away so that none of them could see the tears.

AROUND NOON they passed through the shattered remains of what must once have been a sizable ville. Doc's guess was a town called Kingston, but the effort of recalling so much of his distant past had wearied the old man, and he sat down for much of the time, trailing his bare feet over the stern, gazing at their jagged wake, locked in his own thoughts. Not even Lori could tug him back for several hours.

Ryan realized just how frail Doc Tanner's hold on reality truly was.

"LET'S PULL HER IN," Ryan said a little after two o'clock in the afternoon.

"Hours of daylight left," J.B. protested, looking up at the sky, puzzled. "No storm threatening, so why stop?"

"A vacation," Ryan said, grinning. "There's a clearing to the left there. I can see a waterfall, white over the rocks. Good defense all around. Haven't seen any muties. Let's just stop, like Doc said, and rest up. We'll start again at dawn."

"Gaia, but that's a wonderful idea, lover." Krysty sighed and ran her fingers through her mane of scarlet hair so that it rippled against her skin like a wave of fire.

It was an idyllic place.

Ryan and Jak scouted the region around the landing place while J.B. held the mooring line ready for a swift flight. But they found no trace anywhere of any human footprints. Ryan checked the radiation count, taking a reading that dropped below the orange. Everything that he'd ever heard made him certain that the entire northeast industrial area had been nuked almost out of existence, leaving the place a throbbing hot spot that for a long time actually glowed at night, according to some of the older men and women at Front Royal ville.

The water that tumbled eighty or ninety feet from the lip of an escarpment was fresh and sweet without any kind of chem taste.

There were ample deadfall branches that would make an excellent fire—one with a glowing heat but very little smoke to attract any potential enemies.

Doc lay down on the gently sloping beach of soft white sand and instantly fell asleep. Lori sat beside him, plaiting a chaplet of tiny white and golden flowers that she'd found growing in an abundant profusion near the border of the forest.

Spruce, larch, white oaks and hickories dominated the sloping hillside above the beach, with tiny red squirrels and chipmunks darting fearlessly among them, showing no fright at the appearance of the humans.

"Coming, J.B.?" Krysty asked.

"Where?"

"There," she responded, pointing toward the beckoning shade of the green forest.

"Why?"

"For the pleasure of it, J.B., like Doc said. It's a vacation for us all. Rest and relax and stop your mind running on death."

"I'm happy here, Krysty."

The Armorer was sitting cross-legged in the sand, a few yards nearer the water than Doc and Lori. He had the mini-Uzi cradled in his lap, already halfway through fieldstripping it. His glasses caught the sun, and his fedora was pushed well back on his high, sallow forehead.

"Come on," Ryan urged.

"When we chilled the stickies, I thought I heard something catching on the mechanism. Something didn't sound right. The selective fire blowback's my guess. I've got to check it out, Ryan. You know that."

"Sure. Watch the boat."

The Armorer nodded his agreement, bending happily to his task.

"Jak," Krysty called.

"Yeah. You going to walk?"

"Want to come?"

The boy was still stripped to the waist, his boots off, breeches rolled above the knee. He was paddling in the shallows of the river, one of his lethal little throwing knives poised in his right hand.

"Fishing."

"You'll never get anything with a blade," Ryan said disbelievingly.

"Want to bet?"

Ryan laughed. "I know better, kid."

"Go pick flowers, One Eye. Have some fish grilled for you when you get back."

"Sounds good." Krysty smiled and hooked her arm through Ryan's elbow. "Looks like you an' me, lover."

"Looks like it." Ryan called across to J.B., "Be back 'fore dark."

The Armorer waved a casual hand.

Close together, hips touching as they walked, Ryan and Krysty made their way into the cool, scented gloom beneath the waiting trees.

"Herb the blacksmith, back in Harmony ville, knew lotsa old songs and verses," Krysty said. "Told one 'bout a lost path through the woods. How it was gone, but it was still there for those who had the eyes to see it."

Ryan could see what had prompted her line of thought. The trees were well spaced, with daggers of golden sunlight thrusting through the top branches and dappling the floor of the forest. They could hear the light breeze as it tugged at the fresh green leaves that danced and swayed. The air tasted fresh and clean. Gradually they were leaving the rolling sound of the Hudson behind them.

They picked a path between the trunks, climbing up the slope.

"It's a beautiful day, Ryan."

"Good day for a vacation."

"Look, down there."

They stopped on a grassy knoll that thrust out between the trees, overhanging the beach, giving them a view clear across the river. From that height it shone and glittered like molten glass, barely moving. A little farther above them they could hear the thundering of the waterfall.

Far below them they could easily make out the twin shapes of Doc and Lori, lying close together on the beach, seemingly asleep.

"Oddest love match I ever saw," Ryan said. "I know he's not really two hundred and thirty years old, but he's definitely around his middle sixties. And she's still in her teens."

"You disapproving, lover?" Krysty asked teasingly.

"No. Course not. I'm pleased the old goat's so happy, and the girl couldn't have found a nicer person than Doc. Specially after that double-crazy Keeper she lived with."

"Look at J.B."

Ryan, arm held loosely around Krysty's slender waist, shaded his eye against the sunlight. The Armorer had laid his coat on the sand and was stooped over the stripped segments of his blasters, carefully wiping each one, using a tiny container of oil to grease them. J.B. was in his element, relishing the vacation in his own dedicated way.

"Jak looks like a little boy at play," Ryan observed. "Not that he ever had any kind of childhood."

The white hair blended with the sun-bright sand. As they watched, the lad flicked his wrist. There was a flash of silver from the thrown knife as it splashed into the river. Jak plunged his hand into the water, coming out with something that wriggled and glistened blue-green in his fist. As though he sensed that he was being watched, the boy whirled around, scanning the wall of the forest. He spotted the man and the woman far above him and waved the trout in triumph. Jak shouted something to them, but the words were whisked away on the soft westerly wind.

"Supper should be good, lover," Krysty whispered. "Come on, let's walk some more." She waved to Jak, and then she and Ryan stepped back out of sight of their companion on the beach.

AS THEY MADE LOVE on a bank of light green moss, shaded from the sun, Ryan kept the G-12 at his side. This place was as near to an Eden as anything he'd come across in the Deathlands. But that didn't mean that it was free from serpents.

The foaming stream that fed the waterfall was only a few yards from them, chattering over the rounded stones. A miniature wading bird, wings darted with vivid turquoise and crimson, hopped and picked its way through the water. A gold-throated woodpecker hammered away at a live oak behind them, the thin sound of its rapping beak echoing around the forest. A mutie raccoon, no more than four inches long, skittered over the fawn carpet of leaf mold, ignoring the lovemaking couple who watched it.

"Makes a change to see a mutie animal that's gotten smaller," Krysty said.

"I saw some bear tracks and what I guess is a bobcat," Ryan said. "They looked a coupla weeks old. Mebbe more."

"Gaia, but I hope you're right!" Krysty exclaimed, pretending to push Ryan off her, looking around. "A bobcat on top of me as well as you would be too much."

Ryan moaned in pleasure as the girl laughed. When he was deeply buried in her, she was able to do amazing things with her stomach muscles, lying quite still, yet somehow sucking and caressing him with rippling waves of pressure. He lowered his face to hers, kissing her gently on the lips, tasting sun and salt on her skin.

"I love you, Ryan Cawdor," Krysty whispered. The tip of her tongue danced over his lips, probing between his parted teeth. She sighed as he thrust harder against her, feeling his swelling climax racing closer. She began to pant, raggedly and urgently showing the nearness of her own release.

"Not yet, not yet, not yet," she chanted, head rolling back. The long coils of her burning hair seemed to rise, brushing Ryan's cheeks and shoulders with an odd, sentient life of their own.

"I can't . . . can't . . ."

"Soon, lover, soon . . . yes! Now, you fierce bastard, now!"

They fought to a mutual orgasm, Ryan collapsing on top of her, feeling as though the core of his soul had been sucked out from his loins. He could feel her powerful muscles, fluttering uncontrollably with the power of her own ecstasy.

"Fireblast," he exclaimed. "How d'you like them apples, lover?"

"I guess you don't get many of them to the bushel, huh?"

Ryan rolled off her, wincing at the stickiness. "Where d'you get that expression from? Not many of them to the bushel!"

Krysty grinned at him with the sleepy, contented face of a cat that's gotten the best of the cream. "Back in Harmony. Mother Sonja had a host of old sayings like that. Guess she never figured it'd be used for a real mind-blower like that."

"Guess not."

"Didn't you have sayings like that, lover? Back in your own family."

"Not that I recall."

The smile slipped away, and she saw the tension come snapping back into his face, hardening the lines around his eye and mouth.

"Ryan?"

He stood up, turning away from her. She had a moment to admire the muscular slimness of his naked body, his back, arms and legs seamed with a multitude of old scars.

"Ryan? I'm sorry I touched a nerve."

"Don't signify, lover." He moved to the edge of the water and dipped a toe in it, whistling at the cold. "Feels like meltwater."

"Going to bathe?"

"Hell, why not? Come join me."

She gasped at the shock of the icy stream as she crouched to wash herself. She leaped out suddenly, running on the cropped turf to try to get warm again. A raven, wings carrying the polished sheen of sunlight, floated over the treetops, catching her eye.

Krysty pulled on her silken bikini panties, adjusting them across her hips, easing the flimsy material from the cleft between her buttocks. She hoisted her trousers and tugged on the elegant western boots. The water had splashed her hair, and she ran her fingers through it, letting it float across her shoulders.

"Come out, lover. You'll freeze, and the cold's doing nothing for that . . ." She pointed at his shrunken genitals, giggling at him.

"It'll warm up," he said, some of the toughness easing from his face once more.

"Get dressed, Ryan. Then come and sit here by me. There's another hour or more before we need be heading back to join the others."

He got dressed, leaving his chest bare, relishing the feel of the sun on his skin. Ryan held up his brown shirt, shaking his head at the stain on it, which was nearly black.

"Poor Hennings," he said.

"Seems years past. Can't be more'n a few weeks since he bought the farm. One too many mornings . . ." Her voice trailed away.

"Mebbe we should settle on going west and try to find some of the Trader's old crew."

Krysty rested her hand on his bare shoulder, feeling the skin still chilled by the stream. "What about Virginia?"

"And the Shens?"

"Sure, lover. And the ville at Front Royal where someone's the baron . . . someone who owes you a debt."

Ryan breathed deeply so that his ribs became prominent against the skin of his chest. "It's too many years. Like you said, Krysty. A thousand miles behind. Best leave it there."

But he couldn't hide the note of doubt in his voice. The girl lay stretched out on her back, hands behind her head, looking up at the harsh planes and angles of his face.

"You aren't sure?"

"No. No, I'm not."

"Talk about it."

"You know the story. You heard it down in the swamps."

"I want to hear it from you, Ryan. Now. Your story, your words. There'll never be a better time."

Ryan folded the bloodstained shirt and placed it on the grass, then lay down at the girl's side.

Beginning to speak . . .

Chapter Seven

"PLANT A BULLET anywhere in the domain of Front Royal ville and it'd grow a blaster. That's what folks used to say. By the long winter! It was a good, rich land, Krysty. The biggest ville in all of Virginia. My father said he figured it might be the biggest in the whole of Death-lands. But I don't know 'bout that. The nukes came so thick the sky was black. But they were short half-life mis-siles, most of 'em. My great-great-grandpa took what he saw and held it fast. Great-grandpa got more. Timber and water and grazing. Cattle and horses. Even a few hogs. Deep in the Shens there was sheltered hollows where the rad didn't reach. Great-Grandpa Ryan built and stole and killed and kept."

"You were named after him?" Krysty asked, not wanting to interrupt the flow of words from the man at her side. She felt that he wanted to talk it out, and like she'd said, now was the time and the place for it.

"Surely was. He had chill-cred, did Great-Grandpa Ryan. His son just held what there was. By then, around the mid of the century, there was some trouble from the Walkers and the Takers."

Krysty nodded. "Heard my Uncle Tyas McCann speak of them. Said they was the descendants of the Levelers and the Diggers."

"Never heard nothing 'bout them."

"Go on, lover." She reached out to touch his left hand and felt a reassuring squeeze from Ryan.

"My father took it over around 2050. By then the power was established. There was a rising of the workers on the west side of the ville. Wanted rights to the land they worked. Father put it down. Lots of dead, gibbets on every hill from Nineveh to Oak Ridge."

It had been a dreadful, awesome sight that struck fear into the hearts of every man, woman and child who worked for the Front Royal ville. The bodies hung there, tied with waxed cobbler's twine that didn't rot. The birds picked at the soft tissues of the faces first. The eyes and the lips went, then the cheeks and the tender flesh around the neck. As the slashing wind and rain tore the thin clothes away from the corpses, more of the weathered meat was revealed for the crows and the ravens to feast on.

Baron Titus Cawdor was a tall, broad-shouldered man with fierce eyes and a ready temper. He married the daughter of the baron of a neighboring ville, joining the families. He took over the other ville when his wife's father—an excellent horseman—died in a mysterious riding accident. His wife, Lady Cynthia, was never physically strong, and after the birth of the third child—all boys—she sank into a decline and a wasting sickness, accompanied by a bloody flux that carried her off less than a year later. She was buried in the marble Cawdor family mausoleum.

Morgan Cawdor was the firstborn of the baron's sons. Tall and as straight as a tree, he was everything that his father wished for. He could outride, run, wrestle, shoot or swim any of his fellows. He was kind where his father was cruel, considerate where the baron was a thin-lipped autocrat. Morgan took care to watch over his youngest brother, Ryan, protecting him from any danger.

And the main danger was the second of the Cawdor sons.

Harvey Cawdor.

"Harvey," Ryan said, his voice cold and far away. "Two years younger than Morgan and two years older than me."

"Why didn't your father do something to check him?" Krysty asked.

"Harvey was my bane. He was wicked. Fireblast! But such a bitter, evil bastard!"

Harvey Cawdor was everything that his older brother was not and lacked every one of Morgan's virtues. His sole strength was an overweening ambition, coupled to an iron will to garner what he believed to be his right. His mind was warped and twisted, dwelling in dark corridors that were rank with the lust for power.

"They told me that his birthing ruined him. He was breeched, they said. One leg trailed, like this . . . and his shoulder was hunched and crook'd up."

Ryan limped around the clearing, his right leg dragging a deep furrow, gouged from the soft green moss. His right arm was lifted, and twisted, giving him the lopsided walk of a hunchback. Krysty watched him, face solemn.

"I recall an old tape we had in Harmony. An actor from Europe. The paper was torn and the name was gone, but there was a picture on the label of a warped, bent man, long black hair, and a chain of gold. It was a play about a baron from olden times. Most had been wiped by the pulse. But the start was left."

Ryan dropped his shoulder, sighing as he sat down once more by Krysty's side. "Was this baron like Harvey? Blood-eyed bastard?"

"Uncle Tyas McCann knew the play. He said this baron killed old men and children and married the wife of one of the men he killed. How he could smile and smile and still be a villain."

"Harvey smiled like that. If'n he could find some puppy to blind or a kitten to drown and save and drown again, that was when he smiled a whole lot. I learned early, Krysty, that when brother Harvey smiled it was time for little Ryan to get the fuck out of his way."

The sound of the waterfall seemed to be changing, matching the somber mood of Ryan's tale. It no longer chuckled brightly over the stones. Now it seemed to whisper and mutter of dark plots and inductions dangerous. The afternoon was becoming colder.

Krysty shivered.

"What is it, lover? Want to go back to the others? I can smell woodsmoke. Jak must be getting his fish ready."

"I'm okay, Ryan. Go on."

"What happened to this crookback baron?" he asked.

"Got chilled."

Ryan nodded. "Yeah. Be good if... Where was I?"

"Morgan and Harvey."

She noticed that twice already, unconsciously, Ryan's right hand had reached and touched the scar that seamed the side of his face, jagged from eye to mouth.

"Morgan and Harvey," he repeated. "Morgan always tried to guard his back. Tried to warn our father against Harvey, but his mind was poisoned already and he refused to believe anything bad about him. One day Morgan went out in his hunting wag, with only one servant. It was found bombed out. Stickies did it. But they found boot tracks afterward."

"And stickies don't wear..."

"...boots. Right. The body was torn apart by the explosion. Not enough left to fill the long wooden box. I went and peeked. They put dirt in, Krysty, to make the weight. Dirt, for my fucking brother!''

''Ryan, love, if you don't—''

''No!'' he almost shouted. ''No. I've got to talk this out with someone. Never had anyone before I could tell. If we go back there...to Front Royal, I want you to know everything about it.''

''Go on.''

''I tried to tell Father. But he was old, shaken by what was happening. He wouldn't listen. But Harvey heard what I'd been saying and marked me for an early grave.''

''' 'So wise, so young, will ne'er live long, it's said.' That's from that play. Was your brother married then?''

''Morgan? Yes. Guenema was her name. A strange mutie girl. Eyes like jet. I liked her. I...I suppose I loved her. I was fourteen. Jak's age.''

''What happened to her?''

''She disappeared. Nobody would talk about it. A great wall of fucking silence! They said she was carrying a child and she lived out in Deathlands. But...I doubt it. Harvey would have set his dogs on her trail.''

For a few moments there was silence between them, broken only by the hurtling water as it rushed over the lip of the falls. Krysty leaned back on an elbow, glancing behind them, noticing, at the edge of the trees beyond the clearing, a small cluster of jack-in-the-pulpits, the white spikes bravely erect in the green cup.

Harvey had made his play the day after Ryan's fifteenth birthday. Using bribed and terrified servants he arranged for Ryan's evening meal to be drugged. Then he and half a dozen of the ville's sec men planned to take the sleeping boy. The body would then be weighted and dropped into the moat that circled the main house of Front Royal.

"Not all the servants were in Harvey's pay, and not all loved him. An old armorer called Kenny Morse caught wind of the plan from a kitchen maid. I didn't take the food, and I was ready for them."

Even before Morgan's murder Ryan Cawdor had begun to try to safeguard himself. Kenny Morse had stolen an old .45 Colt from the castle armory for him. Ryan cleaned and oiled it, and spent hours practicing until he could use it with expertise. He was instructed by the diminutive Morse, who risked at best a beating from the baron for breaking his orders that his youngest son was not to have a blaster.

That night Ryan was ready.

"I waited just inside the door of my room. A narrow crack showed me the corridor. It was gloomy. On his way out Morse had removed two of the light bulbs from their sockets. The ville had vast supplies of gas and generators for power. It was midnight when Harvey and his butchers came for me."

The first two shots, booming out of the darkness, killed two of the sec men, warning Harvey and the others that their plan had failed and that Ryan was no lamb, waiting patiently for the slaughterer. The men went crashing back, blood springing from chest and throat, soaking through their trim uniforms.

Knowing that he must now take the offensive, Ryan jumped out, gun braced in both hands, firing twice at the nearest guard. The first round from the old blaster ripped through the upper arm as the man dived sideways, the second hitting him through the side of the face, taking away half of the back of his skull with the force of the impact.

Harvey snapped off two shots with his laser pistol, tracer bullets scything through the blackness and exploding off the wall by Ryan's left shoulder.

"I called him the bastard killer he was. Screamed it, my voice breaking. I was so fucking angry that I'd have torn his face off his skull if'n I could have reached him. Another sec man was flat on the floor, blocking off the exit to the stairs. He was hiding behind the corpse of the second man I'd chilled." Ryan's voice dropped in remembrance of the charnel house scene of death and blood. "His arms and legs were still twitching and jerking."

There was a burst of shooting from a battered Czech machine pistol, but Ryan was moving again, dodging back toward the open door of his turret bedroom. He snapped off another round, the shot flying high, screaming into the black pool of shadow at the top of the narrow staircase. The second round from the Colt caught the guard through the open mouth as he raised his head, peering to see where the boy had gone. It splintered his teeth and angled upward, burying itself in the brain, through the roof of the mouth.

"Harvey shouted to me, then. He'd seen the blaster and knew it held seven rounds. He yelped out that he knew I only had one left."

"What'd you say?"

"Told him I had a spare mag. Didn't, though. Morse only stole one mag for me. I'd fired six and had one left. The fucker was right."

Krysty looked across at the blank, emotionless face of the man she loved. "No other way out? No other door? No window?"

"Fifty feet on stone. Courtyard under the window. You gotta realize, Krysty, that this ville was built way back 'fore the long winter. Based on some kind of old castle.

Harvey would have some more sec men there, faster than goose shit off a shovel. There was only one way out—past my big brother.''

Ryan Cawdor was never a person, even at fifteen years of age, to hesitate when what was needed was instant action.

"I dived out and rolled. Lot of lead came my way, blowing chunks of rock off of the walls. I squeezed my last shot at Harvey, but he was hunkered down and it went high. Had me a real good knife. Fireblast! But I lost it in a firefight close by what used to be Kansas City.''

The dagger was made with the hoof of a stag for a hilt, and it fitted the palm of the hand like it had been made for it.

"I jumped the dead and the dying. They all figured I must have more ammo, or I was fucking crazy. My brother called me a bastard, and I called him a butcher. They were the last words we spoke.''

Harvey was taller and stronger than his younger brother, and he clawed out at him. He drew Ryan close, fingers digging into his flesh. The fifteen-year-old suddenly felt a streak of icy fire across his ribs, and Harvey laughed, breath rank in his face. The knife cut was long and painful, but not deep. The laughter ceased as Ryan managed to bring his own blade into play, slicing into Harvey's upper arm, making him squeal in shock and pain.

"Another moment and I'd have butchered the gimp where he stood,'' Ryan spit, fingers clenching as he relived the moments in that long corridor. "But there was another sec man there, and he came from behind and pulled me away.''

Krysty could catch the faint scent of fish roasting on the beach far below them. But she ignored it, wanting Ryan to finish the bleak tale—to finish it and to exorcise it from his mind.

"I chilled the guard with one thrust to the heart. I felt...a moment of being sorry. His name was George Cross. A good man but... He fell all in a piece, dead before his body hit the stone flags of the passage. But he delayed me for the second that cost me this," Ryan said, touching the patch over his left eye. "And fucking nearly killed me."

As he half turned, Ryan had seen Harvey lunging toward his face, his own eyes exultant with a feral grin of triumph. The younger boy had tried to parry the knife thrust, but was too slow.

"I saw it, Krysty! Saw the knife. I can see it to this day if I close my eye, see the point of his dagger, like a needle tipped with fire. It came direct into my eye." He stopped and turned away from her, looking across the valley toward the sinking ball of the orange sun.

The knife had been well aimed. It slashed into the left eye so that the young Ryan Cawdor could *hear* the steel grating against the bone of the socket.

"No pain. Not a single bit of pain. It felt like hot water on my cheek, where the eye had burst open. No blood. Only a spot or two of blood. I nearly dropped my knife. Or it fell and I snatched it up...I don't remember which. Harvey slashed at me again, went for my other eye. He missed by...you can see for yourself. Opened up half my face like a butcher with a lamb's carcass. Then I bled. Fireblast! But I surely bled then, lover."

Half-blind, terrified and in dreadful pain from the gash across his face, Ryan Cawdor lashed out at the smirking, triumphant face of his crippled brother. He dealt him a lucky punch in the middle of his hooked nose and felt it crumple under the blow like a crushed egg.

"I ran. Down and up and along passages. I was near death from the loss of blood, blinded. Someone helped me. Kenny Morse? I don't know. Suddenly I was out of the house and across the moat. There was snow on my face, melting and running with the seeping crimson all over my neck and shirt. A howling wind blew through the pines on the far side of the valley away from the ville. And I was gone. Fifteen years old and I never went back. Never thought about going back. Not until now." He sat up and pulled on his shirt and coat. The evening chill was rising from the Hudson, and the sun had nearly gone down. "I can smell fish cooking."

"Want to go back? Go 'fore dark?"

"Yeah."

"Help me up, lover. Thanks. What happened back at Front Royal after you'd fled the place? That double-crazy Bochco said your father married again. And what about Harvey?"

"Not much to tell. Haven't heard much fresh until down in the swamps there."

There had been a purge. Harvey had convinced the ailing Baron Cawdor that his youngest son was a murderous renegade and he was named wolfshead so that every man's hand was against him. Several servants believed loyal to Ryan and to Morgan's memory were executed on the old gibbets. Kenny Morse was the first to go, shrieking defiance as his feet were kicked off the stool and he danced in the air.

Pecker Bochco had told them about the cobbles of the courtyard flowing inches deep in sticky blood that clotted and blocked the drains of the entire ville. He had also told Ryan and Krysty about the new Lady Cawdor.

She was a sluttish whore who had been used by Harvey, but whose strength of will and capacity for evil outstripped the halting young man. She seduced Baron Cawdor, persuading the old man of her love for him. Ryan's father, by now, was slipping fast into dementia, finding it hard to tell fact from dream.

Lady Rachel Cawdor was plump and beautiful and just eighteen years old. She fed opiates to the old man so that he slept, then ran light-footed along the winding corridors to the bedroom of Harvey Cawdor.

They found that Ryan's father was more tenacious than they'd expected. He didn't die, despite being poorly fed and treated harshly by the girl-bride. Harvey drew back from butchering the frail old man, but his mistress did not.

One night, under the guise of playing a game of love, she cajoled the baron into letting her tie his hands and feet to the corners of their great four-poster, using cords of silk. She whispered, as she pulled the knots tighter, of the pleasures she would give him once he was her helpless slave. The silk was as thin as cotton, yet as strong as wire, and had been tied so tight that it bit into his wrinkled skin and drew blood from beneath his blackened nails.

Baron Cawdor tried to call out, realizing at that last awful moment that her intention was murder. But Rachel laughed at him, mocking him, even as she knotted a gag around his mouth, muffling his cries for aid.

She told him of her contempt for him as she climbed, naked, astride his chest, gripping him with her heels as though he were a horse. She told him of her lust for his son and of their vile and perverse pleasures together. As she leaned over him her breasts brushed his cheeks, her nipples swollen with her ruthless enjoyment of what she was doing to him. Rachel picked up a large satin pillow, holding it as she wriggled up his body.

Rachel placed the pillow tenderly over his face, leaning all her weight on top of it, whispering as she did so of how Harvey had murdered Morgan and how he had planned to kill Ryan, but the brat had escaped.

She felt the struggles against the suffocating pressure becoming weaker until, with a final jerking convulsion, Baron Titus Cawdor went to join his ancestors.

RYAN AND KRYSTY picked their way down the twisting path through the woods, taking care as the light was fading fast.

"And they have a son?"

Ryan nodded. "That's what I heard. Jabez Pendragon Cawdor. Must be around the same sort of age as Whitey down there."

Krysty sniffed the air. "Gaia, but that fish makes my mouth water! You feeling hungry now, lover? After all your exercise?"

Ryan checked in midstride, turning to look at her, his face a pale blur in the half-light. The patch over his ruined eye seemed blacker than it usually did. He reached out and took Krysty by the hand.

"I'm sure."

"What? That you're hungry?"

Ryan didn't smile. "No."

"What, then?"

"That crazy old bastard Bochco. I've been thinking on the last thing he said."

"What was that?"

Ryan's voice was so quiet that the pounding waterfall nearly drowned it out. Even with her mutie hearing, Krysty could barely hear him.

"The crow shits where the eagle should roost. Return and claim what should be yours."

"I remember."

"It was a scar that had been healed, I thought, for twenty years. Now I know that I was wrong. Now I know where I'm going."

"Where?" But she knew.

"I'm going home, lover. Home."

They walked back to the beach and rejoined the others.

Chapter Eight

DOC TANNER WAS STRAINING at his memory. "Front Royal's in Virginia. There used to be a saying."

"What?" Lori asked.

"Something about the state. They said it in the nineties. Nineteens, not eighteens."

Jak Lauren was leaning against the short trunk of the mast, listening to the old man. "What did they say, Doc?"

"Ah, yes." Confidently he said, "Virginia is for..." Then he lost the thread. "Virginia is for...for... I don't rightly recall."

Jak grinned. "Guess must have been Virginia is for killers."

Doc nodded. "Quite possibly, my white-haired young companion. Quite possibly."

Ryan had told them over the supper of fresh trout that he was determined to go on to Virginia.

"Chill brother?" Jak asked.

"Just might," Ryan replied.

"See your home. I liked that," Lori said, recovered now from the blow to her head.

Doc Tanner smiled at the news. "Sibling rivalry was always an overwhelming motivation, was it not, my dear Ryan?"

Ryan nodded, even though he had no idea what the old man was talking about.

Only J.B. didn't say anything, busying himself with picking bits of fish from between his back teeth with a long, narrow bone. His eyes behind the round lenses of his spectacles gave nothing away.

"You don't seem surprised," Ryan said. "I know I sort of said I would before. But this is for real. I'll go. Even if I go on my own, I'm going back to see my brother."

"Hell, I knew that all along," J.B. said.

DURING THE NEXT DAY, the Hudson River flowed ever more slowly and became wider, the banks shelving away a good quarter mile. As they rolled gently toward the sea, they saw more and more evidence of the devastation wrought by the century-old nuking of the northeast.

They passed the weed-softened remains of what Doc swore must have been a town he called Poughkeepsie. Jak Lauren, for some reason, found that name hilariously amusing, and he rolled around on the damp timbers, holding his sides, laughing uncontrollably. His merriment was contagious, and everyone on the raft began to laugh with him. Even J.B. cracked his cheeks at the sound of the name.

Doc cackled like a rusty hinge. "Guess it always was a funny name."

About four hours later they found themselves drifting toward the wreck of what had once been a gigantic bridge. Ryan spotted it first.

He was standing on the right side of the unwieldy craft, urinating to leeward, shielding himself from the others as best he could. On the raft there was no time or space for any of the niceties of hygiene. As he pissed, it was carried away in a great amber arc, splashing into the flat surface of the river.

"Look at that!" he shouted.

Krysty glanced at him. "Terrific, lover. But what'll you do for an encore?"

"You're envious. But that's—"

"Envious! Ryan Cawdor, you've got—" She broke off, seeing he was pointing around the long bend of the Hudson, far ahead of them.

The river narrowed a little, breaking over the massive piles of the bridge. Rusting girders dangled high above, with a network of thick metal rods holding crumbling chunks of stone.

A bent piece of metal, which looked as if it might once have been painted green, had the remains of some white lettering on it. Whi e Pl ins was all that could be read.

It took all their strength, using the crudely cut branches, to steer the raft around the obstacles. They pushed at the stone piers and shoved away from the maze of fallen metal where the water pitched and foamed, creating strong eddies and currents.

Once they were past the toppled bridge, they were able to relax once more, allowing the slow-moving river to carry them along. Krysty stood at the front of the raft, balancing herself easily against the rhythmic pitching and rolling.

"Doc?"

"What is it?"

The wind tugged at her long hair so that it wrapped itself around her face. She paused, freeing herself, before she spoke again.

"I heard that these parts were filled with people before the big chilling."

"That's so, my dear. Thicker than bugs on a bumper was a current expression. Why do you ask now?" Almost immediately the old man answered his own question. "Ah. Because there is so little sign of human habitation on either bank of the Hudson. Is that not what prompted your question?''

"Yeah. That bridge...and a few ruins on the cliffs. That's 'bout all we've seen for hours. No people. Not since the stickies.''

Doc clambered to his feet, helped by a steadying hand from Lori. His knee joints cracked like miniature blasters. He rested an arm across Krysty's shoulders, gazing rheumily at both sides of the river.

"You cannot possibly imagine the devastation wrought here. Nor, fortunately, can I. If one could have seen the megadeath scenario, then one would have gone stark mad upon the instant.''

For the last mile or so, perched high on the cliffs to the east, they had been able to see a few ruined buildings. They were eyeless wrecks, almost covered by the encroaching vegetation. Most were roofless, walls bleached to an unhealthy white by a hundred years of chem storms. One or two still showed traces of blackening and scorch marks along the upper edges of many of the empty windows.

Ryan joined Doc and Krysty and they glanced behind them, over the high ground to the west of the Hudson. The sun was already out of sight, and dark purple clouds were boiling up, showing the menace of ugly thunderheads at their crests.

"Time to put in for the night. How far from Newyork, Doc?''

"From that sky, there is menace from the west. Perchance we should find shelter. I cannot recall the lie of the land hereabouts, Ryan, but I think we must be closing in on the metropolis. Yonkers is a name that seeps into my mind, though what it was I cannot recall.''

"What 'bout Newyork?" called Jak, who had been dozing near the stern.

Doc hesitated before replying. "The wreckage from that toll bridge back yonder could have overturned our frail barque. The farther south we go along the Hudson, the more problems we shall encounter of that type. Before we reach New York we may need to desert the water for the land."

J.B. also stood up, pushing his fedora back. "Maps show us around fifty miles to go. How far from there to Front Royal? You know, Ryan?"

"Always heard as a kid that Newyork was close to two fifty from the ville."

The Armorer whistled softly, barely audible over the murmur of water bubbling around the front of the raft. "Two fifty. Need us a wag to get there. Never make that distance on foot."

Ryan nodded. It was true. A small party of six people, however well armed and brave, would stand no chance at all in the Deathlands covering a great distance without transport. The Trader had traveled in a convoy of armored war wags, and even then they'd been ambushed and taken losses.

"I'm like to get off this boat," Lori said, screwing up her face like a petulant child, which made everyone laugh at her.

"Let's head in. There's a kind of lagoon ahead on the right. Looks like the whole bank got blasted in. Rad count still shows th'edge of orange. Must have been hotter than fireblast around here."

Doc sighed. "Too true, my dear Mr. Cawdor. Armageddon day must have taken the lives of half the good people around here within ten minutes of the first bomb. Half the survivors within forty-eight hours from injuries and wounds. Then, of every thousand men, women and children still breathing, perhaps one or two might live beyond the next three months.''

"Nuke winter took lots, Uncle Tyas McCann told me," Krysty said.

"Indeed. Projections for that were not, I think, accurate. Many scientists said it would be winter for twenty years. After the bombs finished falling and there was a quiet between heaven and earth, the night and darkness and cold came. But within five years I think our climate was back to normal.''

"It's still not like it was," Ryan said. "Chem storms. Acid rain down south that can take the skin off a man in five minutes. Still places it hasn't rained in fifty years. That's normal?''

"Touché, my dear man. No, things were tipped too far for it ever to be what it was. But it is now as good as it will ever become.''

The six of them slowly steered their raft toward the bank. Jak, splashed in the face by Krysty, licked the spray. "Real salt now.''

"Hudson's tidal here," Doc said.

The raft grounded in shallow water, fifty feet or so from the bank.

By the time they'd managed to haul and wrestle the ungainly craft nearer to the bank, the threatening storm had closed in from the west. Thunder rumbled over the hills beyond the river, and jagged forks of lightning punched across the livid sky.

"Tie it up good and safe, Jak," Ryan called, having to raise his voice above the noise of the racing storm. "Lotta rain upriver, and she could rise and rip the raft away.''

"Best find shelter quick," J.B. urged. "Seen some buildings uphill a ways.''

Cedars, balsams and cottonwoods were mixed together on the gently sloping ground, with animal trails winding between them. The light was poor, but Ryan could make out that the spoor was mainly deer, overlaying something that might have been wolf.

Each of the six carried a backpack. Doc stooped beneath the weight of his, looking tired. The incessant rocking and pitching of the roughly bound logs over the past two days was enough to drain anyone's strength.

Ryan led the way through a bright patch of red-orange flame azaleas, picking his way between the nodding shrubs, ducking beneath some of their twelve-foot-high flowers.

"Where did you...? Ah, I can see it, J.B. Below the ridge there."

Ryan recognized the setup. There had been a house dug into the side of the hill, with enormously thick concrete foundations. Below it, facing the indistinct remains of a narrow road, had been a double garage with up-and-over doors. The nukes had totally removed the house, slicing off the top of the slope behind it like a gigantic cleaver. But the garage remained, set deep like a rectangular cave. Over the years, earth had fallen and been washed down around it, building up gray deposits where shrubs had rooted and even trees now grew. The actual garage was nearly filled with windblown leaves.

"Home, sweet is home," Lori said, dropping her pack and squatting down on her haunches. "Keeper says that."

"Good defense sightlines," J.B. observed, sizing the place up. "Mudslide there left a narrow entrance. One person can guard it easy and watch down the hill. Get a fire going near the mouth of the garage. Yeah, Ryan, it looks good."

THE FIRE SMOLDERED and smoked at first with the dampness of the wood they dragged in. The leaves inside were so dry that they flared and sparked like tinder, but they wouldn't sustain a flame properly. Eventually, though, Jak persuaded the fire to brighten, and it cast its glowing light all around the cavernous building.

Doc and Lori swept the leaves together, brushing them with their hands and feet into a neat pile at the rear of the building. On the back wall, high up, they found a long shelf, hanging precariously by rusting iron brackets. There were a couple of plastic containers containing oxidized nails, screws and clips. Lori found a cup and wiped it clean, then asked Doc to read the bright green lettering on its side.

"It says 'I Rode Colossus,' whatever that means. The little picture looks like some sort of roller coaster," Doc said, adding hastily, "and don't ask me what that means, either, dear child."

The six friends had only been inside the underground garage for about ten minutes when the threatening storm arrived on their bank of the Hudson.

There was a dazzling ripple of lightning, stabbing through the darkness, accompanied by a truly deafening crash of thunder. The sound was so loud that it seemed to echo inside their heads for several seconds afterward. More lightning followed, almost continuous, so that their own shadows danced, knife-edged, on the side wall of their refuge.

"Likely there'll be rain," J.B. said, peering out into the night. "Good job the raft's well moored. Going to be a bad one."

"Best open the self-heats," Ryan suggested. "How many cans we got?"

The Armorer had the most at five, and Lori the least at two.

"Need some real food," Lori said, sitting by the fire. "Saw deer tracks."

Which reminded Ryan of the other spoor he thought he'd noticed as they hurried up the hill toward the garage. The G-12 in his right hand, he walked casually toward the low entrance, squinting around the earthslide that blocked off the outside. There was another rumble of thunder, very close, and vivid lightning, tinged purple. He could hear the hissing and pattering as the first drops of rain began to fall on the ruined path.

Ryan stared for several seconds, lips peeling back off his lips in a silent whistle. He turned to the others inside. "Hey! We got company."

Chapter Nine

THE NOTE OF WARNING in Ryan's voice was enough to bring the others to his side, every one holding a cocked blaster.

"What is it?" Krysty asked, the first one to join him.

"Look for yourself."

The girl took a cautious half step forward, bending so that she could see out under the lip of the roof where the garage doors had once hung.

"Gaia!" she exclaimed, straightening up. A fierce flash of lightning broke outside, making her green eyes glitter with a vulpine glow.

The others took advantage of more lightning to stare outside for themselves, seeing the company that Ryan had mentioned.

"They lovely," Lori squeaked. "But they get wet and cold."

Ryan's only guess was that "they" were some sort of mutie bears. Most of the dangerous creatures around the Deathlands had mutated upward, or sideways, growing larger or more dangerous. But there were exceptions to that.

There were more than a dozen of the little creatures, sitting in a patient row in the teeming downpour, big round eyes fixed on the humans who had taken over their den. They looked about eighteen inches tall, with round potbellies. Their fur was a pale orange, like desert sand,

and it clung to them, matted and sodden with the force of the chem storm. Their ears were pricked up in sharp points, and their stubby front paws were folded across their chests. None of them made a sound.

Ryan glanced all around, peering out both sides in case there were any other, more threatening creatures waiting beyond their refuge. But the rain brought visibility down to about thirty short paces.

The thunder was incessant, pounding at the brain, making coherent thought difficult. Ryan put down his Heckler & Koch, slipping his right hand onto the butt of the SIG-Sauer pistol.

"Where d'you...?" Krysty began.

"Can't leave 'em out there," he replied. "See if'n I can..."

The rest of the sentence was lost in the rumble of the storm. Lightning was constant, making the night seem like it was floodlit. Ryan took a couple of cautious steps out of the garage, keeping his eyes fixed on the nearest of the little furry animals. He held out his left hand in a gesture he hoped would assure them of his kind intentions.

The big brown eyes followed every movement, growing wider and wider until it looked as if they might pop right out of their sockets. Not one of the animals moved as Ryan drew closer.

"Come on, come on," he muttered. The rain was ferocious, lashing in from over the river valley, tearing at his face like thousands of fine wires. Ryan licked his lips, suddenly concerned that this might be an acid rain that would blister and peel his skin. Apart from a hint of salt, it tasted normal. His hair was quickly plastered to his skull, making his face seem leaner and more brutal. It trickled down inside the eye patch, and he shook his head to clear it.

The nearest of the mutated creatures was only five paces away from him. Though they were trembling, the fur quivering, they didn't seem particularly frightened of the advancing man.

Ryan's boots slopped in the loose mud that washed down from higher up the side of the wooded hill.

"Come here, out of the cold," he whispered, bending and reaching out. His fingers touching the wet pelt, feeling its amazing softness. The animal made a thin, mewing sound, but it didn't try to escape, and allowed the man to pick it up.

One by one he brought them into the relative warmth of the cavern. Eleven in all. They were placed gently in front of the glowing fire to dry out. The little animals didn't try to struggle or run away, sitting where they were put, their round heads turning slowly and wonderingly to gaze at the six people. They seemed particularly fascinated by Krysty Wroth's flaming red hair.

Ryan dried himself off, his shirt and pants steaming as he stood close to the warm fire. Lori picked up one of the creatures and cuddled it on her lap, whispering to it. The animal's tiny paws touched her gently on the arm, and its eyes rolled wider and wider.

"Lovely and soft and such fat little guts," she said.

"Fucking cute," Jak said, grinning broadly at the row of animals, perched together, solemn-faced, like hairy, portly monks.

"Yeah," Ryan said. "They dried out yet?"

Krysty stooped and touched one, stroking her fingers across the long fur. "Seems dry to me, Ryan. You ready for this?"

After they'd slit the throats of the cuddly little bears, they skinned them and roasted them over the fire.

The little creatures made real good eating.

Chapter Ten

DOC TANNER BELCHED and rubbed his stomach. "I beg your pardon. Considering how small those little furry bastards were, they had meat as tough as buffalo." He sat down on the beach, tugging at his right boot. He took it off and shook a handful of grit out of it, then pulled the cracked knee boot back on. The wind had risen, and it snatched his stovepipe hat off, sending it rolling along the sand at a fine pace.

"Why not let it be gone?" Lori asked. "It was old and smelling."

"You think so, my dear dove of the north?"

"Sure."

The others watched, amused, as Doc rose to his feet and set off after the hat, proceeding like a stately galleon under full sail. His coat, an uneasy mix of gray, brown and black furs, billowed about his shrunken shanks. His tangled hair skittered across his narrow shoulders.

"Is he really going to dump that hat?" Krysty asked. "I'll believe it when I see it."

"Must be two hundred years old, that hat," J.B. said.

"Like throwing away part of history," Ryan added.

"Get another easy. Look him go," Jak said, grinning.

The wind was teasing Doc, allowing him to get almost within reach of the black hat, then flipping it away so that it rolled on its battered brim, always just below his grasping fingers.

"Go, Doc!" Lori yelled, jumping up and down with excitement.

The hat spun into the lapping edge of the Hudson, subsiding, giving up its flight and allowing Doc Tanner to pluck it. The old man stood there for some moments in silent contemplation, holding the hat and turning it around and around, slowly, head bowed over it.

"He's saying goodbye," Krysty guessed.

All of them stopped what they were doing. Jak was beginning to untie the mooring rope. The river had risen a foot or more during the night, but the raft was still held securely. J.B. was putting the backpacks on the raft.

"Adieu, old companion!" Doc shouted, his voice loud and clear. Taking the stovepipe hat by the rim and running a hand caressingly over the dent in its crown, he spun it far out into the main stream of the Hudson, where it settled like a wing-broke raven, floating the right way up. The river took it, revolving in a stately manner, carrying it away, downstream to the south. They all watched it until it was only a small black blur against the deep blue-green of the water.

As Doc rejoined them, the other five gave him a round of applause and three rousing cheers. Doc's cheeks cracked into a broad smile, showing his strong white teeth. He bowed in an old-fashioned, elegant manner.

"My dear, dear friends. How can I thank you for your generous reception of my cathartic act. That hat was too much a symbol of my past. My long, long past. And now I look forward." He paused. "When I remember to, that is."

HORDES OF PALE LILAC ASTERS thronged the sides of the river as they drifted south. The water was still as clear as crystal glass, and filled with fish of all shapes and sizes.

But after their feast on the small bears the previous night, none of the six felt hungry enough to try to catch any.

"Must be close to Newyork," Ryan said to Doc. "Light'll be going soon. It's so wide here that we might have problems getting a place for the night. And the city's rubble's supposed to be double-bad. So they used to say."

"I heard that in Mocsin," the elderly scientist said. "The sec boss . . ." He shuddered.

Ryan pursed his lips in a silent whistle. "I know him. Strasser. Fireblast, but he was a bastard fitted for six feet of mold."

He remembered the man well. It had been when he'd first met up with Doc Tanner. Strasser had been the sec boss in the ville of Mocsin. The ville of Jordan Teague, the baron. Strasser had always worn black, head to toe, and had a fringe of hair around a shaved skull. Thin was the word for Strasser. Thin body, thin face, thin eyes and lips. Lips that Ryan Cawdor had smashed to bloody pulp with a thrown blaster.

"He talked about New York. He'd been there. Traded there. Drugs and children. He said they were all ghouls, cannibals, night crawlers, blood tasters, dark watchers, death lovers."

"From what I hear, Strasser was right for once," J.B. said.

They passed another ruined bridge, its eastern section more or less complete. The shattered remnants of an old passenger wag hung poised on the brink, stuck there since the missiles had burned its driver to a crisp a century earlier. One day the rest of the bridge would rot through and the automobile would plummet down with it into the ever-patient Hudson.

A few minutes farther on the river narrowed down from more than two miles across to less than one. On their right the banks rose high in a series of wooded bluffs that Doc said he thought had once been called the Palisades of New Jersey.

Now, at last, on the left, the six companions began to witness the silent, twisted horror of total urban destruction.

No trees grew on the eastern bank of the Hudson, other than the occasional stunted ash or sycamore. Ryan's rad counter began to cheep softly, the needle creeping inexorably through the orange and holding not far from the red that showed a dangerous hot spot.

The old Cross-Bronx Expressway vanished behind them, swallowed up in the pale gray mist that came drifting in from behind the bluffs. It wasn't possible to make out anything still standing that even vaguely resembled a building. It was a rolling, melted sludge of concrete wilderness. Nothing remained higher than a tall man in that part of what had been the Bronx.

They could only see two kinds of botanical life amid the ruins: banks of nodding magenta fireweed, rising here and there far above the blasted sections of houses, shops and offices, and an ugly, rank weed—a sickly green color with a tough stem that twined around itself as though it sought suicide by strangulation. As the raft drifted toward the eastern shore, they could see more clearly. The weeds had serried bristles, like the skin of a hog, and they bore seedheads that were circular, letting poisonous yellow spores drift to the earth like malignant paratroopers.

"Earth Mother save us all," Krysty whispered, face blanched with the horror of the vanished city. "Is nothing left?"

"Might be some of the big blocks standing. Central Manhattan was zapped, but a few scrapers were mebbe big enough. I seen vids of them, and they couldn't have been leveled.'' Ryan's voice betrayed his own chilling doubt.

The desolation was so total.

Ryan thought he noticed an unnatural flurry of movement among the rancid weeds that crowded down to the very brink of the water, now only about fifty paces away from where the raft turned slowly on an eddy, moved by a long-submerged obstruction.

''Push it away!'' he called urgently, taking one of the branches himself and poling off, trying to shift back to the center of the current.

''What d'you see?'' Krysty panted, throwing all her weight against the steering oar at the stern of the raft.

''Nothing. Something. I don't know.''

''I heard something. *Heard* it. Like someone laughing. But someone who didn't have a proper mouth. Does that seem stupid?''

''No. Not down here it doesn't.''

''Let's shove off. Be dark soon,'' J.B. said. ''Fog, too.''

''Yeah. Doc says we're only 'bout twenty miles or so from open sea. Be good to make that.''

''Might be safer night,'' Jak suggested, his unruly white hair tied back with a ragged length of red ribbon that Lori had given him.

''Could be,'' the Armorer agreed. ''Map shows river gets double-narrow. Could be chilled from either bank in good light.''

''So, we keep going?'' Ryan called, and he got nods of agreement from everyone.

THE MIST BECAME THICKER, swallowing up the raft in gulps of sinuous gray damp. The long tendrils came in from their right, tasting of cold mud and still, brackish water. The fog had an unpleasant odor that seemed to linger on the tongue as you breathed.

"Where d'you figure we are now, Doc?" Ryan asked, glimpsing a teetering ruin through a sudden clearance of the darkening fog on their left.

Doc rose from where he'd been sitting with his arm around Lori. Pearls of moisture hung in his hair like a chaplet on the brow of a crazed monarch. But his voice was unusually calm and sane.

"Damnably hard to determine, Ryan. No visual clues. Around level with the north side of Central Park, perhaps? Once I sailed clear around Manhattan on a pleasure craft. The sun shone and cameras clicked and whirred. The great buildings like the Twin Towers stood proud and tall, their glass reflecting a thousand bursts of golden light. I felt like a Christian viewing the Eternal City." He stopped speaking for a moment, lost in memory. "And now, it is the valley of the shadow of death. Hobgoblins and foul fiends have inherited the place. It is all despair."

It still wasn't full dark.

The fog seemed to carry its own peculiar light, glimmering like corpse candles in a gruesome mire. The river now flowed so slowly that it was hard to detect any movement at all. Once or twice they heard the shrill metallic calling of seabirds swooping above them. But they flew on with sheathed beaks, not bothering the six travelers.

Krysty told Ryan that she thought she could hear the steady thudding of a gas-powered generator, but the mist distorted noise and she wasn't even able to tell which bank carried the sound.

At one point Ryan was certain he heard a dreadful, shrill, screaming laugh, definitely off the eastern bank, around where West Seventy-second once ran. But nobody else on the raft caught it, and he decided it must have only been his imagination.

"We still going south?" Jak asked a half hour or so later.

"Can't easily tell," Ryan replied. "I'll go to the front and watch the water."

Doc had fallen asleep, his head in Lori's lap, and Ryan stepped carefully over the old man's extended legs, nearly slipping on the treacherous logs. He lay on his right hip, face level with the leading edge of the raft, only a few inches above the dull water of the Hudson. Everyone was quiet, oppressed by the fog and the feeling of desolation all around them.

To his left, Ryan was sure he could make out a rippling noise, like the river lapping on stone. Unable to see either bank, it was impossible to have any idea of where they were in the treacherous currents as they shifted and changed.

The hand that erupted from the water and gripped his left wrist had no nails on its grotesquely long fingers, fingers that had five joints and were webbed halfway along their length. The skin was creased, hanging at the wrist in folds. The touch was cold and slippery, but as tight as a machine wrench.

The face emerging from behind the pincering hand was worse than anything from the deeps of a jolt-spawned nightmare. The jaw protruded eighteen inches beyond the gaping holes of the nostrils. There was no forehead, the naked bones of the skull angling back in pitted ridges. The ears were tiny, pinned flat to the side of the hairless head. The eyes were narrow, protected by blinking hoods of leathery tissue. Even in that insipid light, the eyes burned with a ferocious and demonic glare—less than a foot from Ryan's own eyes.

And the clashing teeth! Row upon row of them, overlapping, sharp fangs that grated on yellow stumps farther back in that wolfish thrusting jaw. The breath was fetid, like an opened grave, and it nearly choked Ryan.

The creature had come up under the bow of the raft in total silence, its attack so stealthy that none of the others had even noticed that Ryan's life was under a desperate threat.

With his left hand pinioned and lying on his right side, Ryan wasn't able to get at either the blaster or the long panga.

The mutie grabbed at the logs with its other hand, bracing itself to lunge at Ryan with its fearsome jaw. Life was a bare handful of heartbeats.

Instead of pulling back, Ryan jabbed his head toward the monstrosity, butting it on the end of the snout with his own forehead. It was a jarring blow. The grip relaxed for a moment, and Ryan was able to throw himself to his side, freeing his right hand. He clawed across for the hilt of the panga, feeling it slide free from the sheath in a whisper of death.

Jak Lauren had spotted the struggling figures and yelled to the others. But help would be too little and too late. Salvation lay in the eighteen inches of honed steel.

The teeth were slashing in at him, and Ryan punched with the heel of his hand, feeling blood gush as the jagged fangs caught the side of his wrist. But the maneuver bought him another precious second, time to swing the panga. He tensed his arm and shoulder, putting all of his power and weight into the downswing.

Instead of aiming at the dripping skull, he slashed at the lean, muscular arm as it rested across the hewn timbers of the raft.

The impact powered clean to his shoulder, and he felt the panga hack through the flesh and bone, burying itself in the wood. The tight fingers on Ryan's own wrist slackened, and he was able to roll free, tugging at the blade as he fell back.

The mutie gave a hissing, bubbling cry of pain, still trying with a manic ferocity of purpose to claw its way onto the raft. Its severed hand wriggled and jerked with an obscene life of its own. Even as Ryan looked at it, the clawing hand toppled over the edge and vanished into the Hudson.

"I've got it!" J.B. shouted, warning Ryan to drop down clear of his line of fire.

But Ryan Cawdor wasn't about to do that. The sudden appearance of the horror had startled him, had frightened him. That didn't happen very often, and the best way of shifting the memory of the chilling, paralyzing fear was to destroy the mutie with his own hands.

"Get down!" Krysty shrieked, appalled at the hideous monster that was now aboard their craft. Blood was coming from the stump of its wrist, but it oozed rather than gushed in sticky gobs of dull brown ichor.

Feeling carefully for balance on the shifting timbers, Ryan readied himself. Feinting at the creature's legs, he altered his aim and cut at the other arm. But the mutie was lightning quick, dodging so that the steel skittered off its reptilian skin, leaving a small gash in the flesh.

"Don't chill it," Ryan snapped over his shoulder. "The fucker's mine. Mine!"

Breath hissing from its snapping jaws, the mutie shuffled forward, its good hand clawing at Ryan. Once caught in that embrace, it would be too late for any of the others to save him.

Ryan ducked and slashed at the thing's legs, barely nicking it below the knee. But his thrust checked the monster's advance, giving another moment of breathing space.

"Shoot it, Ryan," Doc Tanner called in a reedy, trembling voice.

But Ryan's temper had been touched, a temper that he had fought to control most of his adult life.

"Come on you fucking lizard! Come on, you rad-mutated bastard. Come and eat this blade." He beckoned to it with his left hand, watching for some sign of reaction, but the fishlike eyes remained blank and incurious. Even the amputation of one of its hands didn't seem to have disturbed the mutie very much.

The fog was growing thicker.

The mutie slid closer, hand weaving, the elongated fingers opening and closing. Ryan flicked the heavy panga from hand to hand, feinting with the left and then the right. He was growing tired of the standoff.

"Fuck this," he snarled, picking his moment to attack.

He fended off the snapping fingers and dealt a short, savage blow that hit the mutie across the side of the head. The broad blade of the panga gouged a chunk of bone from the upper jaw and snapped off a dozen teeth. Blood seeped from the wound, and the creature staggered back, arms flailing for balance. Ryan moved carefully after it, swinging the panga in a roundhouse blow that severed the end of the snuffling jaws, leaving oozing flesh and torn teeth.

"It's going!" Lori whooped.

"One more," Ryan grated. He tried a last cut at it, but he was short and the blade hissed harmlessly a couple of inches away from the mutie's throat.

The creature seemed to fall off the front of the raft in slow motion, arms waving for balance. Its ruined jaw hung open, and a pale red slime trickled out. The eyes fixed Ryan Cawdor with a basilisk stare.

To his amazement, the creature spoke, even as it was in the act of falling. In a clear, calm voice it said, "Into the long dark."

It didn't make much of a splash as it went into the Hudson, the body vanishing under the water. Though they kept a careful watch for many minutes, none of them saw the mutie reappear.

The raft flowed slowly southward in the direction of the Atlantic Ocean.

Chapter Eleven

AROUND MIDNIGHT the fog cleared away, like a curtain drawn at the opening of a play, revealing the sharp moonlit vista on both banks.

The raft floated on, like some stately royal barge, with Jak Lauren able to keep it easily on course with the steering oar.

On the New Jersey shore they saw no signs of life among the waterlogged wharves and jetties of the old docks. It was obvious that the water level had risen since the old days, with less being taken out for power and industry. Now the surface lapped over the rotting concrete of the walls.

The skyline of Manhattan changed as they moved ever so slowly toward the tip of the island and upper New York harbor.

Now, at last, there was evidence that the lower parts of some of the scrapers had survived even the megadeath nuking of 2001. Doc strained his sight and his memory to try to identify some of the towering hulks that dotted the weed-wrapped wilderness of the city. But there were no landmarks, nothing to judge by. Two monoliths, each at least a hundred feet high, jostled each other close to the southern spur of the vanished metropolis.

"The Trade Center. Has to be. I flew into New York myself, and I would deduce the year must have been just before the second millenium. We circled over Manhattan, just above low cloud. I saw the flat roofs of those great towers jutting above the bank of stratus, and there were tiny people walking on them. I swear that it was one of the most bizarre hallucinations that I have ever suffered from.''

At that moment the moon vanished behind banks of sailing clouds, and the remnants of the city were plunged into darkness.

"Look!" Krysty cried. "Lights! I can see some lights."

She pointed at the flattened debris, almost level with where Canal Street had once run. All five of the others were on their feet, peering into the blackness.

"I see 'em," Ryan said. "Like points of pins. A dozen or more."

"Yeah. Flickering. More a hand's spread to the right." J.B. pointed.

"Like oil lamps," Jak said. "Kind of a gold look to 'em."

Those tiny spots of lights, moving painfully among the rubble, touched every one of the six.

Doc Tanner dredged deep into his raddled memory for a suitable quote. Eventually he said, very quietly, "And whatever walked there, walked alone."

After the attack of the amphibian mutie, no one on the raft felt much like sleeping. The dark water carried them along, now slower than walking, moving toward the dawn.

"What's that?" Lori asked, breaking the predawn stillness.

A small island had loomed out of the opaline mists that hung toward the sea. And there was a building, partly ruined, that stood at its center, bleached to the palest of greens.

"Missile silo," the Armorer said.

"Lookout post for Newyork," Jak Lauren suggested.

"Pretty house, Doc?" was Lori's guess.

"I think I know," Krysty said. "I've seen vid pix from before the long winter. I think I know what it was."

"More'n I do. My guess'd be along the lines of J.B.'s and Jak's." Ryan turned to Doc Tanner. "Come on. Tell us."

"It was a statue. A great statue of a woman, holding a torch in her hand to light the path for the hordes of immigrants who flocked to the land of liberty." He shook his head sorrowfully. "I disremember the words, but it carried a message. Something about bringing huddled masses from the old world to the new. I don't... By the three Kennedys, but the wheel turns and turns again and again. He that is first'o   surely be last. And the present one day will be the o   '

The sun was   g behind the tombstones of the skyscrapers of the city, painting the remnants of the statue with a soft pink light.

"Look upon my works, ye mighty, and despair," Doc Tanner said.

THE WIND HAD VEERED, strengthening with the dawning, raising whitecaps as it poured in from the southeast. It rushed through the gap that men before the long winter had called the Verrazano Narrows.

The current of the Hudson had weakened until it seemed the raft was held motionless, moving neither forward nor backward.

"We'll never make it out to the open sea and down the coast on this heap of shit," J.B. said.

"Best put in. There's low land to the right." Hanging on to the short mast for balance, Ryan stared out to where beaches broke the force of the waters. "Give it another half hour. Wind'll mebbe fall."

It would have been better if the fresh wind had continued to blow.

It didn't just ease; it dropped away completely, leaving them bobbing, becalmed, riding a sequence of sullen, swelling waves.

The sun came up like burnished copper from a sky that showed red-purple from corner to corner. Ryan dipped a finger into the water, then spit the liquid out in disgust. The spun-glass clarity of the Hudson upriver was gone. There was the taste of salt, and iron, flat on the tongue. A bitter nitrate and oil flavored the water.

And they were beginning to see things on the water around the raft. Jak Lauren was the first to notice anything, spotting a jellyfish, its skin a leprous yellow spotted with green patches. Its tentacles trailed behind it for better than a hundred yards. Ryan shouted a warning to the albino boy not to touch the creature as it wallowed near them.

"Heard of a man out in the California lagoons who saw a trailing firefish like that. He touched it and died double-crazed. They said 'fore he bought the farm he started t'bite off his own fingers from the pain."

Almost immediately after that they all clung to the raft as something immeasurably vast moved sinuously under them, just scraping the bottom of the logs with the top of its spine. Lori stuck her head over the side, trying to see what it had been, but the deeps had swallowed it.

They had heard gulls, shrieking and crying, all the way from Manhattan Island, sounding like demented souls condemned to fly the skies for eternity. Now the birds started to come closer, gathering above the raft, beginning to swoop toward the six friends.

KRYSTY WAS SINGING QUIETLY to herself, her pure voice the only sound in the stillness.

"A maid again, I ne'er will be,
Till peaches grow on a cherry tree."

Doc smiled across at her. "I haven't heard that tune in...I guess a coupla hundred years. There's a damned odd thought. It's lovely. You learn that from your kin back in... What was the ville called?"

"Harmony. Herb Lanning the blacksmith knew lots of real old songs. Way prechill. It was his son, Carl, who plucked my cherry. That's when I learned the words."

"Must have been a real good ville."

Krysty smiled at the old man. "Yeah, it was. But all things change. That was why we...why we were moving on."

"Your ville a good place, lover?" she asked Ryan.

"Seemed so, then. Until I saw the skull that was hid under the smiles."

"Life's a deal of hard traveling," J.B. said sagely, surprising everyone. Homespun philosophy wasn't normally what you heard from the Armorer.

Jak and Lori were working with the stern steering oar, slowly propelling the raft toward the western shore, now only a couple of miles away. It was backbreaking, soul-destroying work, and they'd found from painful experience that it could only be done in pairs. Any more and chaos followed with everyone knocking and pushing into everyone else.

It took them close to four hours to move roughly half the distance they needed to reach the land.

The waters around them had gotten more and more polluted. Dead fish and birds hung suspended, rotting and half-eaten, bones coated with a yellow grease. An hour back they'd poled past the corpse of a massive shark—a great white, at least fifty feet from porcine snout to the mangled tip of its tail. It hadn't been dead long, and its flat little eye still rolled incuriously toward the rich violet sky.

"Jaws," Doc muttered, enigmatic as ever.

The beach, sand dunes rolling back toward a line of low scrub, was now less than a half mile off. The sun had sunk well behind the hazy bulk of the land. In the last quarter mile they'd finally broken clear of the stickiest of the watery dreck, but the bitter labor had taken its toll.

Doc Tanner had collapsed, muttering feverishly about painted ships and painted oceans. Lori had fainted fifteen minutes later, slumping on the timbers, banging her head again. Despite her reserves of mutie strength, Krysty had given up, sitting down in a heap, her face white and drained. "Sorry, folks," she said, hoarse with exhaustion. "I've paid all I can find. Got no more. Sorry."

It had been left to Jak Lauren, with seemingly bottomless reserves of stamina in his slight body, J.B. and Ryan, to keep working on the clumsy steering paddle. Heaving it backward and forward, each stroke making the muscles of shoulder and spine scream in protest. Each stroke pushed the raft a scant couple of feet nearer to land.

Now the worst was over. Lori, Doc and Krysty had recovered a little, relishing the cooler breeze coming off the beach. Jak and the Armorer were at the oar.

Krysty smiled weakly at Ryan as they sat together. "I felt awful about stopping."

"Don't be stupid."

"Could have used the power of the Earth Mother. But it..."

Ryan squeezed her hand. "No. I've seen you after you've done that. Not worth it. Only 'bout another half hour and we can get off this bastard raft."

"You know we were talking 'bout Harmony? And your old ville?"

"Front Royal?"

"Yeah. If we get there and you kick Harvey Cawdor's ass out of the land . . . what happens then?"

"Do I get to be the baron? Take over the line? Is that what you mean?"

"Course. Would you take it on? Give up all these mat-trans jumps? Give up all the killing? Settle? That's why I left Harmony in the first place."

Ryan looked around them. "We've talked 'bout this before. I don't know, lover. That's the fucking truth. I just don't know."

"Want to spell me, Ryan?" J.B. called.

"Right. One minute."

"Answer me, lover," pressed Krysty. "I want to know what I'm getting into when we get down to the Shens and your ville."

The jagged cut the mutie had inflicted on Ryan's hand seemed to be healing. He picked at a small piece of rough skin around it, trying to sort out how he wanted to answer Krysty's question.

"A baron holds his ville by his weapons and by fear. That's always been the way of it. I don't know if that's the way I want to live, Krysty."

"It can change."

"You can never turn your back when you're the baron. I was old enough and saw enough before I left Front Royal to know that. You never sit, unless you've got your back 'gainst a wall. You never sleep long and easy. You never trust a smile, Krysty. You have too many enemies and no friends.''

With that he stood up and took the place of J.B. at the steering oar, leaving Krysty Wroth with her own thoughts.

A half hour later, with a grating sound, the raft beached on the New Jersey shore.

Chapter Twelve

THE RAD COUNT HAD SLIPPED well away from the dangerous hot spots of the red area, but it still lingered way over into the orange.

They left the raft, which had grounded on a mix of sand and shingle. They picked up their backpacks, checking weapons, leaving nothing behind, before striking off inland to camp for the night. Ryan led them only a mile into the dunes, not wanting to risk stumbling in the dusk over some double-poor mutie commune farther from the sea.

The evidence of heavy nuking was still to be seen everywhere. There was a great area of sharp-edged glass, twisted and warped into molten, lethal shapes. Ryan had never seen anything like it, but the Trader had told of seeing patches like it down in the deserts of Vada. It was where missiles had exploded in sand, the unbelievable temperatures fusing the mica into the lake of nuke glass.

Nothing grew taller than some stunted alders and willows, their trunks rotting and turning in on themselves. They camped for the night in a clearing on top of one of the sand dunes. They could watch for at least a quarter mile in any direction and not even Krysty could hear or see anything. The wind had turned once more, becoming a gentle breeze from the west. J.B. suggested they not risk a fire, and Ryan agreed with him. It was several degrees above freezing, with a clear sky that held no threat of rain.

Krysty moaned in her sleep, clutching at Ryan, her body trembling. She was so close against him that her scarlet hair, with its own mutated life, folded its tresses around his neck and upper arms, as though it, too, sought comfort.

In the morning he asked the girl what her dark dream had been, but she couldn't recall much about it.

"I was cold. I remember that. Sitting on a ruined harbor on the edge of a gray sea with slick granite rocks that reached out into the water. I was huddled up without any protection. Waiting. I was waiting for something or somebody."

"Me?"

She shook her head, stippled with the early morning moisture like tiny pearls amid an ocean of rubies. "No. Not you, lover. Can't... It was the cold that was worst."

They started off, moving westward, just after dawn. Until the blurred outline of the sun was nearly overhead, they saw absolutely nothing to indicate any life-form. Ryan was walking point, checking the soft earth for tracks and finding none, not even any tiny scuttling lizards around the exposed roots of the dwarf bushes.

"Where's the nearest town to here?" Krysty asked. "What's the map say, J.B.?"

The Armorer tutted through his teeth. "No map for this part. I recall Washington and Philly were around here. Don't know where. Doc? You got any idea?"

The old man was marching along, wrapped in his own world, humming a song about following a drinking gourd. He turned at J.B.'s call.

"My deepest apologies, my dear Mr. Dix. I fear that I was traveling some byway of my own. Could you repeat the question?"

"Know any towns around here?"

"The city of Brotherly Love was... No. We are in a dull area for my memory. When I was born I learned in school of a march to the sea. The blue and gray. But towns...? I fear not."

Ryan looked at the sky. "No sign of any chem storms. I know we're headed in the right direction. We keep on westward, then south. Into the Shens. What kind of nukes they use round here, Doc?"

"All kinds. High yield. Low yield. Air-burst. Water-burst. Low-alt and high. Some neutron stuff."

"Down near my ville, when I was a kid, most roads were passable. Never went that far north or east then. But I'm certain sure that a lot of the blacktops weren't too wrecked."

"That'd be neutron," Krysty commented. "Take out life and leave things standing. The idea was you could come in and take over. Didn't figure on doomsday and everyone gone everywhere."

During the afternoon, they reached the ruins of a major highway, which blocked their path, coursing like a stone arrow from north to south. A couple of hundred yards to their right was a tumbled sign, hanging off its broken support. Jak trotted off, and Krysty followed him. They came back together.

"What's it say?" Ryan asked.

"Garden State something. Begins with a *P* and an *A*, so it might be Parkway. Some roads was called that kind of name." Krysty was seized with a coughing fit from the dust they'd kicked up. "Gaia! Could do with some fresh water."

They crossed the wide six-lane highway and kept moving west.

During the next day and a half, they found the land was changing. The bleakness gradually eased away, being replaced by a greener, softer look. The arid sand was covered in clumps of coarse grass that slowly became gentler turf. Here and there they found small copses of live oak and sycamore. And there were flowers again.

Purple orchis jostled among clusters of delicate starry campions. Huge sundrops overshadowed tiny arrow-leaved violets. The six walked at a steady pace through fragrant meadows, past streams that ran east toward the sea.

They found a fine place to set up camp for the night near a clean stream that ran through a pool, which was like liquid crystal and fully ten feet deep with a rock bottom. Trees grew in abundance, but well spread, so that it would be hard for anyone to come at them unseen, not that they'd found any sign of human activity since they'd come ashore.

For supper they opened more of the self-heats, scraping out the spun-soya contents. The fire of tumbled branches was burning brightly, sending a crackling fount of red-gold sparks bursting into the cool night air.

Krysty got up, stretching herself like a tall, elegant cat. She walked the few paces to the pool, bending and putting her hand into it.

"Not too cold," she said.

"You going in, lover?" Ryan asked.

"Tempting. Lori, you want to wash?"

"Why?"

Krysty laughed. "You kill me, kid. You wash because you get dirty. Right now it's the time of month for me to need to keep extra clean."

"When you get bleeding? Why is it dirty?"

The four men listened, interested in hearing what answer Krysty would give the younger girl.

"It's... Gaia! If you don't know why you need to wash, then mebbe you an' me should talk some, Lori. Get your clothes off and come in the water with me, and I'll tell you some facts of life. Your mother should have ... No, forget that." She turned to Ryan, face flushed in the firelight. "Wipe that grin off, you stupe ape! And stay here and let us get bathed without you ogling at us."

"I shall sink," Lori said. "Too afraid."

Krysty smiled at her. "Never you mind. Looks shallow the upstream end of the pool. Come in there, and you'll be fine."

The two women went together, moving out of the circle of the fire. Doc Tanner broke the silence among the men. "Perhaps we might show courtesy by keeping our backs turned?"

"Yeah. Be decent," Ryan agreed, shifting his position so that he looked away into the forest. J.B. was already facing in that direction. Jak was the only one still gazing toward the sheltered little pool of shadowy water.

"Young man," Doc said sternly.

"Okay! All right f'you two. Got women. I don't. Only done coupla times. Gaudies in Lafayette. Krysty an' Lori are double-fuckable and you stop me looking."

Ryan patted the teenage boy on the arm. "Most things a friend can take. But not my blaster. And not my woman. So turn your back."

"But just wanna have—"

"Jak!" Ryan said threateningly. "Just do like I say."

Grudgingly the albino did, his long white hair now released from the red ribbon. They could hear giggling and then a stifled squeal from Lori as she found that the water was colder than she'd expected. Then there was only the sound of splashing, which drowned out any conversation the two young women might be having.

Very slowly Doc Tanner turned his head, ignoring a glare from Ryan. "Hades! They look like a brace of white dolphins sporting together. My Lord, but it makes me feel young again. I recall Emily and I once, on a... But that's yesterday and today's today."

Ryan also glanced behind. Lori was cautiously trying to push out of her depth, mouth open, blond hair trailing behind her. Krysty's bright red locks seemed huddled together like a tight ball of flame. The brightness of the fire didn't reach to the shadowy pool, and it was hard to make out more than the blurred outlines of the two slim bodies.

Krysty brought her hands together and threw a great ball of water in the air so that the orange light caught it as it burst into a million tiny sparks of fire. It fell and streaked over her face and body, funnelling into the valley between her breasts.

J.B. was honing the Tekna knife against the sole of his boot in a steady, preoccupied way. Jak stood and walked quickly to the edge of the trees, throwing a muttered few words over his shoulder.

"Going to scout some."

"Take care, Jak. Watch for muties," Ryan called, but the boy was gone, sulking off into the darkness.

"IT WAS MAGICAL, lover," Krysty said between pants as she and Lori rejoined the men around the glowing embers of the fire. Both girls had faces that glowed, and their hair hung damply on their shoulders. Lori knelt in front of Doc Tanner and gave him a great hug and a kiss.

"I was in water, Doc! You see me?"

"No. I mean, yes, I did. Wonderful, my dear child. Wonderful."

"Where's Jak?" Krysty asked.

"Told him not to get his young meat heated by watching you two in the water."

"Oh, Ryan!" Krysty exclaimed. "He's one of us, isn't he?"

"Doesn't mean he can... Oh, fireblast!" Ryan felt confused and irritated. "Anyway, he went off to scout some. It'll do him good and we can do with help. Food's low, and we got to find us some transport."

"Yeah, I guess so. The smell of burning wood's so strong from our fire I couldn't smell anything else even if it was fifty paces off."

"Someone's coming," J.B. said with a quiet urgency, grabbing his mini-Uzi and diving away from the fire into a dip in the ground. Ryan snatched up the G-12, moving in the opposite direction, hitting cover even before the Armorer. Krysty, hair flying, was at his side, the H&K P7A-13 blaster in her hand. Lori stood, bewildered, by the fire, until Doc Tanner pulled her to the earth, protecting her with his own body.

The land was quiet.

Ryan squinted across the clearing, just able to see J.B. flattened behind a bank of blooming heather. The Armorer half turned, pointing among the trees to the west.

The logs smoldered and light gray ash trickled down onto the coals with a ceaseless, whispering sound. Ryan thought he caught the far-off noise of an owl hooting, but he couldn't be certain.

Then he saw movement, something that flickered for a moment like a will-o'-the-wisp, visible only for a frozen heartbeat behind the trees. There was no moon, and whoever it was had the cunning to close in on them from behind the brightness of the fire, making it almost impossible for their eyes to adjust and see him properly.

"I see him," Krysty whispered. "Flat-topped willow, right of fire. Crouched. Give me the G-12, and I can chill him."

Ryan passed over the rectangular shape of the automatic rifle with its built-in image intensifier. "It's on triple," he hissed. "Won't lift at this range. No recoil."

The girl steadied the blaster against her shoulder, holding her breath, finger caressing the trigger.

When the attacker stood up, showing himself, his stark white hair was like a siren of light in the gloom. "Don't shoot, Krysty! Found us a wag to ride!"

Chapter Thirteen

THE VEHICLE WAS just over a mile inland. Jak led them through the scattered trees of the forest, across a winding stream and onto a narrow path.

"Saw tracks. Boots. Must have used for water. Not far. Keep double-quiet."

"Smoke," Krysty whispered to Ryan. "Not from our fire. Meat cooking."

They hadn't got much farther before Ryan could also catch the scent of roasting meat, making him lick his lips in anticipation.

"There," Jak said, pointing through the thinning trees, to where the amber glow of flames could be seen.

"How many you say?" Ryan asked.

"Saw five. Old man. Old woman. Younger man, girl and little boy, round eight or nine. The wag's just behind fire."

"Anyone on watch?" J.B. asked.

"Couldn't tell. Didn't want to wake 'em by going close. Saw blasters. Old scattergun and coupla hand pistols. Wag's armored."

That was nothing new. It was difficult to find any kind of truck in the whole of Deathlands that hadn't been turned into a sec wag. When even the brightness of day brought winking death, it was madness not to take some care.

As Ryan moved a few cautious steps closer, trying to make out if the camp was being patrolled, his boots crushed some small plants and the air was filled with the smell of wild garlic.

"I'll go around with Krysty?" J.B. suggested. "Set chrons and go on a time count?"

Ryan nodded. Far as he could make out, the strangers hadn't set a watch. That meant they must feel reasonably secure where they were. Which meant, in turn, that they should be easy meat for Ryan and the others to sneak up on and take.

"Go to the wag. Check it out. Could be someone in there. Doc, Lori 'n me'll take out the five by the fire. No chances. Like Trader used to say. Blast first and weep later. Better we chill them than they chill us."

The G-12 was still set on triple burst. Jak had his satin finish Magnum cocked and ready. Lori carried her little .22 PPK. The blaster wasn't any kind of a man-stopper, but the girl was good with it and it would slow folks down. Doc hefted the cavernous Le Mat. He'd got the hammer slotted for the single .63-caliber shotgun barrel.

Ryan glanced around at them, checking his luminous chron. "J.B. goes in three minutes twenty from now. All ready?" He got nods from everyone. "Move in closer. Careful."

The sweep second hand crept slowly around the white dial. Ryan watched it, also trying to make out what sort of a wag they were going after. It was difficult to judge, as the vehicle was behind the fire, and partly obscured by some bushes, but it looked good. Could be an old Mercedes camper, or maybe even a Volvo body. It was clear that a lot of work had been done on it. Blaster ports had been cut on all sides, and there was evidence that some crude armoring had been welded on.

To Ryan's experienced eye, the wag looked good. The tires seemed solid, and he couldn't see much sign of rusting around the wheel hubs, which was always a giveaway of a wag in poor condition.

"Ten seconds... five... let's go for it. Now!"

Ryan burst through the undergrowth, gun at hip, followed closely by Doc Tanner whooping in a high, cracked voice, and Lori screaming loud and shrill. J.B. came whooping out of the far side of the clearing, followed by Jak Lauren, long white hair streaming behind him, looking like an avenging angel of death and destruction.

Krysty was last, covering the boy as he sprinted to the wag, ripped open the driver's door and disappeared inside.

There was no firefight. The five were jerked from sleep by the attackers and held at gunpoint before they were properly awake.

Jak's recon had been accurate. Nobody was lurking inside the wag. There were just the five of them. The old man had a long straggling beard that reached to his belt. His gray-haired woman mumbled constantly and appeared to be slow-witted. The little boy was very frail, with a congenital birth defect—his hands sprouted like little paddles from the points of his narrow shoulders. His face was bright and alert, but they realized quickly the boy was also deaf.

Two other people—the lad's parents—stood trembling together, eyes staring in shock at the strangers who'd come shrieking at them from the darkness. Meadsville stream had always been a safe site, away from any marauding muties or slaughtering stickies.

The boy's father's name was Renz Boydson, and his wife was called Mixy. Their son had been birthed as Boyd, but most times he was just called Boy. Renz's father was

Jorg, and his woman, who was no relation, answered to Valli.

Renz was a traveling repairman. He was good with tired old machines that seemed past their best: old washers and rad-trans equipment, as well as generators and wag engines. The big trailer that was hidden among the trees held a primitive lathe and a mass of tools he'd been collecting for years.

The Boydsons made a fair living, though they frequently had to run the gauntlet of hostiles or double-crazies around the eastern fringe of the heart of the Deathlands. It was the wag that gave them life, food and security. The chassis was off a Mercedes camper, with parts of a Volvo body grafted onto it. The engine was reliable and exceedingly powerful, but so heavy on gas that Renz had adapted the interior to hold five twenty-gallon cans.

The wag had once belonged to a stupe preacher, who'd got it from a woman trader who'd seen the light through his hellfire sermons.

Renz had got it from the preacher, whose corpse, cleaned of flesh, now rested at the bottom of an old quarry, eight miles from Flanders. A bullet from Renz's Luger had been drilled through the center of his forehead.

Renz, hands in the air, glared at the strangers. His first waking thought had been muties, then he'd guessed that some other trader or traveler had followed them and run the ambush. But these six weren't like anyone he'd ever met. Valli was weeping quietly at his elbow, and he snarled at her to shut up with her sniveling.

The leader was obviously the man with the patch over his left eye. He was tall and well built, wearing dark clothes and a long coat. He was hefting a blaster such as

Renz had never seen. The second-in-command was the small man with the battered hat and the glinting glasses who carried a machine pistol.

"Keep quiet and give us no trouble, and you get to live some more," the man with the eye patch said. "We want the wag. Nothing else."

"Mebbe some stew," the young boy said. He didn't look much older than Boy, but he walked with a terrifying air of crazed menace. With hair like spun snow and eyes like the embers that glowed in the middle of the fire, the boy looked like something built by a mountain shaman for a midnight ritual.

One of the attackers was a dotard who looked even older than Jorg, and he was holding a handgun that had two barrels.

Renz looked at the two women. Despite the danger to them all, he felt himself stirring excitedly. The tall, slender blonde wore clothes that seemed designed to beg a man to take her. And the other, a few years older, had hair like living flames. Both women also had blasters, holding them with ease that only comes with experience and use.

The wind soughed through the branches of a grove of fragrant sassafras trees to the west, brightening the ashes of the fire, stirring dancing spurs of orange and yellow from the smoldering ends of the branches.

"Yer take wag and we'll all done get chilled," Renz said, addressing his words to the one-eyed man.

"You get to live. The keys in it, Jak?"

"Yeah. Juiced and ready t'go."

"Start it up. No, I guess you're right 'bout that stew. Smells good. Krysty, you an' Doc serve us out a bowl each."

The meat was rancid, with a ragged lace of rotting gristle around each piece, but the turnip greens and sweet potatoes were fresh and good. Renz and his family sat together, guarded, watching with sullen resentment. Jorg had begun to moan at his son for letting them be taken so easily.

"Chillers come out the brush and take food and the wag. You sit there and don't do nothing to stop them."

"Shut the flap, you old ass-lapper. They got the blasters, ain't they?"

"You ain't worth doodlysquat, you little fucker!"

"Our food! Our wag!" Mixy groaned. "We got no food or nothing. What's you going to do t'them? Tell me that."

Renz didn't know. His philosophy of life was very simple. If someone was more powerful than you, then you crawled, belly down. If you were stronger, then you beat the shit out of them. These six strangers turned his guts to water.

"Want us t'take the rest of the food?" Jak asked. "There's some dried stuff an' self-heats in the wag. Last us a coupla days."

"No. Leave 'em be. Get aboard. Start her up. Krysty and Lori, go with him. Doc, you too. Me and J.B.'ll watch 'em here."

"How about their blasters, Ryan? Better to take them with us?" Krysty pointed with the toe of her boot to the pile of pistols and shotguns by the fire, where Jak had left them.

"Leave them. Once we're on the way an' the doors are closed, it'd take more than them flea-flickers to harm us. Get moving."

The albino boy led the way, followed by the girls and Doc Tanner. Ryan watched Renz and the rest of the family. Behind him, there was the deep roar of the wag engine as it kicked into life.

Jak clashed the gears, making the heavy vehicle lurch forward. It bumped into the stump of a tree with a rending crack. Both Ryan and J.B. glanced around to see what was happening.

It was all the old man needed to make his move.

He had a knife tied to the inside of his left forearm, and he pulled it out, launching himself at J.B. The old woman dropped to her knees with a piercing scream. Renz, reflexes honed Deathlands-sharp, dived for the scattergun with the sawed-off stock and barrel. His wife reached for the open razor she wore sheathed between her mottled breasts.

The little boy stood still.

Against double-poor stupes it might have worked. Against the Armorer and Ryan Cawdor it had about as much chance of success as trying to beat a prairie rattler for speed.

"Hit 'em!" Ryan shouted, shooting from the hip at the white-haired old man. The burst of lead kicked him into a moaning heap and he rolled into the dying fire. Blood poured from the triple wound in the center of his chest, hissing onto the flames.

J.B. dodged sideways, firing the mini-Uzi one-handed, spraying the group of men and women as he moved. Thirty-two rounds of 9 mm ammo ripped out at a muzzle velocity of just over eleven hundred feet per second.

As the Armorer moved forward, his boots slipped on an empty can and he fell, finger still clamped on the trigger, more or less holding his aim.

Renz and his family were huddled together, and the burst of fire was tight and controlled.

Boy went dancing away, half the side of his head blown off, his paddling little hands groping at the empty air as he fell, dying.

Mixy was hit through the knee and went down screaming in a welter of blood and splintered bone. As she fell, several rounds stitched across her stomach, spilling her guts into the dirt so that they tangled around her feet in crimson-streaked gray coils and loops.

Valli caught five rounds, the lead lifting her clear off her bare feet and sending her seeping corpse smashing into the lower branches of a tumbled oak. A jagged branch went straight through her, piercing her rib cage, holding the woman's kicking, jerking body several inches from the blood-sodden earth.

Amazingly, amid the carnage, Renz stood untouched. He had reached the pile of blasters, but Ryan's G-12 was tracking in his direction.

"Feel lucky, stupe?" Ryan asked, his voice loud in the sudden quiet. To the side of the clearing the wag had stopped, stalling, engine ticking into silence. Krysty led the others out of the main door, guns ready.

But it was over.

"Don't shoot me, you bastard. You chilled everyone in m'family. Even Boy."

"It's okay," Ryan called out. "All right, J.B.?"

"Yeah. Didn't figure on chilling the whole brood, though. Caught my foot."

Ryan shook his head dismissively. The family had been stupid enough to try against armed men, just holding blades. He didn't feel any sympathy for them. That's the way it always was in the Deathlands.

The raggedy man stood and watched, face blank with shock. His whole family had been iced in the blinking of an eye, and it still hadn't really registered. And now his wag was going to disappear forever. A great flow of tears suddenly began to course down Renz's filthy cheeks.

"Take me with you."

Ryan ignored him. "Back in the wag, everyone. Let's move out."

"Fuck you!"

The engine rumbled, gouts of blue-gray smoke hanging in the air, pierced by shafts of silver moonlight. Ryan gestured to J.B. to join the others, backing away slowly himself and keeping the blaster trained on the solitary man. The corpse dangling from the jagged end of the branch finally ceased twitching and hung still.

"Can't make it on my own!" Renz stooped and picked up the sawed-off shotgun, lifting it to his face.

Ryan hesitated, considering chilling the man. But bullets were scarce.

He stepped backward until he was in the open doorway of the wag, never taking his eyes off the solitary figure. Renz was holding the scattergun, staring down at the twin barrels as though he couldn't quite understand what they were.

"Get in, Ryan. I got him covered," J.B. said from behind him.

"Bastards!" Renz shouted, his torn voice ringing harsh through the forest, clearly audible even inside the racketing box of the big wag. Ryan began to close the sliding door.

The clouds had drifted away from the moon, and the clearing was as brightly lit as a stage, Renz at its center. The gun was close to his open mouth, and his eyes were fixed on the door of the wag.

The explosion was muffled.

Even as the door slammed shut, the sec locks clicking into place, Ryan saw the top of the man's head disintegrate in a great spray that looked as black as beads of jet in the moonlight.

"Did he...?" Krysty began, seeing Ryan nod the answer.

"Let's go, Jak," Ryan ordered, holding on as the vehicle began to grind its way westward.

Chapter Fourteen

THE WAG WAS BIG ENOUGH to carry all six comfortably, and each had a narrow bunk. The self-heats in the kitchen area of the wag lacked labels, which made meals an interesting lottery. Near the back, in its own partitioned closet, was a chem toilet. Generally the vehicle was scruffy and stank of old sweat, but during the first morning's driving they bowled along with the blaster ports and roof vents open, all working together to sweep and clean the interior.

The half-breed truck seemed in good mechanical condition. They stopped about ten in the morning because the arrow in the temperature gauge was showing signs of veering into the red. But when Jak checked under the hood he found the reading was false. One of the pistons was worn, and the exhaust roared more loudly than it should have.

"Going t'be heavy on gas," he said. "Good job's cans in back."

None of them knew it, but there was another hundred gallons of precious gas hidden away in the undergrowth near the five corpses.

IT WAS LATE in the afternoon when they reached the fast-flowing expanse of the Delaware River, looking to cross it near the ruined ville of Stockton. The dash of the wag held some fragile old maps, creased and crumpled, which were held together with brown bits of tape and frayed string.

The parts of the maps that would have shown the trails to Front Royal were missing, ragged edges taking them tantalizingly close to their proposed destination. Ryan pored over them at a small table near the open port, the others peering over his shoulder.

"North along the Delaware, toward Easton. Around Allentown and on to... Can't read that name. Doc? Can you make it?"

"My eyes are not, frankly, as sharp as once they were, my dear Ryan. But I believe it must be the town of Harrisburg, and from thence to Gettysburg. By the three Kennedys and the one Lincoln, but there is a name to stir the cockles of memory. That we should be going there after—" He turned away quickly and went to sit down on his bunk, where Lori ran to comfort him.

"Then Frederick..." Ryan continued. "I recall that. The ville's close to there."

"We've got to cross the river first," Krysty said quietly. "Looks wide from that map."

"Lotta toll bridges built in the Shens," Ryan said. "Trade or jack."

"What're we gonna do?" Jak asked, climbing back into the driver's seat. "No jack. What trade?"

Ryan held up the Heckler & Koch. "I figure this is all the trade I need."

Doc wiped his face with his swallow's eye kerchief. "Least we don't have ice to cross the Delaware like...like somebody or other did, but I disremember who."

The highways weren't in bad condition. The surface was cracked and deteriorated, but most of the way it was drivable. Every so often the road disappeared under an earthslip, or was washed out of the world by a swollen river.

Occasionally they'd pass by the tumbled ruins of a small hamlet. Most buildings were totally destroyed, though the central stone chimneys remained standing—fingers pointing upward like graveyard memorials. Now and again they'd come across one or two intact buildings, scorched clapboard rotting away. A doctor's shingle would still be legible, or a rectangular crimson soft drink machine would squat outside the tumbled relic of a general store.

Grass and weeds had taken over most of the land, sometimes bursting through the tarmac of the highway. J.B. took over at the steering wheel from Jak as the day wore on. They stopped to refill the tank from one of the cans, standing in the soft afternoon heat under an azure sky.

They saw more birds, dipping and swooping over a mud hollow, feasting on the lazy clouds of tiny insects. A little way off to the right they could see the remains of a gas station. The building itself had completely vanished under tangling vines, but the metal-and-glass pumps remained, white and maroon paint peeling off in patches.

"Look," Krysty said, pointing farther down the blacktop, where a single human figure stood shimmering in the heat.

"Trouble?" J.B. asked, hand dropping automatically to the butt of the mini-Uzi.

Ryan shaded his eye with his hand. "Road's wide there. No brush close to it. Can't be an ambush. Not one alone."

As a precaution they closed some of the blaster ports, keeping careful watch through the others, and Ryan slid the roof vent across and bolted it. Because of the menace of stickies it wasn't a good idea to give them any way to get at you. Ryan sat up front, riding shotgun with Jak.

J.B. had left the driver's seat and taken up a position by the rear ob-slit.

"Take it slow, Jak," Ryan warned. "Get ready to push the pedal through the metal."

The young albino boy looked up at him, shaking his head. "Wanna tell me how t'wipe my ass, Grandad Ryan?"

"Cheeky bastard. Trouble with young kids now. Too much gall and not enough sand. Let's go, Jak."

The wall lurched forward as the teenager crashed it into gear, making everything in the sweating box of the main compartment rattle and fall.

"He moving?" Krysty asked.

"No. Still where he was. Can't see any danger. Nobody else is there."

"Could be a trap," Doc Tanner suggested from the right side of the wag.

"Could be. One man isn't about to take an armed wag."

Ryan stared through the slit in the wired and armored glass of the windshield. As they moved steadily along the track, he was able to see the motionless stranger a little better.

It was a male, around average height, tending toward skinny. In the Deathlands you didn't very often get to see anyone fat.

He was wearing a light gray coat that hung below his knees, the breeze tugging at its hem. His pants were also gray, tucked into brown laced-up work boots. His hair was cropped to a mousy stubble over prominent ears. His skull was long and narrow.

"Slow it down," Ryan ordered. "Keep your eyes double-wide."

He kept the automatic rifle trained on the man as the wag eased to a crawl. The face of the stranger was turned up, incurious, the eyes locking on Ryan's eye. The expression didn't alter. Ryan spotted the heavy old horse pistol that was jammed into the man's wide belt. It looked as if it'd been used for everything from stirring stew to hammering in fence posts.

Lori was the only one who spoke, staring through her ob-slit at the stranger.

"He got a face like a sheep-killing dog," she said.

J.B. watched through the back of the wag, calling to Ryan. "The crazy isn't moving. Just stands there, looking at our dust."

They kept moving and reached the river near evening as the sun was sinking behind the rolling hills that stretched as far west as the eye could see. After the chance encounter with the mysterious young man, Ryan had ordered them to keep the ob-slits half-shut and made sure the roof vent remained bolted.

There had been discontented muttering about the heat, mainly from Doc Tanner, but Ryan had been concerned that the low bushes seemed to be getting closer to the edge of the highway, making a sneak attack that much easier to mount.

The wag rolled over the top of a low rise, and Jak jammed on the brakes, bringing the vehicle to a shuddering halt.

"What's...? Ah, I see it. Best get ready, friends. Looks like we might have us some trouble here."

There was a battered pair of old Zeiss binoculars hanging from a hook at the side of the front passenger seat, and Ryan took them down. The focusing screw was stiff, the lenses not properly balanced, but he got enough visual information through one eyepiece to make out that the bridge across the Delaware was well guarded. At least a half-dozen figures were standing near it, looking up at the wag, which was poised on the crest of the hill. They were all carrying blasters, which looked to be long-barreled, single-action pieces.

"They seen us," Ryan said calmly. "Shouldn't worry us more'n a mosq-bite. We'll play it this way."

JOSIAH SHUBERT HELD UP his hand, the thumb and seven fingers spread in a warning to the lumbering sec wag to slow down. The blaster ports were all closed, and the driver was hidden by the setting sun glaring off the reinforced glass.

"Whoa down, Renz!" he shouted.

Jak went carefully through the gears, foot holding the brake. His other foot hovered over the gas pedal, waiting for the order from Ryan Cawdor to move out.

Ryan had his visor down on the passenger side. J.B. was covering the rear. Krysty and Lori were on the right of the wag, Doc on the left. All waited, crouched, behind the ob-slits.

"Back early, Renz. Forget something, did ya?"

The wag was inching forward, Jak struggling to keep the powerful engine from stalling on him. As well as the leader of the group, there were six men, mostly on the driver's side. One was by Ryan's side window, picking his nose and carefully examining what he'd excavated. The last of the men lounged against a painted pole that rested on a pair of old barrels on either side of the rickety bridge.

"Roll it down and hand the jack," Shubert ordered, his voice suddenly holding an edge of suspicion, an edge Ryan instantly recognized.

"Go."

Jak stomped down, and the wag jerked forward, slowly starting to gather momentum. The albino had his Magnum resting in his lap, and he snatched it up. Shubert jumped for the running board and hauled himself up. He had a taped .32 in his hand, and jammed it in the narrow slit of the sec window.

"You ain't Renz, ya mutie bastard! We'll chill ya right—"

"Shut it," Jak yelled, shooting the man through his open mouth. The bullet smashed a great chunk of bone out of the back of his head and kicked him into the dirt on the side of the road.

It was the only shot that anyone aboard the wag needed to fire. Ryan had been right in his summing-up of the blaster threat from the men. With their leader rolling, screaming and dying, none of them wanted to be dead heroes.

The armored radiator of the wag tore through the pole barrier, splitting it in two, one half wheeling high in the air and eventually splashing down near the edge of the muddied waters of the Delaware.

Ryan heard the thin sound of a ragged volley from the muskets, but as far as he could tell none of them struck the retreating wag.

"All okay?" he shouted, getting a chorus of positive replies.

The heavy tires thrummed on the planks of the bridge. Jak was still accelerating when Ryan leaned over and tapped him on the arm. "Slow down some, or we'll be in the river."

"Don't worry," the boy said, then grinned, eyes burning with crazed delight.

But he did slow down.

THE NEXT DAY they cut southward across the Blue Mountains, eventually picking up what remained of the old Interstate 78 and following it for fifteen or twenty miles as they came closer to Harrisburg and the Susquehanna River. The road was mainly in good shape, and they barreled along at a reasonable speed. They ran through a couple of heavy storms, rain streaming off the side of the highway, and gathering in deep rutted pools where the top surface had been eroded by a hundred winters and summers.

They saw very little evidence of any settlements near the road, though Krysty smelled smoke several times during the day.

It wasn't until later the next morning that they encountered any people.

Chapter Fifteen

"SOME LOVED NIGRAS and some wanted to chill all the nigras?"

Doc shook his head in exasperation at Lori's question. "No, no, no. And I only used the word 'nigra' because that was the epithet that was current coinage back then. It is *not* a good word, my sweet little child. Not a good word at all."

"Sorry, Doc. But I didn't . . ."

"Gentlemen in the South kept blacks as slaves. Those north of the Mason-Dixon line, as it was known, believed that all men were created equal and should all be free."

"Sounds right," Ryan said.

"Man with the biggest blaster has the biggest hunk of the freedom," J.B. commented, as cynical as ever.

Doc Tanner smiled sadly. "I fear your jaded view of life is too often correct. Certainly the Civil War ended that way."

A young deer had appeared unexpectedly out of the brush in front of the wag at a point where the road was so rough that Jak had to crawl along in the lowest gear. The ports and ob-slits were open, and J.B. felled the beast with a single shot from his Steyr AUG handblaster.

By mutual agreement they stopped at the next safe site and built a fire. The deer was skinned, jointed and roasted.

It was a beautiful spot for a camp. A scattering of aspens, their tops shimmering silver, swayed in the northerly breeze. A stream bubbled nearby in a series of little falls and pools. The whole place was rich with a profusion of wildflowers: hedge nettle, sage and fringed phacelia in a mix of delicate colors and shapes. Lori had woven herself a necklet of white and lavender blossoms, letting them dangle between her breasts as she sat and licked smears of blood from the roasted haunch of the fawn.

Krysty had brought up the subject of the Civil War, knowing from her teachings as a child that they were coming into an area where some of the most intense fighting had occurred.

Doc had been delighted to share his reminiscences with her.

"Those names," he said. "Shiloh and First Bull Run. Some called it Manassas. Stones River and Chickamauga. Chancellorsville and Antietam. The Wilderness and Spotsylvania. The sepia prints by Brady of untidy corpses along a picket fence. Even in Vermont, as a child, I saw men still dying of their wounds from those battles. And the generals. Names that tripped off the tongue like a litany of the gods of Olympus."

"Tell us," Krysty said. "Better than using a gateway as a time machine."

Doc leaned back, picking at his strong teeth with a long thorn plucked from a dog brier.

"There was Grant, above all. Ulysses Grant. And Lee and Sherman and Hood and Nathan . . . I don't recall his other name. But—"

"You ever meet any of 'em, Doc?" J.B. asked. "What kind of blasters they favor?"

"I was only a child. Many died during the conflict and shortly after. But I did meet General Grant. And a sorry meeting it was."

"Why?"

"You ask me why, Ryan, and I shall tell you. Indeed it will give me pleasure to tell you."

Ryan spotted the beginning of the rambling repetition that indicated Doc's memory wasn't yet completely healed. And probably never would be.

"An uncle of mine, whose name escapes me, was one of the physicians attending General Grant during his terminal illness. I visited him on the very day that the great man finally lost his hold on the tenuous thread that bound him to his corporeal self. Once severed, he would be free to roam with the immortals in the fields of Elysium."

"Who chilled him?" Jak asked, picking at the ends of a frayed length of meadow grass.

"A cancer that ravaged his mighty frame. His passing was truly a relief and a mercy after many long days of agony and anguish for all who loved him. It was a dullish sort of day, I recall. I was a lad of seventeen or so. He tried to sit and was staring out at the casement. I kept mouse-quiet in the corner of his chamber. He called out once and then fell back dead."

"What did he say, Doc?" Ryan asked.

"He had a female companion. He said, very clearly to her, 'It is raining, Anita Huffington,' and then he passed away."

Nobody spoke, and Doc stood, stretching his angular frame. Taking Lori by the hand, he said, "Now I think this innocent child and I will walk among the trees and flowers and commune with nature. We shall return within the hour."

"Take care," Ryan said, watching the old, old man go off, still holding the hand of the tall blond teenager.

"J.B. SAID THERE was another river and bridge coming?" Jak asked.

"Not far off. Cross it when we come to it, kid," Ryan replied. "That's a joke, Jak. Cross the bridge, when we come to it. It's a joke."

"Very nearly, lover." Krysty smiled.

Krysty stood—balanced against the rocking of the vehicle—and proceeded to climb onto the support platform beneath the main roof vent. Then she lifted head and shoulders into the open air.

"Beautiful up here," she called out. "You can see ahead for miles. Looks like the main highway's been wasted 'bout a mile on. But there's an older, narrow road to the left."

Jak acknowledged her warning, and four or five minutes later the wag swung off down a bumpy, dusty slope, swaying along the ancient track.

Krysty stayed up on top, her long hair streaming out behind her like a great veil of fire. The land was growing more hilly as they moved farther southwest, and swathes of conifers covered the rolling land.

About fifteen minutes later she shouted down to Jak to pull up. "And switch off the engine a while. I need quiet."

Krysty jumped out through the sliding door at the side of the sec wag and stood in the furrowed dirt of the trail. The others, one by one, climbed out after her. Jak was last, wiping sweat from his forehead with the back of his hand. Ryan joined Krysty, who stood staring intently down the road. Behind them the cooling engine clicked metallically in the stillness of the day.

Ryan was proud of his own keen sight and hearing, and he often tried to match Krysty's mutie-enhanced skills. "What is it, lover?"

"Not sure."

"Far off?"

She nodded, face rapt with concentration. "Yeah. Three, mebbe four miles on. Wind's carrying it toward us."

"What is it, Krysty?" J.B. asked.

"Couple of things. Quarter of an hour ago I'm certain I saw someone using binoculars. Caught the flash off glass. Then I saw nothing else, so I figured it could easy have been the sun off a fragment of broken glass in the undergrowth."

It was a reasonable assumption. The whole of Deathlands was riddled with twisted metal, fallen stone and broken glass.

"But?" Ryan prompted.

"But now I smell oil and fire. Hot iron. Thought I heard shots. If you look a little to the left of where the road crosses the next ridge, near in line with that broken water tower leg..."

"Smoke," said Jak, whose sight was nearly as keen as Krysty's—when the light wasn't too bright to affect his sensitive eyes.

Then Ryan could see it as well—a thin column, its top tinted crimson by the brazen ball of the sun. It was two or three hundred feet high, gradually dissipating near its peak as the wind tore it apart. It was difficult to be sure, but it looked to Ryan as if the smoke had that dark, oily quality that spoke of serious trouble.

"Back in the wag," he ordered. "Close up the roof vent and drop the ob-slits. Don't bolt them shut, but keep ready by them. Any of the blaster ports not covered by someone had best be locked.''

"THAT'S CLOSE ENOUGH, Jak. Hold her here, but keep her running.''

They were about a hundred paces away, and Ryan squinted through the narrow gap in the wired glass at what looked to be a battered truck. The tires were gone, burned to sticky black tar, and all the windows were broken. The piles of charred wood heaped at the bottom of the vehicle still smoked, sending gray coils skyward.

The metal of the wag was rusted deep orange, even around the wheel hubs, and it had settled into the earth.

"Been ambushed?" J.B. asked as the others crowded forward for a look at the wreck.

"Looks that way. Still a lot of smoke. Best wait a while before we go past it. Anyone could be waiting for us.''

They sat and watched, the smoke slowly clearing. There were no bodies visible, which could mean the attackers had taken them prisoner. Or it might mean the wreck held roasted corpses.

"Want me to move on?" Jak asked, sounding bored to the teeth with hanging around.

"Whoever did that can't be far off. Don't forget Krysty said she saw someone spy-watching us. So they know we're here."

There was something about the wrecked truck that somehow didn't sit right with Ryan, something out of place that nagged away at the back of his mind. But he couldn't quite grab hold of the doubt and examine it.

"Okay," he said. "Slow and easy. Double-care, friends."

Ryan saw the two figures first, torn and ragged, stumbling on the broken surface of the road. Their clothes were strips of blackened material and hung off their bodies. Their faces were smudged with dirt, oil and smoke, hair flattened against their heads. Their hands were empty.

"Stop, Ryan?" Jak asked, tongue flicking to lick his dry lips.

"Everyone looking? See anyone?"

The answers rattled in like machine-gun fire. Nobody could see anything threatening from their ob-slits.

"Stop," he said. "Keep double-red alert. Nobody move or open anything."

It was impossible to tell the sex of either of the people who had staggered to a halt in the center of the highway. They were both of average height and lightly built. As far as Ryan could see, neither had any obvious mutie defect.

As the wag stopped, both of them held up a hand, palm outward. Suddenly the one on the left collapsed like a doll, lying sprawled in the dirt.

"Survivors from an ambush?" Krysty said. "You going t'help 'em, lover?"

"Pull alongside them," Ryan ordered. "On my side." He wound down the window a couple of inches. He realized that the person still standing was a woman. The other was a male.

"Help us, mister. Got 'bushed by muties. Came out and blocked road. Set us alight 'fore we could do anything."

The eyes were deep cornflower blue, the voice hoarse and ragged. Beneath all the dirt and oil Ryan guessed she might have been a good-looking woman. Her body was lean and muscular. One firm breast protruded through a tear in her jerkin.

"Help, mister!" moaned the man on the ground, head half-turned to stare up at Ryan. "We'll die if'n you don't."

"How d'you get out?" Ryan asked, still conscious of some incongruity about the wrecked wag nibbling at his gut.

"Luck, mister," the woman replied. "There was a dozen of us. Tried to fight the dead-eyes in th'open. Too many of 'em. Chilled most of us and took a coupla kids with 'em. Me an' Jem runned in the brush. They let us go."

It made sense.

Ryan had lived long enough in the Deathlands to know that the one predictable thing about muties was that they were utterly unpredictable. And he'd seen enough ambushes to know the way death came grinning out of a clear sky. They could be telling the truth about what happened.

"You got blasters?"

The woman held her arms wide, spreading her legs in a parody of the classic sec-search position. The rags were so tattered and thin that he could clearly see she was naked underneath them—naked except for a wide leather belt.

"What d'you think, mister?" the woman said, seeing Ryan eye the man. Other than a similar wide belt, the man was visibly naked under the scorched shreds of clothing.

"What d'you want from us?" Ryan asked. "We can give you a coupla cans of self-heats. Some water. Mebbe old clothes. That do?"

"Take us with you." The man clawed his way to his feet, helped by the woman. He stared wildly in both directions up and down the road. "The muties'll get us if'n you leave us here."

"We don't have the room," Ryan said.

"We can make room for the poor folk, lover," Krysty said behind him.

"It would only be the merest Christian charity, Mr. Cawdor," Doc added.

Ryan turned in the swivel seat. "You say 'Christian,' Doc? That's not a word you hear an awful lot around Deathlands these days."

"Indubitably so, my dear Ryan. But that is a sorry comment on how we live. *Oh tempora* and *oh mores*, indeed. If I may be forgiven the classical tag."

Ryan ignored the ramblings. Looking back at the woman who seemed much the stronger of the pair, he said, "We can't take you." He didn't apologize. Like Trader used to say, it was a sign of weakness.

"Please, mister. You can fuck me. Or fuck Jem here. Any of you can. Make you feel—"

"You want food and clothes?" Ryan said. "We don't have the time."

"No, mister. Just take us with you. Take us for a day, that's all." She was babbling, the words stumbling and jostling each other in her terror. If she was acting, she was very good.

"I told you. Drive on, Jak. So long, lady."

The boy engaged one of the ten forward gears, and the truck began to creep ahead. The woman looked hopelessly at Ryan. He began to wind the window up once more.

"You going t'the Susqua? We can save you."

Ryan didn't answer her, though Jak glanced sideways at him.

"Be a trap there. They get strangers at the toll crossing."

"Hold it," Ryan said to Jak. "Best hear this."

"We can save you. Me an' Jem. Take us on and we can save you all from the chillers."

Ryan reached back and triggered the lever that opened the side door of the wag.

Chapter Sixteen

HER NAME WAS CHRISSY. Jem was her man. They'd been traveling west because they'd heard from some traders that there was a good life in the clean lands toward California. Then the muties had come and ended the dream.

Jem rested, falling instantly asleep under a gray blanket in a rear bunk. She told Ryan all about the squatters who controlled the crossing of the Susquehanna, how they tricked travelers and slaughtered them.

"They're cannies, mister," she whispered.

"What're cannies?" Lori asked.

"Eat meat," J.B. replied.

"We eat meat," she replied.

The Armorer shook his head. "Not human meat, we don't. But cannies do."

"By the three Kennedys!" the girl exclaimed. "Double-nasty!"

"Yeah," J.B. agreed.

"How do they work the trap?"

Chrissy looked at Ryan warily. "I tell you an' you put us off?"

"No. Tell me. The truth." There it was again, like a scab that couldn't be picked. Something about the ambush didn't sit right with him. But what was it?

"They got a lotta blasters. And the road's blocked so you gotta stop. No way around. An' they talk sweet and tell you to get down. Seem okay, but it ain't. That's how they does it."

"When do they hit you?"

"Some kinda word they got. Like one'll say casual that it's bastard cold. That might be the word. You gotta watch 'em. Only way is to step down and talk a whiles. Put 'em off guard. Then you can hit 'em."

J.B. leaned forward. "What if they hit you first?"

The woman seemed caught off-balance. "They...they won't. Not the way they do the chilling. Always same way."

"How far's the river?" Ryan asked.

"Coupla miles."

"We'll be ready."

"RYAN," JAK WARNED.

"I see 'em."

The road came winding down the side of a bluff. The original highway had vanished a couple of miles behind them, slipping away and leaving a jagged edge of concrete and tarmac. Jak had carefully steered the big wag down to the left, where deep ruts showed how other drivers had taken the same course. There'd been a shower of rain, earlier, and it had laid the dust.

Everyone took up their positions inside, blasters ready. They'd all been in on the firefight planning, all finally agreeing that Chrissy should lead them out and then try to let them know when it was best to make their play against the would-be chillers.

The woman and Jem, now recovered, waited immediately behind Jak and Ryan. They'd been offered fresh clothes, but both of them had insisted they'd wait until after the ambush.

"There's around twenty," Jak said, "and I can see a spiked pole 'cross the track. Just this side of the bridge."

At this point, just beyond the southern suburbs of what had once been Harrisburg, the Susquehanna was about a third of a mile wide, and looked like a glittering silver cobra winding through the gray-green land.

Ryan felt the familiar buildup of tension. When he'd been a very young and callow boy, he'd told a stone-faced shootist that he wished he didn't get nervous. The man had looked at him for a moment without speaking, then he said, "You feel that way, means you got nerves. Means you care 'bout getting chilled. Time comes you don't feel that no more is the time you start to die. Might take days or weeks. But you're deader'n a coonskin coat."

Ryan Cawdor had never forgotten those words. Now his stomach was beginning to knot with the anticipation of shooting. Adrenaline was flowing fast, his mouth was dry, and the palms of his hands were slick with sweat. He wiped them on his pant legs.

If the two survivors of the massacre were telling the truth, the ground was going to get larded with several corpses in the next quarter hour.

"Take it slow and steady and pull her up when they tell you," Ryan said.

Jak nodded, concentrating on steering the heavy wag through the bumps and wheel tracks that came together near the bridge.

"What they got?" J.B. asked from the back of the vehicle.

"Looks like a bunch of M-16s. Smith & Wesson handguns in belts. Can't see any gren-launchers or heavy blasters," Ryan told him.

"Best set your G-12 on continuous. Going t'be sharp down there," the Armorer advised.

Ryan nodded. If the girl was telling the truth, then they should have a chance to start shooting and take the squatters by surprise. But if she was lying and they were being set up...

They were about a quarter mile off, Jak keeping the wag moving steadily in low gear. Jem was right behind him. Ryan thought he caught the faint sound of metal on metal, and he swung around and saw both Jem and Chrissy fiddling with their leather belts. Both of them grinned as he turned, keeping their fingers hooked inside, out of sight.

"Nice wag, this," the man said, speaking quickly. "Volvo-Benz, ain't it?"

"Yeah," Jak said. "What was your truck...before the muties got at it?"

Ryan noticed a slight hesitation on Jem's part, but he was concentrating on the bridge and the men ahead of them, who stood in a loose half ring, waving them to a halt. As he listened, Ryan was already reaching for the main door control lever.

"It was an old Nissan. Kind of beat-up, but it ran well."

"Fucking right, Jem," the woman agreed, leaning against the back of Ryan's chair. She was so close to him that her breath stirred the long hairs at his nape. "Jem kept that better'n he kept me. Painted and polished it every day."

That was it!

The wag was easing to a stop, everyone ready to move to the exit to jump down. Ryan's hand was on the door lever.

Without even looking around, he jabbed back and up with his left elbow, feeling it crack home on the side of Chrissy's jaw. A stab of pain shot up his arm, but he ignored it. Dropping the Heckler & Koch from his lap, he drew the panga with his right hand. He turned in a fluid movement and sliced at Jem's exposed throat.

"Trap!" Ryan yelled. "Chill 'em all, outside!"

He was facing the back of the dimly lit sec wag and saw the expressions of shock and horror on his companions' faces.

Jem was on the metal-ribbed floor, his left hand grabbing at the screaming lips of a gaping wound that opened up his neck. The carotid artery had been severed by the keen edge of the panga, and blood was flooding out in great pumping jets. His mouth was open, and he was trying to cry out.

Chrissy was also down, half on her side, struggling to get up. There was a purpling bruise on her left cheek, and a thread of crimson was worming from her nose and swollen lips. "You fucking..." she began.

What caught everyone's eye was what the man and the woman wore on their right hands. Glinting in the poor light with a lethal sheen, the contraptions were made of smooth, dark leather, tight fitting. Each fingertip carried a sliver of curved steel, like a miniature razor, no more than three inches long and a half inch wide. Used together, they were a terrifying weapon. The open sections of their belts made it immediately obvious where the bizarre blades had come from.

From the moment that Ryan Cawdor lashed out at the woman with his elbow to the realization of how close he and Jak had come to losing their lives took no more than five beats of the heart.

J.B. broke the moment of stillness and shock. "Pour it on them," he snapped. "Chill 'em all. Every one of 'em."

Jak tugged the hand brake on, leaped from his seat and started to blast out of the side window with the Magnum.

Both girls eased back the blaster slits and began to fire into the waiting group of men. Then there was the cavernous boom of the Le Mat as Doc Tanner triggered the scattergun, vomiting lead into the faces of the nearest of the squatters.

Chrissy was scrabbling at the metal floor with the steel fingers, striking sparks in her insensate rage. Her eyes were wide open with the crazed lust to kill Ryan, who stood by his seat, staring down at her.

"Fuck you!" she grated. "How did you know? Heard us putting on the snickers?"

"No."

"Then, how the...?"

"Goodbye," Ryan said, drawing the SIG-Sauer P-226 and squeezing off a single round. The bullet hit Chrissy between the eyes, kicking her skull back against the floor of the wag with an echoing thud. Her head bounced once, then rolled to one side as she died.

It wasn't much of a firefight—not from the point of view of the twenty or so squatters waiting outside for Jem and Chrissy to betray the strangers and deliver them into their tender hands. The ob-slits opened and the muzzles of blasters came peeking out, spitting fire and lead.

J.B.'s mini-Uzi and Ryan's G-12 decided the battle almost before it had started. Thirty-two rounds of nine-millimeter stingers flew from the Armorer's machine pistol. The Gewehr fired a burst that sounded like tearing silk.

The gang of assassins was ripped to pieces by the awesome firepower of the two blasters.

Ryan didn't very often like firing the caseless automatic rifle on continuous burst, but he couldn't take a chance that the squatters might be able to take out their tires and then burn the wag. It wasn't fully protected like a proper war wag and was vulnerable to a concerted attack by determined men.

"Hold fire! Gimme a chill count. J.B.?"

"Seven certain, three or four more down."

"Krysty?"

"Agreed with J.B., plus two close in by the wheels. Both head shot."

"Lori?"

Immediately Ryan grimaced, knowing from previous experience what the girl's reply would be. "A lot chilled. Serve the cannies right." Lori couldn't count all that well.

"Doc? How many your side?"

"Pistoled four or five with a single shotgun round, Ryan. Two dead, maybe three."

The running total made it sound like at least a dozen of the squatters had been perma-chilled, allowing for the couple on Jak's side of the big wag's cab.

There was a burst of firing from Doc and Lori's side, bullets pinging like heavy hail off the rough arma-plate. The defenders immediately started to reply, both blasters making light, flat sounds.

"Some running!" Jak yelled, frantically winding down his window to get a clear shot at the fleeing men.

"Leave 'em!" Ryan ordered. "Save ammo. Let 'em go."

Ryan was ramming the twenty-five-round loaders into the magazine clip, feeding the nitrocellulose caseless rounds. J.B. had dropped the empty cartridge mag to the wag's floor, plucking another from one of his infinitely capacious pockets and slotting it home with a satisfying click.

"One crawling away this side," Krysty said. "Looks like a broken thigh. Shall I waste him or let him go, Ryan?"

"Let him be. Jak, get ready to move. Doc, you and Lori go and shift that spiked rail from 'cross the road. Krysty, stay here and keep watch. Me and J.B.'ll get down first and check out the body count. Chill any that are still moving."

"Check," the Armorer said, drawing the small Tekna knife from its sheath on his belt.

"Ryan?" Krysty said.

"Yeah?"

"One thing?"

"What is it? Best get moving and over the river. Might be more of the squatters."

"Sure. But how d'you know?"

"You hear them putting on finger knives?" Jak asked.

Ryan grinned, moving a half step toward Krysty, then wincing as his boots slithered in the sticky pool of the dead couple's blood. "Better get this dreck cleared out 'fore we cross the Susquehanna," he said. "How did I know? It kept nibbling at me that there was something wrong 'bout that burning truck. Then, just as we was coming to the bridge, the woman said something that brought it clear."

"She was talking about how he looked after the wag," Krysty remembered.

"Yeah. You saw it, burned out. Settled in the dirt up to the hubs and raw red rust everywhere, the fire still smoldering."

Krysty looked puzzled. It was Jak who made the connection first. "Sure. Bastards! If'n fire only just burned, it'd be clean metal."

Doc Tanner had been listening with great interest. "I see it now. The oxidation of the exposed metal was old. Days old. Weeks old."

"Mebbe months old," J.B. added. "Could have been pulling that butcher's scam for fucking months. Survivors from the ambush. Get a lift. Then open the throats of the driver and shotgun and let in their mates. Easy as catching a legless mutie.''

"And the way it was sitting there," Krysty said. "Now that you say it... Gaia! What a stupe I was. I can see it in my mind's eye now, and it's obvious it was a real old wreck, set by the track and fired with some brush. Drop of gas and oil and it smokes like a fresh killing ground."

"And they'd have been eaten us!" Lori exclaimed, kicking out at the slumped corpse of the woman. "Cannies!''

"Right," Ryan agreed. "Now you all know what you gotta do. Clean this wag and tidy up out there. Then we can move on again."

It took only a half hour to finish off the wounded men and wash out the bloodied interior of the big wag. Then Jak cranked up the engine, and they rolled south toward the old Maryland state line.

Chapter Seventeen

"I wish, I wish, I wish in vain,
I wish I were a maid again.
A maid again, I ne'er can be,
'Til . . .

"Can't you hold this fireblasted wag steady on the road,
Jak?"

"Sorry, Krysty. Tree felled and blocked us. Had to go
around."

It had taken them three days to get from the Susquehanna, across the northern angle of Maryland and into
the edges of Virginia. The road had been appalling and the
weather worse.

Twice they'd been hit by ferocious chem storms, as severe as anything Ryan or J.B. had ever encountered. The
gales had come shrieking from the east, bringing a biting
salt rain and hail that battered at the metal roof of the
wag. Lightning lanced to earth all around them, filling the
air with the dry taste of bitter ozone. The thunder was so
loud that any conversation within the vehicle had to be
shouted.

At the height of the storms Jak had stopped driving,
unable to see more than a couple of feet ahead. Mud fell
from the skies and streaked the armored glass, coating it
with a thick layer of gray-orange slime.

In the evening of the third day, the wind shifted and ravened from the west. Ryan climbed down from the wag on the leeward side, finding to his dismay that his rad counter began to cheep a warning, the needle sliding into the red.

"Must have picked up some hot shit from beyond the Miss," J.B. said when Ryan told him about it. "Some real glow spots that way. Better keep in and move on when we can."

In one of the places where they lost the highway, they plowed through an old burial ground.

"Where the fuck's this?" Jak shouted, his sweaty hair tangled around his face. It was early in the morning, and a thin slice of sullen sun glowered balefully over a low range of hills to the east of them.

As far as the eye could see, there were great rows of pale stones, most with carving on them and words that had been virtually obliterated by long years of wind, rain and chem storms. Doc Tanner offered to get down and take a look.

The door slid open, and the old man vanished into the hazy dawn. They watched him from the ob-slits, seeing his gaunt figure, stooped like a crow, picking his way among the headstones. He hesitated now and again, hunkering down to peer at the lettering. Once he looked back toward the wag.

"I'm getting out t'join him," Ryan said. "Anyone coming?"

He was underwhelmed by the response. Suddenly everyone had something to do.

"Sorry, lover," Krysty said. "This country's too full of graves for me to want to go look at any more. You go."

The wind was cold and fresh, biting at the skin across his cheeks. On all sides Ryan could see rolling hills, memories bringing back so much of his brief and long-gone childhood: round-topped mountains sprayed thick with pine forest, torn rags of fog lingering in some of the gentle valleys.

Doc was standing with his back turned to Ryan, his hand gently stroking the top of a gravestone. He glanced around at the sound of Ryan's boots crunching on the gravel.

"Welcome to the place of old dying, my friend."

Tears flowed down Doc's furrowed cheeks, washing away the dust in rosy streaks over the silver stubble on his chin.

"Private Joshua Clement. First Minnesota. Fell on the second day of July in the year of 1863. Aged twenty and two years."

"This from the old Civil War, Doc?"

"In my childhood this was possibly the best-known of all cemeteries. Here rest so many good fellows and young. There's another stone there, tumbled in the long grass by time and nuking. Look at it, Ryan, and see how little has truly altered in two hundred and thirty years."

Ryan stooped, cocking his head to read the worn letters. He read it out loud.

"'Drummer Horatio Makem of the 20th Main Regiment. Born in Connaught and died here, aged eleven years and three months.'"

"Children, Ryan. Younger even than that bloodthirsty albino in the truck. So many died here. Oak Hill. The Peach Orchard and Little Round Top. Cemetery Ridge and the Devil's Den. The wounded begging for death. A bullet in arm or leg, Mr. Cawdor, meant cold, blunt steel. The piles of severed limbs quite o'ertopped the tents where the surgeons labored."

Ryan straightened and looked around at the quiet fields and hedgerows, their lines still visible among the tide of fresh vegetation. A wood pigeon was cooing softly in a grove of immensely tall sycamores near a narrow, meandering stream. It was a scene of perfect, idyllic peace.

"You say this was a big fight?"

"A big fight, Ryan?" Doc queried. "Oh, I think that I might say that. Some fifty thousand men and boys were killed or wounded in those three days in bright July. Five years before I was born. Fifty thousand lost, Ryan."

"Who won? North or South?"

Doc Tanner scuffed at the ground where one of the tablets had toppled over. "General Lee hoped for the one great battle that would turn the tide for the South. This was to be it. Gettysburg. The high-water mark for the Confederate States of America. The war was not yet over, but now the die was cast and the count was against the South."

Ryan glanced around, automatically checking for any possible danger, but the dawning was still quiet and peaceful.

"They didn't know that their cause was lost," Doc continued. "They rallied and came again and again into the storm of lead. One cried out to Lee that they would fight on until Hell itself froze over. And then they would go and fight the damned Yankees on the ice. But it was lost."

"Gettysburg," Ryan said, tasting the word on his cold lips. "Heard of it. Old books. So the Union came the way we did, from the north. And the Rebs...that the right name? Yeah, the Rebs came up from the south, yonder."

Doc Tanner smiled gently. "You'd have guessed so, Ryan. Oddly it was just the opposite. Lee came to Gettysburg from the north, and General Meade from the south.

Old Snapping Turtle Meade. That's what he was called. When I was a young tad of a boy and we played Rebs and Yankees, we'd all be our favorite generals. I was Jeb Stuart.''

There was no sign that morning of the madness that swam just beneath the surface of Doc Tanner's shaken mind. He was logical and coherent, pointing out as best he could how the battle had swung backward and forward during the three days, using his silver-topped cane to indicate the hills and folds in the rolling ground around them.

''Thursday, November 19, four months after the battle, a lot of big men came here to dedicate this cemetery as a sort of national monument for the fallen.''

Unseen by either of them, Jak had left the wag and walked through the grass to stand behind them, hearing what Doc had been saying.

The boy began to speak, nervously at first, then with growing confidence.

'' 'Four score and seven years ago our fathers brought forth on this continent a new nation, conceived in liberty and dedicated to the proposition that...all men are created equal.' ''

''Abe Lincoln's Gettysburg Address!'' Doc exclaimed. ''How in tarnation d'you know that, my snow-headed young companion?''

''Pa taught me. Said his pa taught him and his pa before that. There's lots more. Can't recall it now. Bit 'bout the world will little note nor long remember what we say here, but it can never forget what they did here. Meaning the men got chilled. And it ended with something about resolving that these dead shall not have died in vain. That...'' The boy shook his head, the long white veil of hair swirling around his face in the dawn breeze. "Can't..."

Doc Tanner took it over, his rich, deep voice filling all the morning, reaching to the far-off rivers and hills like an Old Testament prophet.

" 'That this nation, under God, shall have a new birth of freedom; and that government of the people, by the people and for the people, shall not perish from the earth.' "

It was a solemn and moving moment. Ryan glanced back and saw that Lori, J.B. and Krysty had all gotten out of the wag and were standing close together, listening to Doc's recitation.

"If I was much given to crying," Doc said, "I would shed tears now for the mindless and overweeningly stupid men who forgot those words of Lincoln. The men, now long dead, who took a dream and flung it into the abyss. The men who took the United States of America and turned it into the Deathlands. I could weep for it, my friends. Truly, I could weep."

Chapter Eighteen

THERE IS A POINT where the old states of Virginia, Maryland and West Virginia all come together at notorious Harper's Ferry. The wag coughed and spluttered its way into Ryan Cawdor's home state, now a scant sixty miles from the ville of Front Royal. The closer they drove to his birthplace, the quieter the one-eyed man became. He sat alone on his bunk when he wasn't spelling Jak in the driver's seat.

It was becoming increasingly obvious that the sec wag wasn't going to make it the whole distance to their destination. The farther they traveled, the rougher the engine sounded, devouring more and more gas.

They stopped for the night, about thirty miles from Front Royal, and Jak dipped a long stick into the tank, holding it angled to the orange beams of the setting sun to try to see the gas level.

"How much?" Ryan asked.

"Not 'nough," the boy replied.

"In the cans?" J.B. asked.

"Drier than an old woman's tits. Guess 'bout ten miles. Mebbe fifteen."

They all looked at Ryan. "You recognize where we are?" Krysty asked. "Ring any chimes from boyhood?"

He shook his head. "Never hunted much north. This trail don't seem much used. Main tracks were south and west of here. Old I-81 was the wide one. Pa had trouble

with guerrillas coming from the mountains to the west.
Shen raiders. They used that interstate with fast wags.
Light armor. Stole horses and cattle and women. Surely
missed the stallions and the seed bulls.''

"But you believe we may be somewhat in the im-
mediate vicinity of your ancestral home?" Doc asked,
scratching his chin, his mind immediately wandering off
the subject. "Why, 'pon my soul, I declare that I have a
dire need of a shave, my friends. Forgive me while I go to
attend to my ablutions.'' The old man vanished toward a
slow-moving stream behind the wag.

Ryan shrugged. "I guess we got to be close. Can't say…
Fireblast! I don't think I'm doing right bringing you along
on this."

Krysty clucked her tongue and moved closer to him, but
he shook his head.

"No, lover. I mean all of you. If'n Harvey once finds
out I'm within a hundred miles, he'll put the dogs out after me. After *us*. And he must be able to call on…mebbe
a hundred sec men or more. As well as having every bastard village and hamlet for twenty miles around under his
heel."

"Wouldn't be here if'n I didn't want to be," J.B. replied.

"And me," Lori insisted defiantly. "We'll killed your
brother together. Shan't I?"

The others laughed at the girl's serious face, Ryan finally joining in.

"Okay, friends," he said. "But when my brother has
us roasting over a slow fire, don't any of you put the
blame on me!"

JAK CAUGHT SOME TROUT and roasted them over a slow
fire of hickory wood, the scent making everyone's mouth

water. The fish were delicious, the tender flesh all but falling off the slender bones.

"What's time, J.B.?" Jak asked, laying back on a shelf of thick moss, legs crossed, his stark white hair spread out behind him like a bride's veil.

"Twenty-five of eight," the Armorer replied, checking his wrist chron.

"We should be moving on," Ryan said, belching appreciatively. "Those fish were double-ace. Hardly ever get fresh eating. Did you have self-heats and spun soya in your day, Doc?"

"What, may I ask, do you consider to be 'my day,' Ryan?"

"Before the long winter, course."

"During my time in the 1990s, I found the quality of cuisine execrable."

"That mean it was good, Doc?" Ryan asked.

"It means it was shit, Ryan." The old man grinned. "Tinned and frozen and packaged and freeze-dried and irradiated and processed. Little better than these appalling self-heats. But remember that my time was also back in the late 1800s, before I was so cruelly trawled forward as part of Cerberus."

"What was food like then? In real old times," Jak asked.

"Ah," Doc sighed. "Like those trout. All food was fresh. Well . . . most food was fresh. Chicken and mutton and beef and turkey. Salmon and trout and bass. Vegetables from your own garden, with no having to take a rad count first. Cream so thick I swear you could cut it with a knife. But what is the merit in such talk? Let us enjoy the occasional marvelous food like these tender fish."

"Had good food as a kid, back at the ville," Ryan said. "Cooks made me a special sort of a pie with apples and oranges in it. Called it 'Master Ryan's Surprise,' they did."

"By the three Kennedys!" Doc exclaimed, leaping to his feet in dismay.

"What the...?" Ryan said.

"Your name!"

"What?"

"Your name," Doc repeated. "Your name is Ryan Cawdor. We all call you by that name, do we not? Indeed we do."

Ryan didn't understand. But he was used to the occasional way Doc's synapses disconnected and produced only babbling. Krysty also stood up, eyes lighting up as she realized what Doc was trying to say.

"Ryan!" she exclaimed.

"You all lost your jack, lover? What's all this about...?"

"About your name, you double-stupe," she said, voice raised. "Tomorrow we'll be within range of the ville."

"And?"

"And if anyone hears the name of Ryan Cawdor, then they'll..."

"Go running to Harvey," Ryan finished, slapping his own forehead with exasperation. "Sorry, friends. Better go and throw myself in that pool to try and get my damned brain working. Yeah, of course. Got to change my name."

"Upon my soul, but I admire a man who likes to speak his mind. Indeed I do," Doc said, grinning. "That's my impersonation of... of someone or other from some old vid."

"I don't know what to call myself," Ryan said.

"John Doe," Krysty suggested. "Used to be the name for chills they couldn't put a name to."

"Thanks, lover," Ryan said dryly.

"Floyd Thursby," Doc offered.

The suggestion was greeted with total silence by everyone. Ryan tried the name on his tongue, finding it felt familiar. "Not bad."

"Like it." Lori smiled. "Floyd Thursby. I can remember that."

Krysty leaned over and kissed Ryan on the lips. "Hey, Floyd, you kiss just like a guy I used to know."

"You enjoy it?" Ryan grinned and pulled her to him, kissing her long and hard.

"Even better when you help," she replied, face flushed, sentient hair coiling and uncoiling on her shoulders.

"Floyd Thursby." J.B. tried the name. "Why not? Where did you pick that one from, Doc?"

The old-timer looked puzzled. "I think... No, it's vanished. Perhaps we shall never know who the real Mr. Floyd Thursby was. It will remain a mystery shrouded in an enigma."

THEY FINALLY RAN OUT of gas a little before noon. Fortunately the rebuilt wag had been giving them plenty of warning, the engine stalling and backfiring repeatedly. Jak, who was at the wheel, had ample time to pick a secluded spot off the deserted blacktop. He eventually parked the truck in a grove of trees, completely out of sight of any casual passersby. They hadn't seen a soul since crossing the Susquehanna, so it looked like a good place to safely store some of their clothes and blasters.

"We go and we look. Find a way—if there is a way—to take out Harvey and his woman. And his bastard son. We need more power, we come back here and collect the rest of the blasters."

The Armorer sighed at Ryan's words. "Surely like to have the Uzi in my hand, going into a hostile ville like this."

"Sec men'd chill us 'fore we got ten paces over the moat."

"Sure, Ryan, sure."

Their secluded grove was a place of quietness and muted grays and greens. A small, furry animal scuttled amid the rustling leaves, darting out of sight behind the wheels of the wag.

"Nice forest," Krysty said. "Any mutie critters around here?"

"Some humans," Ryan replied. "There's still some black bear in the hills, and mebbe some cougar. Pa used to breed wild boars. Big mothers, six feet at the shoulder, with curved tusks that'd rip your belly open 'fore you even saw 'em coming."

"Nice, lover. I'll stay close to you. This all the woods from the Front Royal ville?"

"Used to be. When I was a kid it seemed like we owned half the Shens. Now...I don't know. Just know that we gotta step careful."

"When do we move?" Doc asked. "There's ample daylight left for us to continue with our odyssey, is there not?"

Ryan put his hands to his chin, as if he were praying, trying to decide what'd be best. It was nearly twenty years since he'd been in Virginia. There could have been lots of changes—probably had been. In fact, in the year since there'd been any reliable, fresh news, much might have altered at the ville. Harvey could be dead. So could his wife and son. There could have been a rebellion. It was widely known that precious few barons ever died peacefully in their own beds.

"Wait for dusk," he finally decided.

Most of them slept through that long afternoon.

They all dreamed, locked in their own private memories and thoughts.

Jak was riding a great alligator, fully sixty feet long, with mutie jaws and teeth. Somehow it skimmed above the surface of a vast swamp, covered with rich, waxy flowers in unearthly shades of purple and green.

Lori was wandering naked along swept corridors of gray stone, turning corners, walking and turning more corners. Always the corridors stretched ahead of her, limitless and featureless. Yet she knew that she must keep walking. She was cold, but if she could only find it, there was warmth somewhere for her. Her feet were sore and bleeding and she cried. In her dream, the girl cried.

J.B., his glasses neatly folded and tucked into the protective top pocket of his coat, was immersed in a common and repetitive dream. His lips parted in a faint smile of enjoyment.

He had fieldstripped a Stechin machine pistol and laid the parts out, all clean and oiled, on a cloth of white velvet. He ran his eye over them, naming each part.

"Barrel, recoil spring, slide, barrel bracket, extractor, tip of firing pin..." and all the way through the field manual.

The Armorer sighed with pleasure.

Krysty was dreaming of her childhood, back in the ville of Harmony. She was running through a field of poppies, red as spilled blood, feet bare, a ribbon holding back her vermilion hair. The sun was as bright as a newly minted copper coin. Around her she could hear the laughter of children, pealing sweet and hard like small bells of platinum.

The laughter was getting closer and closer to Krysty.

The sun disappeared behind clouds.

The poppies withered and died.

But the laughter came closer and closer.

When Krysty jerked awake, she was sweating and trembling.

Doc Tanner slept shallow and often, like many old people. His dreams were of the long-gone past, lost and beyond recall.

He was in a book-lined room, which was lit with the soft glow of a brass oil lamp, the background resonant with the regular, measured heartbeat of a walnut grandfather clock.

Doctor Theophilus Algernon Tanner was reading, occasionally pausing to make a note with his quill pen, dipping it into the ornate ormolu inkwell.

Through the open doorway, he could see his wife, Emily, suckling little Jolyon, while baby Rachel, swathed in layers of lace petticoats, played with a plump puppy by the fire. It was a scene of intense domestic happiness, and the old man mumbled to himself, smiling on his bed of dry leaves and soft moss, two centuries away from his dream.

Ryan dreamed of a dagger.

When they awoke, they readied themselves for the journey to Front Royal, leaving their long winter coats in the wag. J.B. reluctantly laid his mini-Uzi on a shelf, and Ryan pushed his precious G-12 and its ammunition under one of the bunks.

It was dusk, a fresh spring kind of an evening with a flock of pigeons wheeling above the tops of the trees. The air tasted green, and already the beginnings of dew lay slick on the folded tops of the boulders.

"That way," Ryan said confidently, pointing to the south.

"Wait," Krysty ordered.

"I hear dogs," Jak said, brushing his hair back from the side of his head.

"Yes," Krysty agreed. "Pack of dogs, coming this way. Fast. Listen. You'll all hear them soon. They're hunting."

Lori heard them next, then Ryan and the other two—a high keening that rose and fell as the animals ran into hollows or over hills in their hunt. Ryan felt the hair on his nape rise at the sound. It was a familiar noise from his childhood. He had heard it when he'd ridden to the hounds after boar, galloping behind his father, stirrup to stirrup with his oldest brother, Morgan.

"What do we do?" the Armorer asked. "I'll get the Uzi out the wag."

"Wait," Ryan urged. "If it's a full pack, then blasters won't be much use. There'll be forty or fifty curs, trained to go for throat or groin. The only chance is to get in the wag and shut the door."

"Then whoever's running the dogs'll take us like rats in a trap," Krysty argued.

"Better than being ripped apart."

"Guess so, lover," she said.

But the pack veered away, heading east. While the six friends stood huddled together, they heard the hunting animals finally catch up with their prey and make their kill.

The screaming went on and on for what seemed like long minutes but probably only lasted for thirty seconds or so. It was a shriek of purest agony. And it was undeniably human.

Chapter Nineteen

"THE MEMORIES ARE flooding back and filling my brain with the past," Ryan said vehemently.

They'd been walking through the evening and into the night, traveling on a twisting network of narrow footpaths. They heard the sound of the pack of hounds, called back by a blaring horn, gradually fading away to the south, toward the ville.

Jak led the way with his good night sight, and at one point spotted the far-off glow of cooking fires. Ryan recalled that there were many small hamlets or settlements scattered around the area.

"They all owed work and land to the ville," he said. "The baron had almost total power over them."

"Almost?" Doc questioned.

Ryan grinned, his teeth white in the moonlight. "Yeah, Doc. Almost. Ville couldn't stop you chilling yourself." He paused. "But your family'd suffer if you took that road out."

One thing had changed in the years since Ryan had fled the region, half-blind and nine parts crazed. There had been a steady infiltration of mutie raiders from the west, and all the small communities now had armed patrols out every night, all local men who knew every twist and turn of the dense forests.

Jak and Krysty heard them coming almost simultaneously. But it was too late.

Short of a full-fledged firefight, Ryan and his group had no way of escape.

The villagers must have heard *them* coming, or seen them through the trees. There were six men, all armed with a variety of handblasters, ranging from an old English Enfield to a target .22 Colt with sawed-off sights. All of them handled the pistols as if they knew how to use them. They had come in on opposite sides, calling out a warning from cover.

"One step and you're all chilled!"

Jak was the only one who went through with a draw, hefting the gleaming Magnum from his belt and waving it threateningly at the trees surrounding them. Ryan snapped out an order for him to holster the gun.

"Don't, Jak. Not now."

"Do like the one-eye says," came the voice, soft and calm.

"Okay, Ry...Floyd!" The albino nearly blew the pseudonym, just remembering it in time.

"Like to see all the blasters by your feet, real slow 'n' easy."

Ryan glanced around. He spotted the six men easily enough, but saw that they were well protected by the trunks of the sycamores. He felt angry with himself for allowing the double-poors to come and take them as easy as that. The only consolation was that they hadn't opened fire on them.

There was also the odd feeling that he didn't need to take any precautions. He was Ryan Cawdor, son of the old baron and brother to Harvey Cawdor, ruler of Front Royal ville and the thousands of acres around it. Why should he not feel safe? And that same feeling had somehow communicated itself to Jak and to the rest of the group.

"Put the guns down," he ordered. He raised his voice to address the leader of the patrol. "We're traders. Our wag ran dry three days back. Been wandering around these forests ever since. Where are we, friend? We were heading for the ville of Front Royal to trade in fish and fruit."

"Baron Cawdor's ville has no need of fruit or fish, *friends*. So you've wasted your journey."

"Are we near the ville?" Krysty asked.

"You mutie? You and the snow-hair kid? Baron don't welcome muties, lady."

"We aren't muties. None of us."

"Step back from the blasters. Now take some care. One at a time you step forward and we'll search you. Make sure there's nobody holding on to a hideaway. That'd be a mistake."

Ryan was impressed with the man's control. It was impossible to make him out clearly, but he sounded only in his late teens or early twenties. He had handled the ambush with an almost ridiculous ease, plucking them all into his net like ripe fruit.

"What's your name and where are we?" Ryan called.

"Hamlet of Shersville, friend. Name's Nathan Freeman. Sec head of our small ville. That's 'nough talk. Old man first."

The search was thorough, and sec men found the knives that Ryan, J.B. and Jak carried, but missed the swordstick that belonged to Doc Tanner.

"Seems okay," Freeman said, still keeping cautiously out of sight. "You can pick up the blasters and come with us. Stay in Shersville a day or two. Then be on your way."

A skinny hunched man called from the other side of the clearing. "Gotta let baron know. Strangers, Nate. Gotta tell him."

"Baron wants to know any danger, Tom. These six won't topple Front Royal. I believe what they say. Let 'em be."

"Cause trouble, Nate. Trouble for you is trouble for Shersville. Trouble for one is trouble for all."

"Damn that fear, Tom!" the leader shouted, suddenly vehement. "The shadow is fucking long. All knows that. But it's not forever. One day there'll be change."

"You speak treason, Nathan," came another voice, older and calmer. "There's many loves you but there's those in Shersville'd see you fall and the chance of wolfs-head jack from th'Baron."

"Shersville don't need such as them. One day we can stand and fall as we are. Not 'cause of fear of the baron and that sluttish..."

"Nate!" Tom shouted. "Watch your tongue, you stupe. Or we'll all dance on cold air for it."

Ryan found the conversation utterly fascinating. There was obviously some deep-rooted and bitter feelings against his brother and Lady Rachel. But there was also intense fear of the chilling power of the ville. The barons Cawdor of Front Royal had always had long arms.

"Said we should report strangers, Nate."

"Yeah, yeah, yeah! I hear you. I say let 'em have their blasters and come with us. Day Shersville can't offer shelter and food to lost strangers is the day Shersville loses all it ever had."

"We are obliged to you, young man," Doc Tanner said as courteous as ever. His hand moved to his sparse silver locks to sweep the stovepipe hat off in an elegant bow, but he let it fall again to his side as he remembered that the ancient hat was now part of the flotsam and jetsam off the New Jersey shore.

"Yeah, we're grateful, Master Freeman," Ryan said. "From what we heard, it sounds like there could be trouble from this baron if you give us shelter. Wouldn't want that."

"Tom speaks over the top. Baron demands we watch the borders for muties and hire-killers. You aren't the first. As for the second... Like I said, six won't take Front Royal. So what's to tell the good Baron Cawdor?"

Nathan Freeman turned and led the way through the bright silvered night, following the trail as it gradually became broader, blending with other tracks until they were on a well-preserved blacktop.

The rest of the villagers straggled along in the rear, talking quietly and urgently together.

"You worried them," Ryan said.

Freeman shook his head. "My mother used to say something about dying on your feet mebbe being better than living on your belly. The ville's been too powerful for too long since Baron Harvey stole it."

"Stole?" J.B. asked.

"Long story. I wasn't even born when it began. We'll get to Shersville and get some food down you. Then I'll tell you."

Ryan had noticed that the man had been staring curiously at his eye patch. When the question finally came, he was ready for it.

"Best I know your names," Freeman said, "so's I can say I made proper inquiries. And I wonder 'bout that wound to your face."

"I'm Floyd Thursby. This is J. B. Dix, Krysty Wroth, Lori Quint, Doc Tanner and Jak Lauren. This?" He lifted a hand to touch the leather patch over his left eye. "Don't much like talking about it. Double-stupe way to lose half your sight."

"How?"

"Rabbit."

"How's that?"

"I was in my twentieth summer, out west, where I was born. Been trapping with my uncle. Both my parents died when I was three. There was a big buck caught in a snare around its foreleg. The wire had bitten deep to the bone and the creature seemed like it was nearly chilled."

Everyone had stopped, gathering around to hear the conclusion of the story. Ryan wasn't a natural-born liar, and he struggled to keep the tale as short and as simple as possible.

"Stooped over it, skinning knife in my right hand. Been a bad chem storm and it was dark, under some trees. Bent low. Fucker wasn't near dead, and it kicked out at me. Hooked this eye out from its socket neat as a stone from a plum. Gouged this down me at the same time." He touched the jagged cicatrix that seamed his cheek from eye to mouth on the right side of his lean face.

"Coney blinded you!" The villager called Tom laughed. "If that don't take the biscuit! A coney spoiled the stranger's looks."

Ryan turned slowly and stared at the man, the moon catching his good eye, giving it a glint of ferocious anger. It checked the laughter so quickly that Tom nearly choked on his tongue.

"No harm meant, Master Thursby," he stammered out, taking a stumbling half step back, stepping on the toes of the man behind him.

"No harm done, friend." Ryan smiled.

"THERE'S STRANGE FRUIT, lover," Krysty whispered as they came within sight of the hamlet of Shersville, a quarter hour later.

Ryan looked where she pointed. Ahead of them, fringing the road, were five corpses. Three had been hanged and two had been crucified on crude crosses.

"Baron Harvey's orchard," one of the older men with them cackled.

"Pour encourager les autres," Doc Tanner muttered.

"How's that, Doc?" Jak asked.

"It means, my dear boy, that the baron believes in visible lessons to those who might consider crossing him."

Ryan stopped in front of the first of the bodies. It was a woman, naked, aged around fifty by the look of the dried, wrinkled flesh. There wasn't enough left of the face to be more certain. Strands of ragged, graying hair still clung to the gnarled bone of the skull. The lower jaw had become detached and fallen to the earth. The eyes were long gone, pecked out by the crows that they'd seen near where they had parked the wag. The hempen rope around the scrawny throat was stained black with ancient blood.

The next dangling corpse was a man. But it was only by the torn ribbons of breeches and jerkin that you could guess it. The body had obviously hung there longer than the old woman; the flesh had turned to crisp leather, tanned and gleaming in the bright moonlight. The hands were bound behind the back, and the ankles were also tied together. One foot was missing.

The third body was smaller, younger and fresher. The eyes were missing, as well as the lips and part of the soft flesh of the cheeks. It was a teenage boy, flaxen-headed and slightly built. Both hands were gone, obviously cut off before the lynching. Smears of thick tar around the stumps showed where a crude effort had been made to stop the lad from bleeding to death before he could be strung up.

"Found a boar with broken legs out in the wild Shens, south of here," Nathan Freeman said, voice as cold as death. "Beast was done and he slit its throat and took a haunch for food for his family. Live on the edge of Shersville. Someone leaked word to the baron and..." The sentence drifted away into the silence of the night.

Both of the crucified corpses were men.

"See this on every road around Front Royal," Tom mumbled almost apologetically, as though he needed to give the six strangers some sort of an explanation for the horrors.

"Been up for weeks, them two," added the oldest of the villagers. "Both gotten catched hoarding food meant for Lady Rachel's horses."

"That's a high price," J.B. said, staring up at the tortured corpses.

"Bad way t'go," Nathan commented. "The hunk of wood for your feet makes it longer. Ropes around the wrists and ankles. Baron wanted nails used, but Lady Rachel said nails made it quicker. Through the tendons and bones at wrist and ankle. Ropes is more cruel, she said. So it was ropes."

"What chills you?" Jak asked, displaying a ghoulish interest in the mechanics of how a crucifixion actually worked.

Nathan pointed. "See the way the head falls forward on the chest? Whole body leans out. Closes up the chest so you can't breathe. You pull yourself up straight. Then the strain's too much so you slump. Goes on until you choke."

"Bastard hard," Ryan said.

"Indeed, Master Thursby," the tall young man agreed. "But the baron and his...his lady have less kind ways."

"Worse than that!" Krysty exclaimed, shaking her head in disgust.

"A man who spit at Lady Rachel Cawdor, for what she'd done to his family, was taken and stripped and his wrists bound tight with whipcord. Then he was placed on a large wooden spike that tapered, becoming wider and wider."

Jak looked puzzled. "Placed? How d'you mean? How?"

"Point up his ass, Whitey," Tom explained. "He gripped with his feet. But he got tired, didn't he, mates? Slipped down a bit. Then there was all the blood and stuff on the spike. He went down farther. And in the end it came clean out through—"

"Enough!" Doc Tanner shouted. "By the three Kennedys! This is monstrous." He turned to Ryan, whose heart sank at the suspicion that the old man, in his rage, was about to call him by his real name. And possibly destroy them all.

"Don't glare at Floyd, Doc!" Lori shrieked, hanging onto his arm and nearly pulling him clear off-balance.

"Who? Don't what, child? Who is..." The light of reason seeped back into the eyes. "I swear I was near the brink of... But let it pass. Master Thursby, I fear that I cannot, nay, will not, spend a night in the shadow of these poor curs."

"Where can you go, Doc?" Ryan asked.

"Back to wag. I knew the trails," Lori said. "I could have found it easy."

"You said it was days off," Tom interrupted, suspicious. "Didn't yer?"

"There's a cache of food," Krysty said quickly. "Mebbe it'd be safer for them, Floyd."

"If'n that's what you want, Doc."

"I can lead you back," Nathan Freeman offered. "Know these woods from a child. On the morrow I can trail and make sure all's well."

"No need, thanks," J.B. said. "We know where the wag is."

"Sure," Ryan added, taking the old man by the arm and leading him out of earshot of the others, Lori following closely.

"We'll be fine, Ryan," the old man whispered. "Be good cover if'n there should be trouble. Don't trust them."

"The young man, Nathan, seems a straight. But I know what you mean. So much fear of the ville. We'll stay there for the night and then leave early morning. Stay at the wag and we'll pick you both up before noon. Is that okay?"

Doc gripped him by the hand. "Ryan...I mean, Floyd. I don't have the power of a doomie to see the future. But I fear that this promises ill. Will you abandon the venture, come back to the gateway and let us go elsewhere?"

Ryan sighed. "No, Doc. Thanks for the warning. But I've come too far, too far to turn back now. Take care. And you, Lori. See you tomorrow."

The slim young girl led the way back along the trail, Doc Tanner walking more slowly, stumbling a little, after her. In a very short time they'd both disappeared into the darkness, leaving Ryan to wonder whether he should have let them go.

Or whether they should all have gone with them to the wag.

You could almost taste the fear when Nathan Freeman led the strangers into the hamlet. Many of the inhabitants were asleep, but most of those were quickly awakened by the noise that greeted Ryan and the other three.

Nathan brushed aside any discussion about whether the baron should be told, and Ryan did what he could to reassure everyone that they would be leaving early in the morning. They were taken to a barn, clean and dry, with ample fresh straw for all four of them to sleep in comfort.

A woman carried in a tray that held cups of warm goat's milk and four wooden bowls containing thick vegetable soup. Her hands trembled as she served them.

They all fell asleep quickly. Ryan awoke only once, around two, when he thought he heard the sound of a horse's hooves, muffled. Though he lay and listened, the sound wasn't repeated, and he was soon asleep once more.

Chapter Twenty

THEY ROSE EARLY in Shersville, and had breakfast by eight o'clock. Ryan had risen earlier, only a few minutes after a pale dawn. He'd pulled on his high combat boots and tucked his pistol and panga in their sheaths. As he walked out of the barn, he nearly bumped into the tall well-built figure of Nathan Freeman, who stood patiently in the deep shadow of the wooden building.

"Good morrow, Master...Thursby." The hesitation before the name was so slight that most men wouldn't have noticed it at all.

Ryan noticed.

"Morning, friend," he said.

"The others awake?"

"No."

"I'd like a chance of a talk, Floyd."

Ryan looked at the young man, noting the peculiar dark shade of his eyes, so dark it was almost black.

"Now?" the older man asked.

"Too many would wonder. After we've eaten. There's bread and there's eggs...and everyone is about their own business. Then we could walk to the river and talk together. Yes?"

Ryan nodded. "Okay, Nathan." He wondered whether he should ask him about the horse he'd heard leaving the village during the night, but decided it wasn't worth it.

THE BREAD WAS NEWLY BAKED, crusty and delicious, its top covered with small, crisp seeds that burst with flavor. The eggs were scrambled with butter and a mix of herbs. Even Jak Lauren, who was not normally a sturdy trencherman so early in the morning, devoured three helpings, wiping grease from his chin and looking longingly at the platter that crackled and spit over the open fire with more eggs.

"Fucking good," he said, belching, earning a reproof from the middle-aged woman who'd been serving the breakfast. She rapped him over the back of the head with the heavy wooden ladle.

"A loose tongue is an affront to an honest woman," she said.

"Where's this fucking honest woman?" he retorted, grinning impishly at her, delighted to see the hectic spots of angry color that sprang to her rounded cheeks.

"By the Blessed Ryan, I'll...!" she began, then put her hand over her mouth and turned away from them, gathering her long skirts and darting into one of the huts.

The four friends sat in silence, looking at one another. It was Jak who broke the stillness.

"Hear that, Mr. Thursby? Hear what old crone said?"

Ryan nodded slowly. Somehow, it didn't surprise him. He knew from plenty of other primitive double-poor Deathlands communities that odd religions were the norm. If Harvey Cawdor was the obscene tyrant he seemed, it made a kind of bizarre sense that some of the older locals might still cherish the name of the vanished son. It was something he needed to think about. And maybe talk to Nathan Freeman about. He stood and went to join him.

They sat side by side, on the bank of the narrow, twisting river. Nathan had said that it didn't have a name. It was just "the river." That was all it had ever been. As there was only the one, it didn't need to be called anything.

The water gurgled over round moss-green stones, forming small pools where delicate silverfish weaved and darted. Ryan watched them, leaning back against the sun-warmed bole of a toppled beech tree.

"Good feeling, Nate," he said.

"Not many of those within a country mile of Front Royal and the Cawdors. Father, mother and devil brat."

"Tell me a bit 'bout the ville and the Cawdors. I don't know this region well."

"Don't you, Master Thursby?" Freeman asked with an odd insistency. "Sure 'bout that, are you?"

"Course. You lived here all your life?"

"Yeah. Father was a local man. My mother came to Shersville when I was around three years old. Never rightly found where we'd been till then. Traveling some was all she'd tell me. Died when I was still a boy. Neighbors raised me."

"The Cawdors?"

"Run the ville since the long winter, so the oldsters say. Old baron died around twenty years back. Whispers tell of his being choked by Lady Rachel. But . . ." He allowed the sentence to drift off into silence. "There were three brothers. One good, one bad and one . . . one that just up and vanished, Master Thursby. He was... I'll come to him last. There was Morgan, who was everything good. Murdered by Harvey, who now runs the ville, who's every evil you could set your mind to. A gross and perverted bastard who shadows the earth he waddles over. Married to slut Rachel. One son, Jabez Pendragon Cawdor. Has every stinking, rotten part of both his parents in him. I can't . . . There aren't words for someone like him."

"The other brother?"

"Ryan Cawdor. Fifteen when he disappeared. Word was of an attempt on his life. That left him . . . Swift and vengeful boy, they say. Some think him rotting in the moat, like many another. But a lot of honest folks still think that one day he'll come riding in from the west on a stallion of pure white. He'll slaughter the Cawdors, take back the ville and the sunshine days will come again to all in the Shens. What d'you think of that, Master . . . Thursby?"

This time the hesitation was plain.

"What do you think about this missing brother, Master . . . Freeman?" Ryan dragged the pause out even longer.

"I think that I believe some things and not others. You know?"

"What?"

"I believe he escaped. I believe he lives. I don't believe in the dreck about a white stallion or a blaster that fires golden ammo. No!"

"I heard a tale, Master Freeman."

"Tell me." The young man picked up a handful of dried cones from a nearby pine tree and flicked them underhanded into the water, staring after them as they bobbed and leaped through the shallows and falls of the narrow river. He kept his face turned away from Ryan.

"Morgan Cawdor, they say, had a woman, and the woman bore a child after the death of her husband. Murdered, we agree, by Harvey. A son, I heard. The mother was mutie."

"She was . . ." the young man began, pale face flushing, dark eyes glaring. He threw the rest of the cones into the water with a barely controlled viciousness.

"She was what? I heard she was a woman with the power of seeing. If there had been a son, could he have inherited that?'' He waited a moment, then answered his own question. ''Perhaps.''

''They say that Ryan Cawdor was desperate wounded when he fled the ville.''

''Do they?''

''They say that a blade from Harvey's fist took out an eye, neat as a stone from a ripe plum—so they say—and opened a cut that ran from eye to mouth along the right side of the boy's cheek.''

Then he turned and looked straight into Ryan's good eye, a fierce intensity in his glittering black eyes.

Neither man spoke for several heart-stopping seconds.

The moment broke into shards of crystal time as a voice wafted to them from the trail that led to the village.

''Nate? You there?''

''Yeah.''

''Seen Tom?''

''No. Saw him late last night. Not this morning. Why d'you . . . ?''

''Missing. Horse gone an' all.''

Ryan felt the short hairs rising on the back of his neck— the familiar warning of imminent danger. Sitting close to the young man, he was aware of Nathan's whole body tensing and stiffening. His mouth hung open, and the breath hissed through the man's teeth.

''We've—''

''I heard it,'' Ryan interrupted.

''The horse? The bastard's gone to the ville.''

There was a cold horror in Nathan's voice and blank, shocked face.

''Couple of hours after midnight. Listened. Didn't hear anything more.''

Freeman stood up, uncoiling with an easy grace. "You heard it! By all the gods, Ryan! Didn't you *feel* it? Didn't you *see* it?"

Ryan also stood, hardly noticing in the sudden, dreadful tension that Nathan had admitted he was indeed part mutie. And he had called him "Ryan." He knew him.

And, in turn, Ryan realized his own guess was correct. He knew who Nathan Freeman was!

"Morgan's son," he said softly. "You're the son of my brother. Your mother was Guenema. I'm your uncle, lad."

"Hell," Nate said. "I guess I knew that all along, Uncle Ryan." His expression changed. "But now's not the time. Gotta move, and fast."

"We been betrayed?"

"Tom. Wants to be sec chief of Shersville. Guess he'll get his way now." The words tumbled over one another in the young man's haste to explain.

"When will they come, Nate?"

The water was covering their conversation from the villager standing a few paces behind them.

"They're here."

"What? Fireblast! We have—"

Nathan Freeman laid a hand on his arm. "Too late. Now I'm concentrating I can hear 'em. Load of sec men, on all sides. They'll take you, even in a firefight. Listen, I can make it through the woods. Get to the old man and the straw-head girl. To your wag. Other blasters there?"

"Yeah. Couple."

"I know paths and ways. I'll do what I can, Ryan. Don't fight. Harvey and Rachel aren't muties. Won't expect you. Won't think it's you, mebbe. Play Floyd Thursby. Stick to your story. Could get away. Watch

Rachel. More, watch Jabez. Warn others. Me and the other two'll do what we can, when we can.''

Ryan's fighting brain was racing. He still hadn't heard any sound of a sec patrol closing in on them, but he'd seen enough of mutie skills in his life to know that his nephew was probably telling the truth. There'd been a blind listener up in the high plains who could hear a kerchief of satin fall on soft earth at two hundred yards.

"Yeah," Ryan said. "Don't charge in after us. If'n we can fool 'em, we could get away free. Foolish to lose lives for nothing. Wait and listen, Nate. That's the best.''

Then Ryan heard them—horse-mounted sec men, clattering along the main blacktop through Shersville. He knew they'd be good mounts. Front Royal had always been famed for the quality of its horses. Right back to the time before the long winter.

"Gotta go," Nathan whispered. "Just meet the man I dreamed of for twenty fucking years. And we gotta part.''

"Watch your back, Nate," Ryan said, quickly shaking hands with his nephew. The grip was brief but firm.

The young man leaped at the river, balancing for a moment on a large flat stone near the center, then hopped to another, smaller stone. With a splash, he reached the opposite bank. Pausing for a second and waving a hand to Ryan, he then disappeared into the dense screen of bushes.

Ryan turned away to make his way back to Shersville, where the sec men were already in control.

FOR A MOMENT Ryan's head whirled, and he felt himself transported back to his fifteenth year, battling for his life in a blood-slippery passageway in the stone heart of the ville. The uniforms of the sec men were unaltered: maroon jerkins, with breeches tucked into high boots. They wore helmets that hugged the skull, and some wore goggles. They were armed with the same M-16 assault rifles that Ryan also remembered well enough from his childhood—trusty weapons that had served the barony well over the years since the endless chilling.

Krysty, Jak and J.B. stood in a group outside the barn, surrounded by at least thirty of the guards. The old man, Tom, preened himself nearby. He was grinning broadly, chest out like a little pigeon, bursting with pride at his own achievement.

The leader of the sec guards was a sergeant, tall and with shoulders nearly as broad as the doors on the barn. He saw Ryan coming toward him and grinned.

"Hurry up, One Eye. That's four plucked and two to go."

"Where's Nathan Freeman?" Tom yelped.

"Who?" Ryan said.

"You know, you bastard!" screeched the venomous little villager. "Make him tell," he whined to the sergeant.

The sec man spit in the mud, not bothering to hide his contempt. "Baron says you get to be sec chief of this dung heap until someone better comes along. So zip up that mouth of yours or I'll shut it. I decide what happens."

"And what's that, Sergeant?" Ryan asked. "We're travelers who only arrived in the Shens a day ago. We hoped to move on."

"Came in a wag?"

"Yes."

"Where? Where's the wag?"

"Ran dry way back north. Dumped it. No chance of gas around here?"

The big sec officer laughed. "Not for the likes of you scum. Baron controls all gas for fifty miles around."

"Why are you here with this army?" J.B. asked.

"Old runt said you was armed and dangerous. Said there was two more of you. Old man and pretty little girl. True?"

Krysty stepped forward and smiled at the sergeant. "Do we look dangerous? Our two friends have gone to try to make their way back to the wag. But we fear they might be lost in the forest."

"Don't waste all that fucking charm, sister," the sec man said, the smile vanishing. "Got my cock and balls blown off by an old anti-pers mine ten years back. Don't fuck a lot now. We'll get moving." He shouted an order to the patrol, standing stone-faced in a maroon circle. They snapped to attention and began to shepherd Ryan and his companions toward the road, where they saw a couple of horse-drawn wagons with barred sides and roof, obviously built to accommodate prisoners.

As he passed Tom, Ryan whispered to the old man. "One night you'll feel cold steel in your groin."

The villager turned as white as a sheet and tottered, hand going to his heart.

Ryan smiled at him as they were led into the wagons. The three men were put in the first cart, Krysty in the second one.

THE SKY THREATENED RAIN. The air felt cool and damp and the breath of the horses hung about them like fog. They could see mist filling the hollows on the other side of the wide valley, leaving only the tips of the trees emerging from the pale blue haze.

The sergeant was at the head of the convoy, followed by a dozen mounted sec men. Then came the cart with the men, and a dozen more troopers, followed by the wagon with Krysty, and another dozen horsemen at the rear.

Oddly there had been no attempt made to disarm them. Ryan had seen the eyes of the sergeant home in on the butt of the SIG-Sauer, but it remained in its holster. He guessed they would lose their arms when they reached the ville.

For Ryan it was a journey deeper into his own past.

Every rattling turn of the wheels brought him closer to the ville. Every now and again he'd recognize some bridge or building or turn of the road. Once a massive wild boar thundered across the trail, making half the horses rear and whinny, throwing a couple of the sec men. Its eyes were vicious rubies, and Ryan saw fresh blood on its curved tusks.

They also passed more signs of the tyranny of Baron Cawdor and his family. Eight corpses. One in chains at a crossroads gibbet, not a shred of flesh remaining on the dry bones. Three on makeshift gallows, one a woman. Three crucified, two of them children, whose frail little bodies looked no more than six years of age. And the charred remnants of a corpse, smoldering in glowing metal links at the center of a heap of ashes.

It took close to two hours for them to finally reach the massive ville of Front Royal. And when they did, Krysty stared out in disbelief. The ville was just about the biggest building she'd ever seen in her entire life. It was like pictures of medieval castles in the old books she'd read as a child in Harmony. The brick was weathered to a glorious golden hue that shone, even on such a dull morning. The windows were mainly narrow slits, as in most armored wags. But high up on one wall was an arched window that looked as if it were made of colored glass. There was a wide river around the outside with only a single bridge that crossed it, which could be raised or lowered on chains from inside the ville. Through the archway, under a spiked gateway, Krysty could make out a central courtyard, where armed men patrolled. For at least two hundred yards on all sides of the squat building, the trees and bushes had been hacked down to prevent them being used as cover by any would-be attackers.

She realized then why the Cawdors had been able to control so much of the Shens for so many years. With a hundred armed sec men and a ville of this strength, it was impossible to conceive of the baron ever being humbled.

Krysty began to feel very frightened.

As soon as the wagons had rattled over the cobblestones of the bridge across the sedge-crusted moat, they reined in to a halt. The four friends were hustled with an overfirm politeness through a studded doorway, along a narrow corridor, past other guards and into a large chamber.

"One at a time into there," the big sergeant said, pointing at another door. "Everything off. There's a bolt on the inside, in case you worry about your privacy or whatever. There's clothes and boots on racks on the walls. All sizes. Leave everything there. It'll be boxed up and kept for if . . . for when you get out of the ville."

"Blasters?" J.B. asked.

"Watch my lips, short-ass. Everything. Know what that means? It means ev-er-y-thing. Far side there's another door. Go through it and wait. Don't try to fuck off anywhere else. You'll be watched. And don't forget to unbolt this door before you go on through. You read me?" He glowered at J.B.

"Sure you don't want us to unhook our balls in there, so we can all be the same?" the Armorer replied, never one to be faced down, even when he was at least a foot and a half shorter than the sergeant.

The sec man stared, stone-eyed for a moment, then nodded and laughed. ''Mebbe that old coot back in Shersville had something, little man. Mebbe you're more than . . . Mebbe we'll talk after the baron and the lady've spoken to you. I hope so. That jest of yours could turn sour.'' He looked at the others. ''Now who goes first?''

''Me,'' Ryan said.

He pushed the door shut behind him, not bothering to slide the heavy iron bolt. If the sec men wanted to get in at him, a single bolt wasn't going to hold them off, and the far door had no lock, anyway. But to make up for that the farther doorway was encircled by what he recognized as a sophisticated metal detector in top condition. The only better one he'd ever seen had been in a double-class gaudy house down in Norleans, years ago.

The sets of clothes that lined the wall, which looked like sucked-out corpses, were in the familiar dark color that was worn by most of the interior servants of Front Royal ville. They had a strip of black on the lapels, with a neat red star that showed they were guests.

His mind raced with what was happening. The last time he'd seen his brother, Harvey, it had been through a welter of streaming blood. The air had been filled with murder. Now, after so many years, he was about to meet up with Harvey Cawdor once more.

If he recognized Ryan as his missing brother, then death would follow as surely as night followed day. But would he?

That was the question that occupied Ryan as he pulled off his steel toe-capped boots and replaced them with the soft leather ankle boots. He placed all of his clothes in a large canvas bag, putting his weapons on top of it—the long panga and the slim-bladed flensing knife, with the 9 mm SIG-Sauer on the very top.

He tried to recall what this part of the ville had been used for when he'd been there, but time had blurred the edges of his memory. Some kind of storeroom, he thought.

"Rutabagas," he exclaimed out loud, remembering now that there had been a great dump of yellow turnips in the room. They'd been piled high in the corner where the boots were stacked near the farther door. He'd used it when playing hide-and-seek with Morgan when he'd been about nine years old. He'd carved his name with a battered horn-hafted knife on the side of the door. Ryan went and peered to examine the frame, but it had been rebuilt and painted several times and there was no sign of his initials.

Dressed and ready, he now had to go and face the next room in the ville, and hazard the chance of being recognized by his brother. Ryan took a deep breath and pushed the door open. The chamber beyond was dimly lit, and he blinked into the darkness.

A voice bubbled out from above and behind him. "Welcome to Front Royal, brother."

Chapter Twenty-One

BROTHER!

He knew. Harvey Cawdor knew, had known all along! Someone had recognized Ryan, had spotted the blind eye and the torn face and put two and two together. It had all been a setup to take him off-balance, to get his weapons away without a fuss. The gentle approach.

Ryan winced, waiting for the crushing impact of a .45-caliber bullet between his shoulder blades. Or would it be slower?

"For any man that comes to our home is surely our brother, is he not? Or our sister. If he is a woman she is . . . then she is not our brother but our sister. Then our sister and our brother are all men and women who visit us." The muddled sentences dribbled away into a gurgling, chortling laugh, which sounded like thick gruel boiling on an open fire.

Ryan turned around slowly, fighting for control as he realized he was not down and doomed. Not yet.

His eye was quickly becoming accustomed to the smoky half-light, which was generated by flaming torches placed in wall sconces around the room. There was a balcony that ran clear around the second-floor level. This had been a small dining room when Ryan had been a child, and there had been music—mandolin, dulcimer and banjo—played from the balcony.

Now Harvey Cawdor, baron of the ville, stood there with his woman at his side.

"We welcome you, Master Thursby, to Front Royal. You will understand that we must take precautions—" he stretched the word out to an absurd length, as if he savored every elongated syllable "—precautions . . . against them that trespass against me. You saw our crop of flowering trees as you came here, Master Thursby?"

"Yes, Baron." Ryan made a half bow to the shadowy figure.

"Good, good, good. You see, dearest, that here is a man of culture and understanding who will be welcome. Not some ragged and double-poor fucking bastard who would covet everything I own!"

Ryan took a deep breath. The change from the effusive and elegant welcome to the foul words—delivered in a rising and hysterical scream—was totally unexpected, bringing to Ryan the realization that his older brother might well be full-crazy.

"Where are the other visitors, brother? Brother Thursby?"

At that moment the door opened again, and Krysty Wroth came in, wearing a dark blue blouse and knee-length skirt of the same Front Royal livery. Her ankle boots were of plain untanned leather with a low, stacked heel. She'd used a piece of thin cord to tie back her cascade of hair. Even in the poor light of the vaulted room it still blazed like a coronet of living fire.

"Brother, wel... Come... sister. Sister welcome. Is she...?"

Ryan heard a woman's voice for the first time, pitched low, but with the crack of a command to it. The bulky figure of the man shifted sideways a few steps, until it stood directly beneath one of the torches.

Then, at long last, Ryan was able to properly see his brother. He had the same clumsy, shuffling, crablike walk with the right leg trailing and the right shoulder lifted in an unsightly hump. His face was partly in shadow, but Ryan could detect that there was some malformation of the mouth and nose. After so many years it gave him a thrill of vicious pleasure to see that his parting punch into his brother's hooked nose had been so brutally successful.

But above all of this was the astonishing way that Harvey Cawdor had grown grotesquely fat.

Not plump. Not just obese. But grossly, obscenely fat. He wore a flowing gown, like a cerise bed sheet, but it couldn't conceal his size. A quick guess put him around the 350-pound mark. His clothes were covered in delicate filigree embroidery, in woven patterns of silver and gold. His chubby hands were smothered in rings, one with what looked like a human eye set in a stone of amber.

Lady Rachel moved, with an infinite grace that caught Ryan's attention, to stand near the lord of the ville. Her face turned away from the light to peer down into the gloomy cavern of the hall at the man and the woman. She was taller than Harvey Cawdor, slim and elegant, wearing a gown that looked like black velvet, soft as sin. Her hair was cropped to her narrow shoulders, dark and lustrous. Her cheeks were very pale, and her eyes had vanished like gemstones of midnight jet in the hollows of their sockets. She wore no facial makeup, and her fingers were long and strong without any jewelry.

"Is the woman mutie?" she asked in a soft, caressing, melodious voice.

"No, she's not, Lady Rachel," Krysty replied in a loud, ringing voice, startling Ryan as he felt it wash over him like a breath of fresh air. Only then did he realize that the room carried the scent of some floral incense. One of his father's serving women had used something like it. The odor was clinging and sickly sweet, like the rotting meat that attracts the most beautiful of butterflies.

"Where are the others of your party, Master Thursby?" the lady asked. "There are two more men and then two more that have fled our hospitality into the unfriendly Shens."

"True, my lady. Doctor Theophilus Tanner and his...and Lori Quint. I am Floyd Thursby, as you know, and this is Krysty Wroth, from the ville of Harmony." He turned as the door opened once more. "This is Jak Lauren from the far south of the Deathlands."

The woman on the balcony gasped aloud. "Azrael! His hair, husband!"

"Mutie. A mutie, here in the heart of my ville. Take him, guards! Slit his throat and in the boar pit for my precious pets."

"He is not a mutie, great lord," Krysty said. "His hair is natural. Where he comes from it's as common as red or black hair."

Harvey Cawdor laughed, shaking like a massive cherry jelly. "'Great lord!' Rachel, did you hear? The red-hair is... I like her, like her, like her." His voice edged up the scale toward a falsetto shriek that made the torches dance and flare into bright flames.

At that moment, as quick and neat as ever, J.B. came into the room, glanced up at where the lord and lady of the manor stood and folded himself into a bow so deep it held the taint of parody. Fortunately neither of the Cawdors seemed aware of that. Ryan introduced him.

"John Barrymore Dix, from Cripple Creek in the Rockies. A man with a great skill with all blasters and weapons."

"Could use him, Rachel," a slobbering Harvey said. "Lotsa blasters going home, sweet home on the range. Need a good man to put them together again, again."

"Now that we've seen you, you can eat with us," Lady Rachel Cawdor called down. "And you can all tell us more about yourselves. Then we can decide whether you . . . what happens to you."

There was a third person behind the ornate pillars of the balcony, indistinct and shadowy, with a pale round blur of a face. The clothes were as dark as Rachel Cawdor's, with what looked like a chain of gold around the neck. It held a single large amethyst, cut so that its facets reflected bolts of violet light across the room.

As quickly as he appeared, the person vanished, moving with a gentle ease, not making a sound. Ryan looked again at the space where he'd been, doubting his own sight. But he noticed that Krysty had also seen him.

She mouthed the single word "Jabez" to Ryan.

Suddenly the audience with the rulers of Front Royal was over.

Rachel had begun to show signs of a strange unease. Her hands fluttered around her mouth, like startled birds, and she rubbed at her lips, chafing the skin of her cheeks. When she spoke, her voice had dropped, becoming rapid and urgent. She told Ryan and the others that they should wait for the sec men, who were posted at each corner of the large hall, to take them to their quarters for the night.

"We eat at six in the evening. Don't leave your rooms, or you'll be killed on the spot."

It was said with a chilling finality. Ryan watched them go, his brother shuffling haltingly like a mountain of blubber after his wife. One thing was sure: Lady Rachel Cawdor wasn't someone to screw around with.

Chapter Twenty-Two

LOCKED AWAY in the heart of the castlelike ville of Front Royal, Ryan and his friends found that the day passed with infinite slowness.

They had been taken away by the sec patrols, along winding passages, up and down narrow stone staircases, to what Ryan thought must be the third or fourth floor of the fortress. Each of them was pushed firmly into separate rooms, the doors slamming shut behind them, keys grating in locks.

To his amazement Ryan found that he was in a chamber that had once been his nursery. The pictures on the walls of stags and boars being torn apart by ferocious hounds were gone, and the draperies were now of plain blue material. The window, which was barred, looked out over the scum-covered moat across the strip of cleared land to the rolling waves of the forest ocean.

Shelves—mainly empty—lined the wall that had once held Ryan's toys and the handed-down model blasters and soldiers of his two older brothers. Morgan's toys had been well used but serviceable. Harvey's had been generally in mint condition, but with sly damage: a leg severed from a soldier, or a wing cut through on a USAF F-4C Phantom.

There had been something about the shelves, something that Morgan had once shown him. There was some way to get behind it into the room next along the corridor, which had once been used by an earlier baron for his illicit affairs with serving maids. There had been a simple catch, Ryan remembered, but it had been too high and too stiff for him to reach easily.

There was a sliding panel in the center of the heavy oak door, and as Ryan glanced at it, the square moved back silently. An eye appeared briefly, staring in at him. Then the eye was gone, and Ryan thought he glimpsed the violet flash of an amethyst before the panel closed.

If there was a hidden doorway between his room and the next one, it was dangerous to try to find it with someone manning the spyhole. Ryan went back to the window, looking out toward the west over the blue haze of the distant mountains.

He knew Jak Lauren was in the first room along the corridor, and he thought Krysty had been put in the chamber on his right, the chamber that he remembered had the connecting door. It was a possibility worth hanging on to.

Several times during the afternoon he saw or heard someone watching him.

There was a rainstorm at four o'clock. He could hear a bell chiming the hour from the central tower of the ville, a sound that once again plunged his mind back twenty years to his childhood. He remembered standing in this very room, staring out through the window—before it was barred—watching a bald eagle, with a monstrous wingspan of more than twenty feet, pluck a young foal from the meadow and carry it off, whinnying. The mare had run below in hopeless, desperate circles.

His thoughts went to Doc and Lori, out there in the sheeting rain that came slanting in gray clouds from the west. The trails were so complex that he feared they would have become lost, though the girl sometimes displayed an uncanny sense of direction. And there was also the hope that Nathan Freeman would have been able to find them and lead them to the wag. But what could they do against the massively invulnerable pile of stones that was the ville of Front Royal?

"Not much," he muttered to himself.

JUST BEFORE FIVE a tray was brought in by a young man with hard eyes and the kind of formal clothes that a sec man wears when he wants you to know he's a sec man. There was a cup of milk on the tray and some biscuits.

"Baron and Lady Rachel eat at six," he said. "You'll be ready."

"I'm not going anywhere," Ryan replied.

"No. You're not," the sec man said. He backed away to the door, shut it firmly and turned the key in the lock.

Through the brief gap, Ryan noticed a pair of crimson-uniformed sec guards with their M-16 carbines carried at port arms. Despite his gross personal appearance, Baron Harvey ran a tight ville.

Or Lady Rachel did.

There was another flurry of a storm around five-thirty, with surging clouds of dark green and purple skating across the pale blue sky. Lightning crackled through the dark chem clouds, throwing violent shadows across the room where Ryan waited patiently.

The door opened at five to six.

Krysty smiled at him from the corridor. "Don't know 'bout you, lover, but I could eat me a mutie buffalo, horns an' all."

"Pretty mouth, lady. Shut it or lose it," said the sergeant who'd brought them in from Shersville. His eyes met Ryan's stare, and he came close to a smile. "You 'nother wants to try me, One Eye?"

"I'd kill you," Ryan replied, voice quiet and neutral.

"You reckon?"

"I know. You're big and strong, but you're also soft. You gotten used to breaking the arms of women and kids."

"If the baron says what he usually says, we'll have a chance to see if you're right, One Eye."

"I'll wait."

"Threats are cheap." The sergeant grinned, but Ryan could hear that the edge had gone from his voice. The arrogant confidence had been eroded a little by Ryan's calm manner.

"Not a threat. It's a promise. One day you'll learn the difference."

J.B. and Jak joined them in the passage, each with a trio of guards at the shoulder. J.B. made the fortress clothes look like a neat military uniform. The albino boy had already ripped the sleeves out of his jerkin and wore the breeches low on the hip to give himself greater freedom of movement.

"This way," said the sec officer, heels ringing on the stone flags.

They ate in what had always been the old banqueting hall of the ville. Ryan's father had told him that the region around Front Royal had mainly been hit by missiles that killed but didn't destroy. Ryan later came to understand that the missiles had been neutron bombs. It explained why the ville itself was in such remarkable condition for a prewinter building.

The table was the same. Hewn from two pieces of an enormous oak tree, it had been sliced through and joined to give room to seat at least twenty a side. The four "guests" sat together, Ryan and Jak opposite Krysty and the Armorer, at the far end of the table, farthest away from the log fire that crackled and spit brightly and noisily. Sec men, as silent as statues, stood at regular intervals around the perimeter of the hall, and more watched from the gallery on the second floor. The light came from a dozen multibranched candelabra on the table and burning torches spaced along the four walls of the room.

"No elec?" Krysty asked. "Must have."

"Yeah. Most is wind- or water-generated. Storage batteries in the cellars. Always been a tradition here at the ville to use candles and lamps and torches like those."

"Stand for Lord Harvey Cawdor, Baron of Front Royal and his wife, the Lady Rachel!" a voice bellowed from near the fireplace. The four friends stood up, chairs scraping on the rush-covered stone floor.

In the brighter light of the great hall, Harvey Cawdor was even more grotesque than at first sight. Ryan upped his guesstimate of his brother's weight to four hundred pounds, contained in a billowing coat with horn buttons. It was a dark maroon color and seemed to have used up enough material to make a fair-size tent. The clothes were designed to try to minimize his deformities, but nothing could conceal the crooked back or the dragging leg.

The wide belt of polished snakeskin held two small holsters with the gleaming butts of twin Colt pistols peeking from them.

Harvey took a reinforced carving chair at the head of the long table, waving a hand to his wife to sit on his right side.

Rachel Cawdor was in her middle thirties, and it looked as though she worked hard to keep her appearance down in the twenties. The reward was that in the half-light of the big chamber, she could pass for twenty-nine. Maybe.

Her black hair supported a narrow silver coronet that sparkled with diamonds. The piece was a Cawdor heirloom, and Ryan felt a flush of surprising anger at seeing the murderous slut flaunting it. Her dress was a blue velvet so deep that it could be taken for black. A silver brooch shaped like a long-necked flamingo, its tail a mass of different colored precious stones, decorated the low front. She nodded to Ryan and his friends, totally ignoring her husband. On her arm was a small purse of scuffed black leather, at odds with the rest of her immaculate appearance.

The chair to the left of the baron remained empty.

"Is . . . ?" Harvey said, getting an almost imperceptible shake of the head from his wife. "Ah, no matter, matter is energy is mass and matter. Doesn't matter to me. No damn matter."

Once they had both seated themselves, Ryan and his three friends also sat down. The table was so long that they were twenty yards away from Rachel and the baron.

Harvey Cawdor clapped his hands and servants, dressed in the livery of the ville, appeared bearing platters and tureens and great serving dishes. Ryan had somehow expected it would be the same blue dinner service with the willow pattern design that he'd eaten from during his childhood. As the meal began, he realized why that no longer existed. The Baron Cawdor was an intemperate and violently clumsy eater.

There was no question of soup followed by fish, followed by game, followed by salad, followed by a main course of meat with desserts and then cheese and fruit. Everything came at once. The servants lined up at the far end of the table while their lord and master ladled out slopping portions of anything that caught his eye. He piled it all into a bowl in front of him that must have been able to hold five gallons of liquid or thirty pounds of solid food.

At that distance it was difficult for them to see what precisely went into the bowl, but the servants eventually made their way to the guests' end of the table. Lady Rachel only indicated a small portion of steamed fish for herself, with a spoonful of sugar peas. She took only water to drink.

Ryan had rarely seen a more spectacular array of food. There was steak and great hunks of horsemeat, marinated in white port wine, lamb cutlets with a red fruit sauce; pork, overfat, smothered in honey and wild ginger; flounders, served with toasted almonds; bowls of shrimps, wallowing in a pepper sauce and crabs, still in their shells; meat that Krysty identified as turkey, pallid and waxen, dripping with melted goat's cheese and crushed peppercorns; tomatoes and onions in sour cream, sprinkled with mushrooms and little green berries; a thick gray-brown soup that had, unnervingly, dozens of hard-boiled eggs bobbing greasily around in it; potatoes and rutabagas and beans, minced and fried in gravy.

There were also bowls of fruit, cooked and raw, mostly in sweet and sickly sauces that drenched them. There was water to drink, or a thick lilac-colored liqueur that had an unusual taste.

"Like something a gaudy whore would bathe in," J.B. muttered, struggling to conceal his disgust at the scented flavor, opting for the water instead. He followed Rachel Cawdor's example and took only a portion of boiled fish and a side helping of vegetables.

Ryan chose a steak, finding it grievously underdone, blood seeping from the meat before he even laid a knife into it. He ladled some fried beans on the side and discovered they'd been soaked with grated red chilies that almost took the skin off his tongue.

Krysty contented herself with a chipped goblet of springwater and some of the potatoes, which had been fried in butter. She also took a couple of slices of the whole wheat bread from the wooden board, which was carried by an elderly man with trembling hands who kept his head bowed and didn't look at any of the guests. He repeatedly muttered, "Thank you, my lord, thank you, my lady, thank you..." regardless of the sex of the person he was serving at the time.

With a shudder, Krysty noticed that the old servant's hands had been branded several times, and his fingers and knuckles showed the unmistakable signs of having been brutally broken more than once.

"Food good, Brother Thursby?" Harvey Cawdor bellowed from the murky distance at the head of the table. His face and beardless chins were beslobbered with runnels of grease, carrying particles of several different courses of the meal. His piggy little eyes had almost vanished behind rolls of fat.

"Yeah, Baron Cawdor."

"Dreck," whispered Jak Lauren. "Eaten better from a double-poor swampie's chuck-out pile."

"What did the whitehead say?" Rachel Cawdor asked, blazing eyes focused on Ryan.

"Good food, my lady," he replied.

"I have lost the taste for food, Master Thursby. I no longer get any pleasure from the act of eating."

Her voice was low and uneven, and her hands folded over each other, fingers writhing like ten white snakes.

As they watched, ignoring the grunting and wallowing of Harvey Cawdor, the woman fumbled in her black purse and took out a circular mirror with an ornately sculpted edge where tiny dragons fought amid a tangled forest. It was another of the Cawdor heirlooms. She also removed a small sliver of polished steel and a tiny brown vial, which was tightly corked.

"Jolt," Jak mouthed to Ryan, but the one-eyed man had already recognized what was happening. The woman was probably addicted to the hallucinogenic mix of coke and mescaline. Not everyone who took jolt became quickly addicted. But once you were well hooked, then you were on a steep and icy slope that carried you down faster and faster. All the way to the bottom. If Lady Rachel Cawdor needed to snort some lines of jolt in the middle of a public meal, then the bottom of the slope couldn't be that far away for her.

While Harvey Cawdor snuffled and grunted his way through his trough of food, his wife methodically began her preparations for doing the drug. Ryan and the others continued to eat quietly, occasionally beckoning to one of the silent servants for more bread or vegetables.

Rachel eased the cork from the narrow neck of the small tinted bottle, tipping a half gram or so of the sparkling white powder onto the scored surface of the mirror. She concentrated on the task, oblivious to the glances of her guests. Gripping the thin section of surgical steel and using it to chop and grind the jolt into smaller grains, she eventually arranged the drug into a half-dozen, neat, ordered lines across the glass.

"Anyone want a sniff?" she asked, two spots of bright color highlighting her spare cheekbones. When everyone had shaken their heads, she rummaged once more in her purse, triumphantly pulling out a narrow tube of carved ivory.

She carefully inserted one end into her right nostril and closed the other with a thin forefinger. Lowering her head over the mirror, she sniffed up one of the lines of jolt, moved quickly to the next line and then the next. Eventually all six lines of the iridescent powder had been snorted.

Her body shook in the characteristic tremors that gave the drug its common nickname. Rachel's breath came in sharp gasps, and her eyes rolled back in their sockets. Her husband totally ignored her convulsions, busy as he was with rending strips of meat off the carcass of an unidentifiable fowl.

"Oh, yes, yes," she whispered, her breathing slowing down again. She licked the mirror clean with a long, feline tongue, then tucked all the jolt paraphernalia back into her purse. Looking up, she became aware that the eyes of the four strangers were on her.

"Good, my lady?" Ryan asked politely.

"Better than good, Master Thursby," she replied, licking her lips very slowly as she looked at him. "It is better than anything. Better than the most wonderful fucking you could imagine. Better than pain. Better even than death."

"And we know how much you enjoy death, don't we, dearest mother?"

None of them had heard the newcomer arrive in the hall. Ryan noticed immediately how the servants backed away, eyes cast down. The old man with the bread salver came within an inch of dropping it, face angled to the stone floor.

The light from the numerous beeswax candles danced off the polished orb of amethyst at the end of the gold chain around the young man's slender throat. He was dressed in a coat and trousers of black velvet, and black boots. In his belt was a small high-velocity dart gun that fired a cluster of razored metal projectiles only a half inch long, their shafts barbed to make withdrawal difficult and damaging.

"Jabez," the woman said delightedly. "You have come to join us?"

"Of course. We have guests so rarely and they stay for such a short time."

Ryan looked curiously at his nephew. Harvey's son was in his late teens, of average height and build, with a face that seemed oddly unbalanced. The right side was higher and more angular, the corner of the eye twisted and pulled down as though the young man was continuously blinking. Jabez's complexion had a deathly pallor, as if the light of the sun were never permitted anywhere near him. His hairline was receding, hair cut short and of a nondescript brown color.

"Come kiss me, son of my loins," Rachel Cawdor said, reaching out for her only child.

While the others looked on, Jabez strode the length of the table, stooped and kissed his mother on the cheek. A dutiful, filial kiss. As he straightened he caught Ryan's eye on him and smiled—which sent a chill down Ryan's spine.

"More, Mother dearest," the boy said, leaning and gently lifting Rachel's face to his. He lowered his mouth onto hers, pressing it over her parted lips. As he leaned across her, he allowed his left hand to drift over the front of her dress until it cupped Rachel's right breast. Lady Rachel Cawdor made a helpless gesture of resistance, then gave herself up to him.

When he finally released her, Jabez's mother was flushed and panting, smiling up at her son and holding his hand in hers. Even from where he sat, Ryan could see the unmistakable bulge of an erection pressing at the front of the lordling's breeches.

"You have traveled far, Master Thursby, I hear," Jabez Cawdor said, turning away from his mother and totally ignoring his gormandizing father. Baron Harvey Cawdor ate on, never lifting his eyes from his bowl.

"Gaia!" Krysty exclaimed, pushing her plate away in disgust at the blatant behavior.

"Eat it," Ryan said in a low, urgent voice. "Don't let him know it matters." Raising his voice he said, "We have traveled many miles for many years, my Lord Jabez."

"And you have lost an eye. How careless."

"It is common enough in Deathlands," Ryan replied. "And an arm or a leg or even a mind."

As though he were bored, Jabez sat and beckoned over his shoulder to the servants to bring him food, taking only chunks of pork. His father also called out, in a voice muffled by the dribbling mush he was eating, for more meat. When he finished a plate he would knock it from the hands of the particular servant with a grunt of rage that rose high and thin like the scream of a gelded animal.

Down at the other end of the table there was no conversation between Jak, J.B., Krysty and Ryan, each locked in his or her own thoughts.

Ryan's mind was whirling at the visible madness that ran the ville. Harvey was a double-crazy who would eat himself into the grave within the next few months. His wife was psychotically withdrawn and obviously dependent on jolt. From the junkies Ryan had seen, the woman would also be dead within the year. And that would leave her incestuous son, Jabez.

The security at Front Royal was tight, primed with fear, and it would be hard to find a way of slaughtering his brother and family. Their insanity was both a plus and a minus. It needed careful consideration.

"A rabbit, Master Thursby?"

"You're well informed."

Jabez persisted. "Thieves are blinded in parts of the Deathlands, Thursby."

"Yeah."

The voice was soft, insistent. "Are you a thief, Thursby? You and the killer and the two muties? Killers, are you? Are they killers, Mother? Should I take them where it's quiet and ask them?"

Rachel didn't answer, but Harvey looked up, glancing, eyes bright amid the smeared food, and shouted to his son, "I'm eating, you filthy little bastard! Fuck off! Go on, get away from our table before I—" The anger faded as quickly as it had risen.

"What'll you do, Father?" Jabez asked. "Thursby the killer and his friends are listening."

"They can leave after breaking their fasts tomorrow morning. I'm bored with 'em. Hear me, Thursby? You can go tomorrow."

"Thank you, Baron Cawdor." Ryan's mind darted. That meant they must do what they could during the night. There was that secret door between his room and Krysty's...

"More of those eggs," Ryan's brother bellowed, struggling to look over his hunched shoulder for that particular delicacy.

Rachel was sitting back in her chair, waving a hand dreamily to and fro, humming to herself. Like her husband and her son, the woman marched to the beat of a different drummer.

"Your hair is beautiful," Jabez said, pushing his own seat back so hard that it crashed over onto the floor. Ryan felt a pang of concern.

The young man moved with a lethal elegance, allowing his hand to drift over the carved chairs, gesturing for the old man with the breadboard to step out of his way. When he reached Krysty, he stopped, his eyes flicking between Ryan and his mother. There was something about Ryan that bothered him; that was clear. As long as he didn't start to make some connection...

His hand darted out like a striking adder and tugged at the cord that kept Krysty's flowing scarlet hair bound up. It tumbled about her shoulders in such a cascade of light and color that even the baron was distracted from his eating for a moment.

"So pretty, pretty, pretty," Jabez whispered. "Tonight I'll come and visit, but not a word to Mother." He giggled like a little child sharing a secret. "She gets so jealous."

Jak laid his fork down on the china plate, his knuckles whitening on the hilt of the table knife. J.B. caught his eye and made a subtle, cautionary movement with his hand.

Ryan watched Krysty's face, seeing the green eyes narrow, then close. The girl was fighting for inner control against the hand that rested on her shoulder, then began to caress her nape. Jabez was staring beyond Krysty's head, smiling gently at his mother, who now sat up straight and looked at him, emotionless, slate-eyed.

"Your hair is the most beautiful hair I've ever seen. So soft and... Aaaaarrrggghhh!"

For a splinter of a second Ryan thought Krysty had succumbed to the temptation to use the awesome power of her Earth Mother against Jabez. Then he realized that the young man had been startled and terrified by Krysty's sentient hair, which had coiled and tangled around his fingers. The scream made everyone in the room look up, including the doddering old man who carried the bread.

His eyes fastened for the first time on Ryan, and his mouth sagged open in shock.

The hand shot out and pointed. "By Jesu and the martyrs! Our prayers are answered. Lord Ryan himself has come back!"

Chapter Twenty-Three

JAK LAUREN HAD GONE for a sec man with a table knife, cutting the man's forearm to the bone before he was clubbed to the rush-covered floor.

Ryan, J.B. and Krysty didn't resist.

Trader used to say that there was a time to fight. But more important was the time you decided not to fight.

The only casualty had been the old servant who'd blown the whistle on Ryan Cawdor.

Following the cry that identified the one-eyed man as the missing son of the ville, there was a moment of utter silence. Everyone reacted in different ways to the shock.

If Ryan had been counting the beats of his own heart, he would have reached twenty before anything happened in the banquet hall.

Harvey Cawdor lifted his porcine face from his dish very slowly, staring at Ryan with an expression of growing horror.

Lady Rachel unfolded her hands and carefully laid each one—as if it were a rare piece of porcelain—on the linen cloth in front of her. Her face didn't alter as she absorbed the news.

Jabez Pendragon Cawdor took a dozen slow steps backward in the direction of the fireplace. His eye blinked rapidly, and his hand began to creep toward the dart gun in his belt.

"Ryan? My brother?" Harvey muttered, shaking his head stupidly, bits of food spraying all around him. "How can...?"

"Dead," Jabez said quietly. "You're dead." Then loudly, "Dead for twenty years! Bones and blood, but you shall stay dead, Uncle!"

He drew the blaster and aimed it at the center of Ryan's chest, finger white on the slim trigger, lips peeled back off his yellowed teeth in an expression of tigerish delight.

Ryan had known this moment would come one day. If you lived your life by the blaster, it was certain that eventually you'd die by it. You'd hear a cold voice out of the darkness telling you not to turn around, or meet it face-to-face. In the end, they were both much the same.

He heard Krysty, sounding a far way off, calling his name, but he sat there and looked into the eyes of his nephew, waiting for the shock of death.

Which wasn't to be that day.

The old man moved first, lightning fast for his age. Mouth working, he stood there, stunned with everyone else. "Lord Cawdor, forgive me!" he shrieked, like the eldritch howl of a midnight banshee.

He threw himself at Jabez Cawdor, clawing at the young man's face. Ryan heard the distinctive hiss of the dart gun, and the servant's body jerked backward like a gaffed salmon. With arms flung out, he toppled over, blood frothing from his open mouth, darkening the front of his uniform.

He lay there, legs twitching, dulled eyes staring blankly at the vaulted ceiling of the hall as if he'd never noticed it before. His lips moved as he tried to speak, and he struggled to turn his head toward Ryan. He said something that might have been "Sorry," and then he died.

Jabez spit at him and wrestled with the stubborn mechanism for recocking the blaster. The sec men started to move in, and Jak leaped to his feet, brandishing the knife.

The stones would have been awash with blood if Lady Rachel had not acted. She raised her hand and snapped out a command that checked her son's murderous rage and stopped the sec men from opening up with their carbines.

"Alive," she shouted. "Take them all alive! Chain Ryan and lock up the others. Triple guard."

So it happened. Jak was carried away unconscious, bleeding from a gash on his temple. The others walked—escorted by sec men—back to their chambers.

On the way, Ryan looked around and saw that the tall sergeant was still in charge of them.

"One question," he said.

"What?"

"The old man who died."

"Yeah. What of him?"

"Who was he? Didn't recognize him."

"He knew you, didn't he, *Lord* Ryan Cawdor? You didn't even try to deny it. You sat there like a kid messed his pants."

Ryan shook his head. "Didn't intend to come and dine with Harvey. Wasn't the plan."

"What was?" The sec officer held up his gauntleted fist to halt the escort. "Come on, Lord Ryan. You'll tell me sooner anyway."

"I'll tell you anyway. Why not?"

"Murder the family and then rule yourself as the baron of Front Royal?"

"Yes to the first and mebbe to the second. You still didn't tell me his name."

The sergeant moved closer, grinning. "You'll like this, Lord Ryan. Remember little Kenny Morse?"

"Course. If'n it hadn't been for Kenny, I'd have died at fifteen. He saved me from my brother."

"And you know what—"

"He was murdered," Ryan interrupted. "I heard that recently."

"That was his brother, Will, just betrayed you in there. Funny, isn't it?"

"No."

SOME MILES AWAY, deep in the forest of the Shens, Nathan Freeman was leading Doc Tanner and Lori Quint along winding paths. Picking his way carefully, he stopped frequently to listen for any sound of man or beast. They were heading toward the rambling fortress of Front Royal.

THE CHAIN AROUND RYAN'S THROAT bit into his skin and was drawn so tight that breathing was difficult. It held his head still, strained up and back. The steel of the handcuffs was pitted with age, but the action was greased and clicked home, and squeezed so hard that the ends of his fingers were swollen and sore. But he'd felt worse.

At least the sergeant hadn't taken the opportunity to give him a beating, merely checking that the cuffs and the throttle chain were secure. He fixed the end of the links to a heavy iron ring that was built into the stone of the wall.

"Now you wait, my lord."

"I wasn't going to move, anyway. Could you put out the lamps? They'll disturb my sleep."

The man laughed at that, tweaking him by the cheek with the thick leather glove. "If you weren't who you are . . . and if you weren't going where you're going . . . I swear I could almost like you."

"When will my brother come?"

The sec man sniffed as he straightened up. "Baron's not well, seeing you come up like a skeleton out of the tomb. Had himself some drink, did the baron. On the morrow he has to ride out to Fishers' Hill. There's a hunt fixed. Boars. Baron wouldn't miss that. And it'll give you a day to sweat on it."

"Tomorrow night, then?"

"Figures. There, I've dimmed all the lamps but one. Need that to watch you through the judas hole in the door. Sleep well, Lord Cawdor." Somehow, that time, there didn't seem the same element of sarcasm when he called him by the title.

The door closed with a solid thunk, and Ryan heard the key turn in the lock. A double bolt slammed home. The sec man had told him that the other three were also locked in their rooms, but none of them was to be tied. And Jak had recovered consciousness from the blow to his head.

They would all take their turn being interrogated by Baron Harvey Cawdor.

There was a warm glow from the lamp that stood on an old, polished round table near the barred window. The draperies had been closed, leaving only a chink near the top. It was full dark outside.

From where he lay on the floor of the chamber, Ryan could hear the noises of the ville as life went on. He guessed that the news of his return would already have raced through the big building until the meanest scullery boy would know that Ryan Cawdor was back at Front Royal.

"Oiled and ready to tear some ass," Ryan said out loud, managing a wry grin. He was resigned to that fact of his imminent death. It was simply a question of how and when. J.B., Jak and Krysty would also perish. That was also destined. There was a slim chance that Doc and the girl might get away. Ryan hoped so. He liked Lori, but he was coming to love the eccentric old man.

The only hope left now to Ryan was that they might get careless at the end and give him a chance to at least settle the old debt by killing his brother. He could do it easily enough with his bare hands, given just a couple of seconds and a scant yard of space.

Somewhere he could catch the distant sound of a piano playing, and he wondered who was at the keyboard. An aunt of his had come to the ville when Ryan had been eight years old, an immensely tall, skinny woman whose name escaped him. It was some sort of flower, he thought. She'd loved dancing and had teased the solemn young boy by snatching him as they'd passed in one of the long corridors. Pressing him to her flat, bony chest, she'd called out, "Heel and toe, heel and toe, one-two-three, one-two-three. Lovely, Ryan, lovely."

As the wasting sickness that had killed her had begun to set its teeth in her body, she'd grown more melancholy. Once she'd been playing an old tape of music, a dance tune called a tango. She'd looked up at him from the thin birdlike face, with eyes bright and fevered, the bones scraping at the inside of her skin.

"They say the tango is a merry rhythm, Ryan. It is not. It is infinitely mournful."

She'd died a week later and been buried in the family plot with the rest of the line of Cawdors, back to the long winter.

Ryan didn't recognize the tune the piano was playing. After a while it ceased, and he slipped into an uneasy sleep.

The rattle of the spyhole woke him, and he peered across the room. The lamp was burning low, near to guttering out, and the chamber smelled of oil. There was a momentary flash of brighter light as the door opened a narrow crack and then closed again. Someone slipped through the gap, and for a split second Ryan allowed himself a glimmer of hope, knowing the foolishness of such a thought.

He heard a voice, speaking with a frighteningly cold intensity. "On your life, trooper. I'll spill your heart blood myself. Not until I knock to be let out. Understand?"

One of the sec men murmured his assent as the door closed.

There was plenty of light for Ryan to immediately recognize Lady Rachel Cawdor, wearing the same dark clothes and carrying the same worn leather purse. Without a word she knelt at his side, drawing a slim-bladed stiletto from her belt. The point rested for a moment on the material of his pants, just above his groin. She began to push, the steel slicing through the material, touching cold on the flesh of his stomach.

"Now," she said.

Chapter Twenty-Four

THE KNIFE WAS VERY OLD. Ryan had never seen it before, but he knew that the ville had once housed a remarkable collection of early weapons of all sorts. The hilt was silver, heavily embossed with floral decoration, and the blade was steel.

He tried to relax against the sharp pricking of the knife as she moved it lower and lower. Despite himself, Ryan winced and tried to ease himself down, avoiding the steel as it brushed the top of his penis.

Lady Rachel Cawdor laughed delightedly, a soft, gentle sound in the stillness of the room.

"So brave, brother-in-law, yet so like all men. Filled with stupid pride until your pathetic little pricks are threatened."

"Harvey wouldn't like me spoiled."

She patted him on the cheek, running a sharp nail along the jagged scar that furrowed his face. "He did that. And the eye. He talks of it. When he sleeps, racked by horrors, he talks of you. He knew you'd come back one day. Knew it. You're his walking nightmare, Ryan Cawdor."

He didn't speak. The knife was still poised, like a honed nemesis, ready to descend and hack at his manhood. She was very beautiful. Ryan corrected that thought. She *had once been* very beautiful. Now she was raddled by the jolt.

"You can't move. I could do anything to you, dear brother-in-law. Anything. I could rape you. Use that cock of yours, then cut it off. I could kiss you. Make you kiss me. Make you use your tongue on my body. Would you like that, brother-in-law?''

She was leaning across him, her breath running faster. The front of her dress gaped open, and he could see her breasts, the nipples erect with desire.

''What would you like, Ryan?''

''I'd like you to die, and take your husband and that sick little bastard of a son with you.''

He waited for the thrust of the knife, but nothing happened. Ryan had closed his eye, and he opened it when he heard her laugh. She had sat back on her heels, the velvet dress hitched up between her knees, showing a smooth expanse of pale thigh.

''You talk big for a helpless one-eyed man, Ryan Cawdor.''

''Why've you come?''

Rachel's dark eyes were almost invisible in the half-light. ''I wanted to see you. Wanted to see you before that sottish husband of mine had you thrown to his boars or his dogs or whatever unoriginal way of chilling he picks.''

Ryan didn't reply. There was nothing to say. He'd read pulps where the captured hero talks to the mistress of the villain and uses his charms to persuade her to release him. Life wasn't at all like that. Steel cuffs held him helpless, and the chain around his throat made it impossible for him to move. Tomorrow they'd come and take him to Harvey, and then he'd be dead. The best to look for was a quick passing, which was why he'd tried to provoke the woman into wasting him with her knife. That had failed, and there wasn't anything else left.

''Don't want to talk?'' She was becoming more nervous, hands moving, head turning from side to side. He recognized the symptoms from the dinner table. The woman needed more jolt.

"Need a snort," she said, voice as taut as a bowstring. "Need something to rest my mirror on. You'll do, brother-in-law."

She took the knife again and slit his clothes, opening the jerkin and pulling it back across his flat, muscular stomach. Then she cut through the crotch of his trousers. Placing the knife on the floor, she tugged his trousers over his thighs. She touched him, very gently.

"Oh, my dear relative, I've cut you. A tiny ruby that glistens here. Should I kiss it better for you, Ryan?"

Despite the effects of the jolt on her appearance, Rachel Cawdor was still an attractive, skilled woman. Ryan tried to pull away from her, fighting for control.

She laughed. "Very good, Ryan. But I shall win. Like all men..." she began, then bent once more to her task.

When she lifted her head again, the woman was grinning. "There, brother-in-law, that wasn't so awful, was it?"

Ryan didn't reply, feeling soiled by the contact, certain only that he would kill Rachel Cawdor if he was given half a chance.

"Bad loser," she said. "While you're here like this I might give myself some..." She stopped, and her body suddenly twisted with a violent shudder. "Oh, the cramps are... First things first."

Rachel took out the little brown bottle and uncorked it. Holding the mirror in her hand, she looked round the room for somewhere to set it, eventually placing the chill metal on Ryan's stomach. She cut the powder into finer grains, then formed it into several narrow lines.

"Forget the fucking, after all," she breathed, breasts rising and falling. "This is..."

The ivory tube in one nostril, the other pinched tight, she again lowered her face toward his body. She sniffed up the lines of jolt, her body trembling with the powerful sensation of the drug. Only when the mirror was clear did she sit up again, face wreathed in a broad smile.

"Now, what shall we do, Ryan?"

"Get out," he said.

"Worried the mutie redhead'll find out you enjoyed me doing you? I might go tell her right now."

"That jolt'll kill you soon," he said.

"I can stop when I like."

"Like everyone else can. I seen the stiffs from coast to coast. Heart gives up the effort. You're dead, bitch."

"Harvey won't live long. His heart's near finished, brother-in-law. Then I rule the ville."

"What about your son?"

"Jabez? The darling does everything I tell him to do."

"Like fuck you?"

At last he got through her guard. She slapped him hard across the face so that his head banged back against the wall. She snatched up the knife and stared at him, eyes open wide in an insensate rage.

"You don't...don't..." she stammered, spraying him with her spittle. "I'll...Jabez loves his mother. That's all."

Rachel put the dagger down once more, leaning close to Ryan so that he could almost taste the scent of her sour-sweet breath. With a swift movement she sat astride him, her weight on his groin. Her left hand tangled in his hair, pulling so hard that it brought tears to his eye.

"Keep very still," she hissed at him, her white face inches from his.

Her right hand stretched and touched the leather patch over his blinded left eye, easing it upward.

"No!" he cried involuntarily.

"Ah, so the brave hero has his weakness. I only want to see what good work my dear husband did on his little brother. There..."

Ryan closed his right eye. He knew what Lady Rachel was seeing. He'd seen it often enough in pools of water or in polished metal or in mirrors. The empty, raw socket, the skin puckered, red and scarred. Often the scooped cavity would weep a little. A clear liquid, as though it wept for the missing eye.

He winced again as she laid her thumb on the skin at the very corner of the eye. "What does it feel like, Ryan?" she whispered.

He screamed. For the first time in countless years, Ryan Cawdor screamed in helpless, mindless terror, feeling the jagged nail probe into the deeps of the empty eye socket, pushing hard against the agonizingly delicate skin. The pain went on and on as she turned her finger around, still keeping her iron grip on his hair. Through the mist of raw red pain, he could hear her laughing at him.

Ryan jerked so hard at the handcuffs that blood sprang from the ends of his fingers.

A millenium of suffering crawled by until at last she took the finger away. He could feel a warm liquid coursing down his cheek, but he didn't know if it was tears or blood. It touched the corner of his lips and it tasted salty.

Her weight moved off him, and he blinked open his good eye. Rachel stooped and adjusted the patch back over the blank socket.

"So much blood, brother-in-law. Such a deep scar, isn't it?"

Ryan didn't trust himself to speak, knowing that his voice would shake with his pain and anger.

"I think I shall go and kiss my son a fond good-night. After all, I doubt you could please me with this—" she touched him contemptuously with the toe of her dark blue shoe ''—this worm.'' She giggled, the jolt coursing through her body, making her hyperactive for a brief few minutes. ''Know what I do if I see a worm in my path, brother-in-law? I crush it beneath my heel. Perhaps... No, it would be a waste. If it was Harvey's pathetic worm, then...''

''Why stay with him?''

''He is the baron, Ryan. You know what that means. After I throttled your father, Harvey stopped sleeping in the same bed as me, fearing for his wretched life. And he is right. Now he will soon die. There have been two attacks already, and the doctor says he cannot live through another.''

''In twenty years you could have...''

The woman shook her head, bending to collect her dagger and thrust it back into the sheath at her belt. ''Not until Jabez was old enough. This ville runs on fear, Ryan. And now you've come back. All my life here you've been a shadow on every wall. A listener behind every door, the poison in every dish, the fear in every dream.''

''Now I'm here.''

''The older servants prayed to you. We flogged and branded them and still they believed that one day you'd come back and save them all from... Harvey and from me. They call me the Lady of Pain, you know, Ryan. Me! This time tomorrow Harvey will return from the hunt. You and your friends will die in a fine public ceremony. Soon Harvey will die, and Jabez and I will run the Shens. And there will be no more shadows!''

Her voice soared like an eagle as she ranted at the bound man at her feet. She kicked out at him in a vicious temper, her feet cracking into his ribs, leaving deep purple bruises.

As quickly as it had come, the anger left her, the wild swinging of moods that was typical of a jolt junkie. She stood panting, her face growing blank. "There, brother-in-law, you made me... Relatives shouldn't anger each other."

"Goodbye, sister-in-law," he managed.

"I came to see you," she said, pausing near the door, "to see if you might be of use. You could have killed Harvey. That would have been pleasant, wouldn't it? All the double-poor stupes that live on our lands would have flocked to worship at the shrine. Ryan, the miracle baron of Front Royal. You could have had me as well, brother-in-law."

"Why not?" he asked. Behind her the last of the lamps was guttering out, making her shadow dance, shift and vanish.

Rachel smiled. "No, Ryan. Not now. You should have been the baron. You and I could...once... Not now. I know men, Ryan. I know you. You might agree, to save your skin, then break my neck without a single backward glance. No. You aren't weak enough."

She pulled at the door handle, pausing a moment in the brightly lit opening to glance back at him. Then the door slammed shut, and Ryan was left alone in silence and in darkness.

The blood congealed on the tips of his fingers, around the nails and on the grazes around his throat from the tearing of the rough iron chain.

As the night wore on, Ryan managed to slip into an uncomfortable slumber, waking often from the pain of his position. He wondered how the others were bearing up, thinking specially of Krysty Wroth.

Ryan also wondered about Lori and Doc Tanner.

Chapter Twenty-Five

"BY THE THREE KENNEDYS!" Doctor Theophilus Tanner exclaimed, tripping over the gnarled root of an ancient live oak. It had rained, briefly but fiercely, and the ground had become soggy and treacherous. The low clouds veiled the moon, making it difficult to see more than ten feet ahead.

"You okay, Doc?" Lori asked, helping him to his feet and wiping ineffectually at the smears of mud on his black coat.

"Yeah. Just this path doesn't run straight for more than twenty yards at a time."

Nate Freeman looked back over his shoulder, face a pale blur ahead of them. "Want to get nearer than this to the ville 'fore sunup. We're close to Shersville here, and they might have patrols out, watching for me to head home."

The clouds parted, and the moon broke through, bathing the region in a bright silver glow. Doc looked around him, admiring the beauty of the forest, the rain glistening off the boles of the endless ranks of trees.

"How far?" he asked the young man.

"Sunup or the ville?"

"The dawn's early light."

"Two hours."

"The ville?"

"Three. If we don't all keep falling over our feet like clumsy old stupes."

"You'll watch your mouth or..." Lori threatened crossly. But Doc patted her arm.

"No, my dear heart. Nathan is right. I must take more care."

"Should have fetched the fast blasters." The girl sighed.

"Safer in the wag," Freeman argued. "You go through your plan to try and get in the ville then that mini-Uzi and the gray rifle'd have you in the moat 'fore you could say, 'Blessed Ryan spare us.' Know what I mean?"

Doc was thinking about the plan as they walked briskly through the Shens. Part of it had been his, but he kept forgetting bits of it. He was to be a traveling quack who was calling at the ville to treat any minor ailments and to draw teeth. But he'd lost his bag of tools. He could remember all of that. But Nathan hadn't liked the idea.

He'd wanted to wait and see, to try to sneak some news from those in Shersville who were still loyal to him. But even the young man had admitted that there had to be a real risk that Ryan's cover had been blown inside the ville. Doc had asked how long he thought Ryan would live once Harvey knew who he was.

Nathan had replied by simply snapping his fingers once.

So, that was why Doc and Lori were going in. For news. And if that turned out bad, for a try at a rescue.

"How?" Doc mumbled to himself. And after a little while he realized he didn't have an answer to that question.

The swordstick helped the old man over some of the rougher parts of the trail, and Lori was always at his elbow with encouragement.

"Path here goes through a swamp, so step careful. Mud's near bottomless on both sides. And we're closest we come to my home village. Fast and careful and quiet's the way."

Ironically it was Nathan Freeman who nearly brought disaster upon them all. He had looked back to make sure that his two companions had safely negotiated a tumbled willow tree that was rotting across the path, when his own foot slipped and he crashed to the ground. In falling he clutched at a low branch of a stunted elm tree, which broke in his grasp with a loud report that sounded like a Magnum going off.

"That you, Beau?" called a voice. It was a thin, whining sort of a voice, like a querulous old man asking when his supper would be ready.

Nathan drew his blaster from his belt, a double-action Smith & Wesson Model 39 handgun. Dropping into a crouch, he waved to Doc and Lori to take cover behind him.

"Beau? You fallen in the fucking water 'gain? I'm not pulling yer out if'n . . ."

"Hi, there, Tom," Nathan said, straightening up, holding the pistol on the hunched little figure that had appeared out of the rags of mist that hung over the muddy water. "Thought I knew your voice, my trusted old friend."

Doc and Lori also stood up, seeing that the other villager was paralyzed with fear. The old man was literally shaking in his boots at the sudden appearance of the man he'd betrayed.

"Ramjet! Nathan, is . . . ? I didn't know you was going t'come back. Me an' Beau . . ."

"Here," Nathan said quietly, beckoning to Tom. "Come here."

The little villager stumbled toward Freeman, wringing his hands like an abject penitent. "Didn't mean trouble,

Nate, you know that. Hell, we bin friends longer than most. I taught you to shoot an' told..."

"Shut up, Tom," Freeman said. "Kneel down here, in front of me."

"I'll get my breeches fouled in the dirt, Nate. You know what Becky's like if'n I get muddied up. I'll just stand."

"Kneel. That's good. Now get your mouth open real wide, Tom."

"What for? I don't... Urrgh..."

Doc looked away, knowing what was going to happen. Lori also guessed, and she clapped her hands together delightedly, eyes sparkling in the moonlight. "Yeah," she said. "Do it, Nate."

The little villager knelt in the slime, hands together, looking up at Nathan Freeman. The muzzle of the heavy automatic pistol was jammed in his mouth between his broken and stained teeth. His eyes were as wide as saucers, and he was moaning to himself.

"Close your lips, Tom. Suck on it, real good, like it was mother's milk. Good. So long, Tom."

The gun bucked, the sharp edge of the foresight cutting open the man's mouth. The explosion was muffled, sounding no louder than a man slapping a mosquito off his wrist. Out of the corner of his eye, Doc saw a hunk of bone burst out of the back of the scrawny villager's skull, landing with a plopping noise in the water on either side of the trail. A fine spray glittered in the moonlight for a second, like a ballooning fountain of fireflies, mushrooming from the hole in the head. The dappled mess of blood and brain tissue pattered in the dirt. The body jerked violently backward, legs kicking in the air, the mouth hanging open.

"Help me roll him into the swamp, Doc," Nathan said, holstering his smoking piece.

Tom's clothes held pockets of air, and at first it didn't sink, floating like a sodden log in the scum-covered water. Nathan glanced around. He found a broken branch from one of the willows and used it to push at the corpse, hold it under. He watched the bubbles, some bursting with crimson centers. When they stopped, he let go of the branch and threw it away. The body stayed beneath the surface.

Without a word, Freeman turned away and led Doc and Lori onward.

When they reached the screen of trees that fringed the open space in front of the fortress of Front Royal, it was a little after sunrise. The dawn was brilliant, the flaming disk of the sun lurching over the eastern horizon, coloring everything with its crimson light. The ville looked as though the stones glowed with a dreadful inner heat, and the water of the wide moat lay like congealing blood.

The drawbridge had just been lowered, and villagers were beginning to enter, hurrying past the dozen guards that lined the main gateway. Nathan looked worried.

"Normally only a couple of sec men there. Smells of trouble."

"Then I venture to suggest that we might consider our entrance as a matter of some immediacy. Time is of the essence, my dear young man, would you not say?"

"Yeah. I'll wait up here. You get out with news, take the trail runs due west. But don't go as far as Shersville. I'll pick you up. Don't look for me. I'll find you."

They heard the brazen howl of a trumpet from within the gates and the baying of a pack of hunting dogs, a sound that Doc and Lori recalled only too well from their arrival in the Shens. The girl shuddered at the noise and clutched at Doc's hand for comfort.

"Baron might be going hunting," Nathan said. "Nothing stops for that. Nothing. After the wild boars he breeds in the cellars of the ville. Best keep under cover until he's gone by."

Doc Tanner parted the branches of leaves and peered out at the fortress, grim and invincible, surrounded by the bloody aura of the rising sun.

"I doubt either of you are familiar with the poetic works of Mr. Edgar Allan Poe? No, I thought not. Poor man. Tragic life. My grandfather on my father's side knew him slightly. This scene recalls one of his verses, concerning a haunted palace."

"I like you reading poems, Doc," Lori whispered, glancing proudly at Nathan. "Doc knows millions of poems, doesn't you, Doc?"

"Perhaps hundreds rather than millions, my dear chickadee," Doc replied.

"Tell me the poem you said. About a haunting palace."

"It starts about a fine castle, like the ville here, that was once a place of great riches, splendor, pomp and circumstance. Then it fell upon bad times."

"Go on," she whispered. Nathan Freeman half listened, watching the road into Front Royal for the best moment to move.

"But evil things, in robes of sorrow,
Assailed the monarch's high estate;
(Ah, let us mourn, for never morrow
Shall dawn upon him, desolate!)

"Then it goes on about how the wonders of the olden times are sunk forever and locked into the grave, as they are here. The crimson of the rising sun is so strong in recalling this verse."

"Something's happening, Doc. Look. Horsemen and the pack of dogs. Stay still and keep your voice low."

First came a squadron of mounted sec men, their uniforms tinged with dazzling scarlet by the dawn. Then came a huge mutie stallion—the biggest horse Lori and Doc had ever seen, not that the girl had actually ever seen a live horse in her entire life. Mounted on it, wrapped in a silver cloak that the sun streaked with bloody splashes, was an immensely fat man. He wore a feathered cap that nodded and danced.

"Lord Harvey Cawdor, baron of Front Royal," Nathan whispered, unable to hide his hatred.

Then came a pack of twenty or so dogs, slavering black hounds with narrow muzzles and long legs. They were controlled with whips by a half-dozen mounted grooms. At the rear came another squadron of sec guards.

They cantered by, only a hundred paces from the hiding place of the three companions, who watched them pass.

The sec men were laughing at some shared jest. From the tone of the laughter, it was a cruel joke. Doc Tanner continued his remembered poem by Poe.

"Somehow it is even more suitable now that we have seen that procession of death," he said.

"Tell it, Doc," the girl urged.

"And travelers now within that valley,
Through the red-litten windows see
Vast forms that move fantastically
To a discordant melody;
While, like a rapid ghastly river,
Through the pale door;

A hideous throng rush out forever,
And laugh—but smile no more.

"Watching the front of that dreadful pile, lit by the vermilion rays of the rising sun, seems as ominous and frightening as the haunted palace of that verse." Doc's rich melodious voice had carried the poem well, sending a shiver down the back of both listeners.

Nathan suggested that it was as good a time as any to try their luck. With the baron out of the way for the day, heading toward Fishers' Hill, it was unlikely he'd be back before sunset.

They made their farewells quickly, then the old man and the pretty girl strode confidently out of the cover of the forest, joining other commoners on the road into the ville.

"You outlanders? Beyond Shens?" a stout young woman asked, dragging a trio of snot-nosed brats behind her as she wheeled a barrow along the rutted trail. The rickety cart was loaded with a mixture of mud and potatoes, heavy on the mud. Her accent was so barbarous and rude that it took all of Doc's frail concentration to understand what on earth she was saying to him.

"I regret that we are not fortunate enough to enjoy the benefits of a domicile in these attractive parts."

"What? You talk like a double-stupe mutie!" She spit to show her disgust as they joined the lineup at the drawbridge.

"He's not for here," Lori said, doing her best to ease the sudden tension.

"Yeah. Bin here 'fore?"

"No, never," Doc replied. "You know the ville well?"

"Should do. Bleeding scullery maid here for eight bastard years. Cleaning shit an' sodding grease off whoring plates. Then I landed these little pissers and me man went off south. Now I sell what I can."

The sec men were passing everyone through at a fair speed, seeming to recognize them as regulars. But Doc noticed that one of them was already eyeing Lori and himself, muttering to the guard next to him.

"Secs are busy today. Someone must have farted in front of her ladyship."

"No-o-o-o," jeered an elderly man at their side, who carried a string of diminutive onions on a long pole across his shoulders.

"How come you know so much, Eddy Pungo? Riddle me that."

"Hasn't heard? Course not. You's not gotten daughter in ville. Your man left you, dinne?"

"A stone an' a stick can make me sick, but words don't ever harm me, Eddy Pungo. You got news, then tell us."

The old man looked both ways, then leaned toward her, casting an anxious eye first at Doc Tanner and Lori, seeming to recognize them as being harmless. "Ryan. Ryan Cawdor."

The woman laughed, a short, coughing kind of a laugh that made her disbelief obvious.

"True," the old man insisted. "Girl says so. Seen the secs taking him and some friends. Tried to raid the ville."

"Lord Ryan come back? One eye an' all?"

"Ssh. One eye an' all. It's him all right, like the old stories say."

"What has happened to him?" Doc asked, hoping that the fluttering in his chest was only an attack of nerves.

"To Lord Ryan, stranger? I hear he was 'trayed. A servant, brother to Kenny Morse, gave him up from shock. Now he's bound and waits death when the baron comes back from his hunting."

"Oh, dear!" The woman with the barrow sighed. "Fucker, innit? Wait twenty years or more for the lord to come and release us. Then next day stupe bastard gets chilled by Baron Harvey and us no better for it."

"No worse, no worse. Gotta look it that way. That's why gate's crawling with secs, as thick as lice on a horse blanket."

Soon enough it was Doc and Lori's turn to face the guards on the cobble-lined approach to the main entrance to the ville. Up close Doc realized what a difficult operation it would be to try to take the fortress.

"Could use a Peacemaker or a Minuteman missile here," he said.

"What's that, stranger?" a sec man barked. Doc hadn't even realized he'd spoken out loud, and he became confused.

"Don't wish to cause any fuss or alarm. Sorry if I spoke out of turn, only the volume of a given mass of gas is inversely proportional to... to something or other."

Two more of the sec men turned their way. "What's he saying?" asked one, a brutish looking bully with a number of unhealed sores across his upper lip. "Heard him say something about wanting gas."

"No, that wasn't quite..." Doc Tanner paused, fighting hard to gain control of his wandering wits, knowing that for the first time in many, many years, the lives of others rested with him.

Lori was holding his arm so tightly that it was hurting him, but it suddenly seemed to be his sole contact with reality and sanity. With an effort the old man pulled himself together.

"I am Doctor Tanner and this is my—"

"I'm his assistant," Lori put in quickly, remembering from the planning session in the abandoned wag that this was to be her role in their attempted deception.

"Yes, my assistant. I wish to gain entry to this eminent ville." The splendidly rounded vowels rolled out from between the immaculate set of teeth.

"Why?"

"I am a traveling medicine man."

"What d'you do?" the sec man asked. Now there were six of them around the strangers, mostly there to leer at the blond vision that was Lori Quint.

Then Doc recalled something of the spiel he'd contrived as they'd walked through the forest. "Hallelujah, my brothers. I'm here to help to heal the sick and make the lame walk. To aid the blind in obtaining the miraculous gift of sight and the deaf to be able to worship at the shrine of the muse of orchestral sound. If your piles itch or your skin flakes or your glands swell or your kidneys leak or your lungs wheeze or your teeth ache, then let Doc Tanner be your hope and your blessed salvation."

He ended on a silence that seemed respectful. The old man thought that he might have missed his true vocation.

"I have missed my true vocation," he said, not intending to speak out loud. Fortunately his tumbling speech had fascinated all of the guards, and nobody listened to his comment.

"You say you draw teeth, old man?" asked a skinny man with a stubbly beard sprouting amid a lake of warts.

"I do, indeed. But sadly all my tools were taken when we were attacked by muties some days ago. They took all our possessions."

"We got tools in the guardhouse. Come in. Our sergeant's been moaning for days and nights about a tooth that ails him."

Doc was brought sharply back to earth. "Draw a tooth for your sergeant? I don't...I mean to say that it's not—"

"Not what, old man?"

Doc swallowed hard, wondering why his mouth had become bone-dry. The crowd pressed around him, and he heard Lori squeak as someone goosed her. He struggled to hang on to his unique role as the savior of the group. Everyone was depending on him.

"If the tools are suitable?"

There was a disturbance in the throng, with men and women staggering sideways. A tall man appeared in an immaculate uniform, gesturing for the drawbridge to be kept clear.

"With the renegade caught, we have to watch for any spies or enemies," the sergeant barked at the sec men. "And who the sweet crucifix is this?"

"Traveling quack-salver," the corporal replied. "Says he can treat bad teeth."

"Then get him in and he can treat mine. Pain's burning my brain. Is the gaudy with him?"

"My assistant, Captain," Doc Tanner said. "Did I hear you mention some renegade?"

"Only the missing Ryan Cawdor, come sneaking back like a diseased rat after barley. But he's locked safe. And by dawn tomorrow he'll likely be another fruit a'dangling in the baron's prize orchard yonder."

WHEN THE PLIERS SLIPPED on the sergeant's rotten tooth and Doc heard the ominous crunch of broken bone, he knew that he and Lori were in deep trouble.

Chapter Twenty-Six

KRYSTY HAD WATCHED the departure of Baron Harvey Cawdor and his entourage for their day's sport in the Shens. By peering through the window of her room she could just see the road that wound out across the drawbridge, vanishing into the trees on the far side of the moat.

With nothing else to do, she had sat on an old-fashioned stickback chair by the open casement, watching the men and women from the surrounding villages file in to sell their produce.

And she saw the silver-haired old man in the cracked knee boots and stained frock coat, who was accompanied by the tall blond girl with the wide smile. For a moment Krysty stood and leaned on the sill, hoping to try to catch the eye of Doc and Lori. Then she withdrew into the room as she realized that they were playing a dangerous game, hoping to infiltrate the ville in some secret guise.

A few minutes later she could hear yelling and cursing, floating up from the guardhouse just inside the main gateway. She hoped it wasn't anything to do with Doc and Lori.

She'd heard something of what had gone on in the chamber next door to hers during the darkness of the night. Krysty's part-mutie birthright had given her certain peculiar skills, including enhanced sight and hearing. The visit of the Lady Rachel Cawdor to Ryan had been largely audible to Krysty, though some parts of it had been left to her imagination, not that much imagination had been required!

Once it was daylight, the tall redheaded girl had devoted her energies to examining her prison in the most careful detail.

She'd spotted the interconnecting door immediately. But it was sealed with an old iron bar, secured with a huge brass padlock. She rocked it with her hands, but the bar was rooted in the stone wall and hardly moved at all. The window opened on the moat, but it was a drop of forty feet. Though it didn't have any heavy security bars, the window frame was split into eight by metal rods. With a great effort it would have been possible for a small, skinny person to wriggle through. But for someone of Krysty's height and build, it was unthinkable to escape that way.

The main door into the room was locked and bolted from the outside. There was no judas hole for the sec men in the corridor to spy on her, but she could hear from the sound of boots and quiet conversation that there were at least a dozen guards in the passage.

The room was eighteen feet by fourteen, with no other exits or entrances. There was a fireplace, but the chimney was blocked off with stone and concrete. She even checked the stone flags on the floor, rolling back the coarse woolen drugget. The furnishings were sparse, and seemed very old.

A carved wooden chest at the foot of the double bed opened at her touch, revealing a pile of cloth. The smell was unpleasant, like damp earth. Krysty pulled the top bolt of cotton out of the trunk and unfolded it. The cloth was spotted with speckles of green mold, which carried the rich, moist odor. She wrinkled her nose as realization came to her. It was a cerecloth that had been used as a shroud or winding sheet for a corpse. Though, by the look of it, the cerement had done that duty on several occasions.

The chest also held a number of iron and pewter vases, which were cold and dusty with age. A wardrobe at the head of the bed on the left was completely empty, except for the stub of a pencil and an empty can of fly killer. A faint message had been scrawled on the inside of the door: Cathy Supports Lynx.

Krysty wondered who Cathy had been and how long ago she had supported Lynx, whatever that was.

A mahogany cupboard in one corner, with a deeply ornate acanthus design, held a lidded chamber bucket, which Krysty had used and emptied into the filthy water of the moat.

There was a tapestry on the long wall behind the head of the bed. Faded green and blue, it showed a sailing ship, partly dismasted, running for shelter before a terrifying storm. Massive white breakers curled under the schooner's quarterdeck, and sharp-fanged rocks waited at the base of towering cliffs. It was a mournful and desolate picture that fitted Krysty's mood of bleak pessimism.

Since leaving Harmony, Krysty Wroth had been bowled along, bouncing from adventure to adventure, constantly flirting with death, but never finding herself locked in its embrace. Now it was changed. They were prisoners of a ruthless and crazed baron, locked away, weaponless, in the center of a fortified ville that swarmed with sec men. Only Doc Tanner and Lori Quint had offered any prospect of help, and she'd just seen them both stroll into the gaping jaws of the grinning tiger.

Krysty felt very much alone.

They brought food around noon, a hand-turned wooden bowl of vegetable soup, with some scummy slices of potato floating in it, and a hunk of coarse bread. They didn't give her even a spoon to eat with, nor did any of the three armed men speak a single word to her.

There were no books in the room. No tapes. No pix, no sounds. Using some of the skills taught her by her mother, Krysty eventually lay on the creaking bed and willed herself into a semitrance, slipping easily into sleep by relaxing herself from her toes upward.

The day crept by.

IT WAS NEAR DUSK when she heard the distant baying of the pack of hounds drawing steadily nearer. The fading light made it difficult to make out details, but she thought that Baron Harvey was slumped in the high saddle of his horse, his pretty cloak caked with gray mud. The whole party was subdued, with none of the chatter and singing that you would normally expect with the return from a successful day's hunting.

There was the bloodied corpse of a large pig of some kind, its curling tusks gleaming yellow in the dusk. Its throat had been slit, and there was what looked like a scattergun wound in its flank. It had been flung into the back of a cart, which rattled over the cobbles into the keep of the ville.

The guards brought another meal, identical to the first except that there were some shreds of stringy pork lurking in the slimy depths of the bowl.

Through the open door, Krysty could see the sergeant who'd brought them in from Shersville. She noticed a crust of dried blood on his lower lip, and the side of his jaw seemed swollen. Even as she looked at him, he lifted his hand and touched his face, wincing as though it were damnably tender.

"A good hunt for the baron?" she called out.

"He fell at a thorn break. Came home tired and in the foulest of tempers. And I feel much the same, so just shut your mouth and keep it that way."

"Won't he see us tonight?"

The sec officer sighed. "I told you to... No, he won't. He's gone to his bed. But don't worry, Red. One more night t'live. Be thankful. This time on the morrow you'll either be chilled, or you'll wish that you were."

And the door slammed.

KRYSTY WAS AWAKENED by a faint grating sound that seemed to originate behind the head of her bed. She sat up, trying to work out what the time was and what had caused the noise. The sound was repeated. It had a peculiar, hollow resonance to it that echoed through the room.

The girl swung her long legs off the bed and stood facing the ancient tapestry, which stirred as if a breath of wind had tugged at it. Though the window was flung open, there wasn't a breath of air in the room. The night was sultry and humid; Krysty could hear thunder rumbling off to the north.

The tapestry moved again, and the glow from the single oil lamp in the room cast dancing shadows across the faded material. The grating stopped, but Krysty could hear the squeak of an ungreased hinge. There *was* another entrance into the room, hidden by the huge wall covering.

Whoever was coming into the room was moving with a marvelously light foot. Krysty made a guess, calling in a low voice.

"Come in, Jabez. Why not use the proper door to the room? Frightened you might be seen visiting a mutie in the middle of the night?"

A hand appeared at the edge of the fabric, gripping it tightly. At her words, the hand vanished for a moment, then the tapestry was pushed aside and the young Lord Jabez Pendragon Cawdor stepped softly into Krysty's prison room.

He wore a jacket of plum-colored velvet, slashed with white ermine. His chest was bare beneath it and, Krysty noticed, utterly without hair. His trousers, made of raven-black satin, were loose and baggy about the knees, like something out of a child's book of Sinbad the sailor. He wore fur slippers on his feet. His dart gun was in his belt, his right hand hovering near the butt.

"Only a mutie could have known it was me," he said quietly, looking around the chamber suspiciously. When he was satisfied he and Krysty were alone, he perched on the edge of her bed, one foot dangling.

"Who else could it be? Your father? To move so quiet? Your mother? I think not. Her liking for jolt would keep her to her room at night, unless she had some vital errand." Krysty stared at Jabez as she spoke, looking for a clue that he knew about Rachel's nocturnal visit to Ryan.

But the pallid face betrayed nothing. The distorted eye blinked furiously. His left hand toyed with the beautiful amethyst set in gold at the end of the long chain about his throat.

"Blood and bones! You are one of... If you were not marked for death I could..."

Krysty felt her pulse rate rising. There was something truly sinister about the young man who sat so relaxed on her bed. There weren't many reasons why he might come to see her at this hour. And none of them were good.

"What is it?"

"I came to see you. To see if my brief and interrupted memory of you was correct." He paused, but she didn't reply. "And it is," he concluded lamely.

"You've seen me. Now you can go."

"Ah, no. That's stupid of you. Stupid to anger me."

"You know I'll be dead by tomorrow, lordling," she mocked. "You think any threat can frighten me? Go and sleep with your mother, like a good little boy. Go on."

Jabez drew the dart gun and leveled it at her. "It can be tomorrow. It can be now, you flap-mouth slut! It can be easy or I can make it hard."

Krysty continued to deliberately provoke him, feeling her own tension mounting, knowing she was flirting with an instant chilling.

And not caring.

"Hard, Jabez? I can't believe you can make anything hard, least of all your pathetic cock."

"Bitch!" he screamed, taking a half step toward her and squeezing the trigger of the blaster. But his feet slipped on the edge of the large carpet and threw his aim. The cluster of darts hissed venomously across the room, burying themselves in the door of the wardrobe, missing Krysty by a hand's breadth.

She backed away from him, whispering to herself, watching Jabez Cawdor through slitted eyes. "Earth Mother, help me. Aid me now, Gaia! Help me and give the strength and the power."

"Prayers won't help you, slut! I'm going to open your belly and rip out your tripes. But first I'm going to show you how a Cawdor can fuck. Sit on the bed and keep your hands still. No, take off your clothes. Fast! Before I waste you, here and now."

Moving as slowly as she could, Krysty concentrated on slipping into the trance of power, the way her mother,

Sonja, had taught her. The dark blue top came off, revealing her splendid breasts. Still chanting the invocation to the Earth Mother, the girl started to unzip her pants, slipping off the low boots and kicking them into a corner of the room.

"Faster!" The slit barrel of the dart blaster gaped at her as Jabez waved it angrily.

"Give me all the power. Let me strive for life," she was whispering, eyes closed now, feeling the familiar surge. An almost indescribable sensation flowered in her loins, spreading like a slow fire through her belly and thighs into her chest and arms and down to her ankles. It finally filled her head with a scything hiss, as though her brain were floating. She felt unbelievably light and potent.

Jabez Pendragon Cawdor, baron designate of the ville of Front Royal, saw none of that. He saw a sexually attractive young woman with a wonderful body, who had stripped naked at his bidding and sat patiently on the big bed, waiting for him to take his pleasure.

He licked his lips as he stared fixedly at the junction of Krysty's thighs, at the curling nest of blazing pubic hair that tangled and concealed and aroused.

"Lie down," he said, voice trembling.

"Don't," she said, now calm, her breathing steady and relaxed. It would be better if Jabez left the room without touching her. But if it happened, then she was ready for it.

"Beg for mercy, whore. It adds to my pleasure. Beg." Clumsily, holding the dart gun in his right hand, the young man shrugged off the rich velvet jacket, kicking the slippers to one side. "I don't hear you begging, you useless mutie slag."

"Come then," Krysty whispered, holding her arms out to Jabez.

"Blood and bones! You'll weep for death this very night." He unlaced the satin pants and tossed them to the floor, grinning as her eyes fell on his near-erection. The blaster was steady in his hand as he knelt on the bed and leaned over her.

Krysty was ready.

Chapter Twenty-Seven

WITH A SHORT, STABBING BLOW from the heel of her hand, Krysty Wroth crushed Jabez's larynx, rendering his vocal cords useless. It was a savage and crippling attack that flung him onto the floor, his mouth flopping open in a silent, anguished scream. His eyes opened wide, the drooping lid flicking up like a window blind suddenly released.

Krysty's most awesome mutie trait was her ability, under certain circumstances, to call on a reserve of incredible muscular power for a short time. The cost was dreadful, and always left her exhausted and drained for hours after. Therefore it was an ability she hardly ever used. But she knew the baron's son intended to rape her in the most violent and humiliating way, and then kill her. She didn't have to be a doomie to see that.

Her right hand jabbed at the arm that held the dart gun, snapping both radius and ulna above the wrist. One splintered end of bone protruded through the skin, surrounded by flags of torn and bloody flesh. The fingers opened in a spasm of shock and pain, dropping the dart gun to the stones, where it landed with a hollow, metallic clang.

Krysty was barely in control of her own body. The devastating power of the Earth Mother was released in such a rush that it almost blanked her mind: all that registered was that she had to kill this man in the most absolute and total manner.

Jabez struggled to his feet, chest heaving as he battled for breath. His eyes stared blankly at the staggeringly beautiful woman who stood across the bed from him.

He shook his head in disbelief at her speed and brutal strength. Jabez had always relished giving a good beating to a serving maid, smiling at her screams as his whip cut patterned welts over the soft skin. They were so weak, women.

Krysty punched out at his other arm, snapping it like a dry twig at the elbow joint.

Now a red killing mist swamped her mind, closing off any reason or sense.

Or mercy.

Short jabs with fists clenched broke five ribs on the left side of Jabez's chest and four on the right. None of the savage punches traveled more than six inches. The man staggered back against the wall and tried to scream for help, only managing to make a sound like a newborn lamb bleating weakly for its mother.

Krysty grabbed his dangling left hand and crushed it between her palms.

At this point, Jabez Pendragon Cawdor fainted, slumping in her arms, his blood smearing the stone floor. He lay on his back, legs outstretched. Krysty looked down at him, eyes blank and cold, breathing faster.

As though in a trance, she measured her aim, leaped high and came down with both heels on either side of the left knee, springing the joint so that the patella popped out like a metal bearing between finger and thumb.

Jabez stirred at the appalling pain of the injury, but before he was jerked back into consciousness, Krysty repeated the attack on his other knee, destroying the joint.

Had he lived, Jabez would have been a helpless cripple, unable even to crawl.

Had he lived.

Krysty stood, panting. Her eyes were half-closed, and she was swaying on her bare, blood-smeared feet. She glanced down at the naked, broken, unconscious man lying crookedly on the gray stones of the bedroom floor.

If any of Krysty's friends had seen her at that moment, they would have backed away from her, horrified that she'd been seized by a killing frenzy. She touched Jabez with a toe, and he jerked away from her. She laughed quietly, an ugly, tinkling little noise, like a cracked silver bell.

Jabez's eyes flickered open, and she heard a choked groan of purest pain. She could see the pulse that fluttered unevenly in his throat, just beneath the ear.

As she stared at him, the mutie power of her mind stripped him to the soul. She saw the stunted, evil core of Jabez's being, when pleasure came only through the pain and suffering of others. She saw the festering slime that a religious person might have called the soul. And was appalled.

Jabez Cawdor stirred, head rolling to one side. A thin trickle of bile, tinted with blood, drooled from his open mouth.

Krysty lashed out with her heel, hitting the heir to the ville of Front Royal at the base of the nose. Cartilage burst, and the septum shattered into a dozen splinters of jagged bone. Gouts of blood spewed in the air and all over Jabez's naked chest. The power of the kick jammed the shards of bone high into the soft spaces of the skull, driving them into the brain.

RYAN HEARD NOTHING of Krysty's fury from where he lay
in his own room, watching the light fade away. He'd heard
the clattering of hooves on the cobbles in the morning and
the excited yapping of the hounds. A bowl of gruel and
some crusts of dry bread had been his only meal, given to
him so cautiously that he'd lapped at it like an animal. He
knew nothing of the disastrous and farcical entry of Doc
Tanner and Lori Quint into the ville.

And he knew nothing at all of the visit of Jabez Pendragon Cawdor to Krysty Wroth. Not a hint of the young
man's hideously violent chilling.

The sec men hadn't bothered to leave Ryan any lamps
lit in his prison room. Despite the discomfort of his binding and the imminence of his departure from life, Ryan
still managed some sleep, dozing until the links of the
chain around his neck jerked him awake.

But something else had disturbed him. He lay still, eye
open, straining to listen. It had been a creaking noise, like
a piece of wood being slowly split in two. There was silence, and then another, sharper sound. In the blackness,
Ryan could make out a narrow strip of golden light shin-
ing in the middle of the shelves.

Where he knew the secret door was hidden!

A figure moved against the thin rectangle of pale yellow, then the door closed and the chamber was in total
blackness. Ryan tried to wriggle into a position where he
might at least try a kick at whoever had entered the
chamber.

"Come on," he whispered. "Come on, you bastard!
Come on."

His hearing was better than most, and he strained to
listen to the pounding stillness. Bare feet moved with an
infinite caution on the cold, dusty stones of the room.
And the ragged breathing sounded like that of a man at

the farthest edge of exhaustion, only a knife blade from collapse. The steps hesitated again, and then stopped about five paces from him.

"Ryan."

The touch of a moth's feathery wing brushed at his hearing—Krysty's voice, seeming to come from a great distance, from somewhere in the deeps of the ville.

"Lover?" he said. "What is it?"

"The power of...of the Earth Mother came...to...to me. Was as though Gaia herself took possession of..."

The words faded away.

"What is it? What happened? Fireblast! If only I was free I could... Krysty, tell me what's happened. Tell me."

She came closer, and he finally felt her hand on his arm. "Ryan. Oh, but...I've killed Jabez Cawdor."

Since he already anticipated death within the next few hours, Ryan wasn't too shaken by her words. The murder of his brother's only child didn't make a whole lot of difference. The Trader used to say that a man could only get himself chilled once.

"How? No, make that *why*?"

"Came in to rape me. He was the most evil...evil bastard I ever met, Ryan. So I took him. Wasted him."

"Had it coming, lover," he said.

Then she broke down, lying across him, hanging on as if she were drowning, her tears wetting through his clothes. The girl's whole body was shaken by sobbing, the sound muffled as she pressed her face to his chest. Despite being bound and helpless, Ryan tried to comfort his woman, muttering softly and kissing the side of her neck. He could feel that her long, sentient hair was coiled tightly at the back of her head in a defensive bundle.

"Tell me 'bout it."

Krysty fought for self-control, sitting back on her heels, trying to steady her breathing. "Chilled him. But ... that isn't all. The power was worse than I ever knew."

"How d'you mean? Worse?"

Her voice was so quiet that Ryan could barely hear it, but he eventually made out what she was saying. And the flesh crawled on his nape at the horror of it. She hadn't just killed the young man. She'd slipped into a blind frenzy and ripped his body apart.

Ryan tried to speak and found that his voice had gone, choked in a fearful dryness. He'd seen Krysty use her power before, and witnessed the awesome strength at such times. But to rend a corpse limb from limb ... He swallowed hard and found words again.

"Don't ever get angry with me, lover," he whispered.

He felt her relax a little, the hair loosening at her neck. She even managed a muffled giggle at his weak joke. "Try not to, Ryan. If we live that long. What can we do?"

"Nobody outside in the passage heard?"

"No. I'm good at it, lover."

"I know. Are there bars on your window?"

"Some. You can lean out, but I doubt you could escape that way."

"They fear magic in the Shens. Always talk of shamans and wizards. I know that Harvey was always terrified of such things. You could sink the ... the body in the moat and say you fell into a deep sleep and babble about demons and spirits possessing Jabez. The door's locked?"

"Yes. On the inside. And there's some old shrouds and some chunks of iron in a chest. I could weight the bits."

"Do it. At least it might take the blame away from you. Who knows, lover? Can you do it? You're not too weak?"

"I can try. By Gaia! What I want most is to sleep for a month. With you, Ryan."

"Don't forget. He came in and was babbling some sort of shit that sounded bad. You blacked out, and when you came around Jabez was gone. Just a lot of blood on the floor."

"I'll try, lover. Will Harvey and his bitch-wife fall for it?"

Ryan smiled in the darkness. "If they don't, things can't be worse for us. And if they do... Who knows, Krysty? Who knows?"

Chapter Twenty-Eight

HARVEY CAWDOR LOOKED like a man in the last stages of some dreadful ague. His whole body quivered and shook, his chins flapping from side to side like enormous dewlaps. His face was as pale as parchment, and a thread of spittle trailed from one corner of his thick lips. Sweat glistened on his pallid forehead and trickled over the pudgy acres of his cheeks.

"Just blood?" he asked brokenly. It was the twentieth time he'd repeated the question since Ryan and his three friends had been dragged from their rooms just after dawn, and hustled into the main hall of the mansion. Harvey sat in his wide-armed oak chair, wearing a loose cloak of aquamarine, lined with sleek black fur. His straggly hair was uncombed, and his fingers were ringless.

Rachel sat next to him, face blank, hollowed eyes locked onto Ryan's single good eye. Her fingers played with the silver catch on her scuffed leather purse. She wore a black robe with a tiny gold star-cluster brooch on her breast. Rachel had said nothing since the news of the bizarre disappearance of her only child.

"Only blood? How can that be? How can a grown man vanish and leave just a lake of dried blood?"

"He raised demons, Baron Cawdor," Krysty answered quietly. She'd recovered something of her normal strength, but she was still pale and shifted nervously from foot to foot as though she feared she might fall.

"You told us that," Rachel spit, finally stirring from her lethargy.

"The door was locked from within. The window barred so that no human could leave. No body floats in the moat. I cannot...can't...she's a witch, that flame-haired gaudy whore! Killed my little boy. Butchered him and made his body disappear like fucking smoke. Ah..."

Harvey looked at the sergeant of the sec men, who stood at the side of Ryan Cawdor. "The chimney in the room. Was it searched?"

"There was no chimney in that room, Lord," replied the guard.

Baron Cawdor fell silent. Ryan looked around him, his memory conjuring up long-dead faces and times, mostly not worth remembering: banquets with a whole pig being roasted on a spit by a red-faced lad; jugs of beer being hefted by muscular women from the kitchens of the ville; the unforgettable taste of overripe venison with sweet potatoes and crimson berries; music floating down from the gallery that ran around three sides of the vaulted room.

In the stillness he could hear the faint sound of the baron's hunting dogs, howling beneath the central keep of the house. And the keening noise of the ferocious boars that his brother bred for his own sport.

Jak Lauren was on the end of the row, his white hair tangled and greasy, his red eyes darting around the room. He caught Ryan's glance and flashed him a lightning grin.

J. B. Dix stood next to him, arms folded across his chest, pale face turned incuriously toward the baron and his woman. Despite the passive appearance, Ryan knew from long experience that the brain of the Armorer would be racing, calculating angles and odds, looking for a chance. Half a chance.

Anything.

Ryan had been doing the same. Ever since his true identity had been revealed, he'd known that death stood a heartbeat away from them all. A bloated assassin like Harvey would not blink at spilling more blood. And in all the world there was nobody he wanted chilled more than Ryan.

But now the four friends were helpless, unarmed, and overwhelmingly outnumbered by the army of sec men that patrolled Front Royal. The butchering of Jabez had been a tiny entry on the credit side of their account, but their own debiting came ever closer.

The sergeant coughed, catching the piggy little eyes of his lord.

"What is it, man? Speak up!"

"The old man and the girl?"

Harvey Cawdor stared blankly at the sec officer. "What?"

"The old man and the young girl, my lord. She has yellow hair and he—"

"I know who you mean, you fucking double-stupe! What of them?"

The man shuffled his feet and looked down, his hand going to his bruised and swollen jaw. The expression on his face said clearly that he wished they'd never started a conversation.

"He broke one of my teeth. Pretended he was a real doc. We got him and the girl in the guard cells."

"What has this to do with the wizardry and deviltry that took my son from me? Are you saying they're witches, as well? Shall we burn them?"

"No, I don't . . . I mean, my lord . . . What shall we do with 'em?"

"Flog them and turn them out of the ville!" Ryan's brother picked irritably at the chipped blue varnish that decorated his chewed nails.

"They could be traitors and friends to these four," said Rachel Cawdor, leaning forward in her seat, eyes staring above and beyond Ryan's head.

"I don't think so, my lady," the sec man said. "The oldster's barely three bullets in a blaster and the girl's a near-dummy. I say flog 'em out of the ville."

Harvey shifted his enormous bulk and belched, glowering at his sec officer. "You say that, do you, Sergeant? I've a mind to flog *you*. Cut your ears off. Slice the lids from your eyes. Peel off those fucking lips. What then? I've heard the girl is pretty, Sergeant. What d'you say to that, man?"

The sec man swallowed convulsively. "Yes, she is. I'm sorry, Lord, that—"

"Shut up," Harvey muttered, his violent anger passing as fast as it had risen.

Ryan glanced at the line of grim-faced guards, each of whom carried his M-16 at port arms. The windows were flung open, letting in the clean morning air. He could hear a young child crying to his mother for attention. There was the crack of a slap and a scream from the toddler. Another slap rang out, and then silence once more. A young brindled puppy wandered in, looking around for a familiar face. It ambled over to Jak and rubbed itself against his legs. The boy stooped to pet the animal, chucking it under the chin. It was an oddly normal scene, hardly one where four people were about to be sentenced to their deaths.

"I think it was some black magic that took my son," Harvey Cawdor said, levering himself to his feet. "We've heard how he came to question a prisoner. And she...or someone...raised a devil, who lifted my dear Jabez to the realms eternal."

Ryan's hands were still cuffed behind him. Krysty, sensing that the word of doom was coming, took a half step forward to be beside him and rested her hand on his arm. Jak ignored the baron, continuing to stroke the puppy that now rolled on its back to have its stomach tickled.

J.B. stood at ease, the dawn's light glinting off his spectacles, his fedora pushed back off his forehead.

"My order is . . . Sergeant!"

"My lord?"

"Chill that fucking dog!"

"Now, my lord?"

"Now, man!"

The sec officer gestured angrily to one of his men on the far side of the hall. The guard was tall and skinny, the blaster looking as if it weighed him down. Ryan could almost smell the sec man's fear at being picked on in front of the baron.

"Move away, Jak," he said quietly. For a moment he wondered if the boy was going to try to make an issue of it, but after a split second's hesitation, Jak stepped away from the puppy, shaking his head, the pure white hair seeming to float in the shafts of light streaming from the high casements of the hall.

"Chill it, Trooper Vare," the sergeant ordered.

The young man had his M-16 set on continuous fire, and his finger froze on the trigger, pouring all thirty rounds into the fawning dog. The bullets kicked and sparked from the stone floor, ricocheting and whining off the far wall, tearing an old tapestry into colored rags.

The puppy disappeared in a spray of blood and jagged bone that frothed in the air, splattering the sergeant. He staggered back, hands clawing at the warm slush that blinded him, spitting out crimson hunks of phlegm onto the flagstones. Ryan closed his eye, wincing at the burst of violence, feeling Krysty's fingers tighten on his arm. He heard Jak's voice whisper an obscene threat to the sec man, but it was drowned out by a great guffaw of laughter from Harvey Cawdor, his rolls of fat quivering under the bright silk robe.

"Wonderful, Sergeant. Triple fucking A. There's magic. Like Jabez. The disappearing dog. Wasn't a sec man blowing our son apart like that? Course not. Course not. Nothing left to hunt for."

"Get on with it," Rachel grated from between clenched teeth. It was obvious to Ryan that she was craving a line or two of the white elixir of life. Once jolt had the noose around your soul, it pulled it tighter and tighter until you finally snapped.

"Wait, bitch. I said 'hunt.' Hunt." Harvey's thick pink tongue ran over his fleshy lips, and he giggled to himself. "You always liked the thrill of the hunt, didn't you, brother?" Ryan didn't answer him. "Yes, you did. And I love it. My dogs love it. Even my trained boars love being hunted, using their sharp tusks to rip open bellies and throats. Ah, yes. The hunt."

"Hunt them?" Rachel said, suddenly alive. She gave Ryan a look of such intent that it puzzled him, not understanding what lay at the back of her vicious and ambitious mind. Seeing his blank face, she turned away from him, biting her lip in disappointment.

"Yes, hunt them. Sergeant, get everything ready. We shall ride out at noon. Horses, weapons. All the sec men that can be spared from the ville's defense. We eat at eleven."

"The dogs, Lord?"

"Of course, cretin! Make sure they have no food today."

"The old man and the girl?"

"The old what? Oh, them. Keep them. They can do us no harm. I'll question the girl tonight. I shall be in the mood."

"The prisoners?"

"Feed 'em. We are kind, brother, are we not?" Again Ryan ignored Harvey. "Give 'em clothes and boots. Keep them locked up and bring them to the drawbridge at eleven. They shall have an hour's start. Escort them out to the Oxbow Loop. We'll hunt them in there. String out a patrol so they can't break back. This will be..." He hugged himself gleefully.

"No blasters, brother?" Ryan asked.

"Last time you gave me this, Ryan," Harvey spit, touching the puckered scar that deformed his mouth and nose. "A fair trade for your left eye." He stepped closer to his brother, right shoulder hunched, leg trailing. To Ryan, he resembled a mutated, brilliant-colored spider.

"Give us blades," J.B. demanded.

"Blades, little man? You might cut yourself." Close up, Ryan could see from his older brother's eyes that he floated in a sea of tranks, his ferocious temper spurting through on occasion.

"Scared might find an' take throat out?" Jak said.

The sergeant raised a fist and moved toward the boy, who dropped into a fighting crouch. Harvey squeaked and cowered back, hands tangled like a praying monk.

Jak's white face stared menacingly at the sec man. "Not little whelp, bastard," he hissed. "Not forget." He beckoned to the tall officer, fingers waving softly like the fronds of a virulent sea anemone. The sergeant stopped, hesitating, looking to the baron for orders.

"Leave...him," Harvey stammered. "He can...he is... Why not a knife each? One hunting dagger for each man, and for the redhead witch."

Ryan dropped a deep bow to his brother. "One knife against all your men and dogs. Still the white-bellied coward, brother."

"I could have you all torn and burned," Harvey Cawdor protested, his voice a petulant squeak.

"That would show your fear even better, fool," Rachel whispered. "Close your mouth and let us go to our rooms. I have..." The sentence dangled in the dusty dawn light of the long, vaulted hall.

To have a knife was better than anything Ryan Cawdor could have hoped for.

He'd sensed a new spring in the steps of his three friends. J.B. nodded to him almost imperceptibly as they parted company in the upper corridor. Jak whistled a song Ryan had heard before, something about feeling on fire. And Krysty recovered from the horror of the dark night that had seared her soul. She almost glowed as she walked away from the hall. To be burned alive had faced them all. Now they had a chance.

Four blades against thirty or so men who had M-16s, horses and dogs.

That was their chance.

The Trader used to say that if you found yourself with no hope, or odds of a million to one, you took the long odds.

"Long odds," Ryan said to himself as the sec men slammed the door of his room, having chained him once more to the wall.

THE MEAL WAS SOUP and fresh bread. Good soup, rich with vegetables. And half a loaf, still warm on the outside, sweet and crumbling on the inside. They freed his hands to eat but left the chain around his neck.

One of the guards stared curiously at him. "You're truly Lord Ryan Cawdor, aren't you? My father spoke well about you until his death."

"It was speaking well cost him his life," the other young sec man mumbled. "Baron set him waltzing on air on the river road, these five years past."

"If Harvey is such a blood-eyed chiller, why not rise against him?" Ryan asked.

"Would you swallow the barrel of a blaster? First man to say treason dies. And then the second. The baron is careful and ruthless. It would take a great rising and his death. And his lady's."

The sec man was nudged by his friend. "Enough. Too much. Lock him again and let's get out of here 'fore we do the oxyjean jig like your father did."

Ryan could just see the edge of the rising sun through the window. His guess was that it was around eleven o'clock. The sky was a light blue-green, tinted with flecks of orange cloud. Far below him he could hear the excited yapping of the hunting dogs, sensing that they were to be set free on a hunt. Ryan closed his eye and tried to relax, but the sound of the door opening disturbed him.

Oddly he wasn't all that surprised to see that his visitor was Lady Rachel Cawdor.

She stepped toward him, eyes bright in the sunlit room. The lady had obviously been enjoying several lines of jolt, and her whole body seemed to tremble with an eager anticipation.

"Your life is measured in short hours, brother-in-law," she said.

Ryan nodded, wondering why she had come yet again to see him.

"Don't you realize you're going to die?" she asked, drawing nearer to him.

"We all are," he replied.

Rachel sighed. "If we could... But that's all water under the mill. You're twenty times the man your brother...that blubbering pile of lard... It can still be done. I can have him done to death. Half the ville would dance on his grave."

"Replace him with me?" Ryan asked. "The long chill is sweet compared to that."

"But now Jabez has been taken by... By who, Ryan? Not wizards. Tell me how it was done. Where is the boy's corpse?"

"Hell, bitch. I hope."

She nodded slowly. "You and I could rule the Shens and beyond, Ryan. I picked wrong with Harvey. And now he... I came for a last chance for you. Will you join me?"

"If I'm going t'die before dark, then I can go with that. It's paying the price to live with yourself on your own terms. Not something a murderous slut like you can understand. Just fuck off, and leave me be, Rachel."

"You scorn the chance to be one of the lords of life, Ryan. Then I leave you...."

A line of verse came back to Ryan that Doc was fond of using: "To the pleasure of my high vices, that I'll have to pay for at higher prices."

"You think dying in the jaws of his dogs is going to be funny, you double-stupe? I wish I could ride to watch, but

Harvey'll take his funning, then come back for the yellow-head girl in the cells. And life, Ryan Cawdor, will go on.''

She stooped over him, and he felt the brush of her lips against the stubbled skin of his cheek, as cold as the tomb, her breath carrying the sharp flavor of jolt. Then she straightened and walked quickly to the door. She paused a moment with her hand on the latch, as if she were about to say more, but she turned away without another word and left him alone.

KRYSTY BUCKLED the sheathed knife onto her leather belt.

Jak drew his and tossed it a few times into the air, feeling for its balance before sheathing it at the small of his back.

J.B. tested the edge against the palm of his hand, stooping and pressing the steel against the stones of the courtyard, trying out the tension of the blade.

Ryan also drew the dagger that he'd been given. It had a handle of narrow strips of hide, bound around a steel hilt. The blade was single-edged, very sharp, around eleven inches in length and two inches broad at the haft. It was a workmanlike hunting knife.

He thought that it would probably do.

Chapter Twenty-Nine

THE SUN RODE HIGH in the heavens, its brassy glare beating down pitilessly on the forests and streams of the Shens.

Ryan was the first one out of the rattling cart, jumping down, stretching, feeling the freedom in his shoulders and wrists. His eye was caught by a flicker of movement high in the wrack of lemon-yellow clouds. He stared up at it and saw it was a massive mutie hawk with a wingspan of about twenty feet and a hooked beak that would take the arm off a man.

J.B., Jak and finally Krysty stepped onto the dusty lane. The mounted sec men gazed blank-faced at them, their rifles slung across their shoulders on webbing straps. The sergeant with the damaged mouth was in charge of the patrol, and as they had clattered along from the ville, he told Ryan a little of what to expect.

"Oxbow Loop's where the baron does his manhunting. It's 'bout two miles across. Be men blocking off this end, so the only way's in. River's too fast and wide to swim. Muties on far side, if'n you want to try it. Rain we've had'll make it swollen and twice as fast as usual. Lotta trees in there. Streams. No buildings. One trail to a gas store for the ville's main generators. Nothing to help. Nobody to help. And nowhere to go. Nowhere. Best time was a breed, coupla years back. Made it for better'n two hours. And killed a dog.'' There was a note of grudging admiration in the sec officer's voice.

Ryan knew his brother would be along with the pack of hounds in about a half hour. And more sec men. Dinner had taken longer than Baron Harvey had anticipated, and the hunt would now begin as soon as the sonorous bell in the tower of Front Royal tolled once for the hour after noon.

LORI QUINT LAY BACK on the narrow bed, knees tucked up to her chin, watching a gray-brown spider as it wound its way across the ceiling. She was wondering who that immensely fat man had been who'd appeared for a moment in the doorway, licking his fleshy lips and muttering in a monotonous and obscene whisper. She'd only managed to catch the words ''Later, pretty bitch.''

It was more than enough to make her restless and fearful. The sudden booming of the bell in the tower above made her jump and cry out in shock.

OUT IN THE DEPTHS of the woods, only four miles from where Ryan and his friends waited, Nathan Freeman also heard the noise of the ville's bell chiming out the first hour after noon. He wondered where Ryan was and what had happened to the old man and the beautiful girl with hair like summer wheat. A little earlier he'd detected the sound of horses moving on the old Oxbow Road.

The tall young man adjusted the Smith & Wesson Model 39 at his hip and began to walk toward the sweeping bend of the river.

BARON HARVEY HAD BEEN assisted into the saddle of his huge stallion while ville servants tucked the silver-and-maroon cloak about his crooked shoulders. The pair of matched Colts were settled snugly on both sides of his belt. His thinning hair was protected from the baking sun by a feathered cap of crimson velvet.

He sat atop his mount, beaming happily and vacuously around his demesne. The pack of crossbred Rottweilers and Dobermans was behind him, moving excitedly, muzzles thrust into the warm air, sniffing. Now that the hunt was close, they made little noise. Their handlers moved among them, occasionally striking out with short-hafted whips to keep them under control.

The tranks the baron had gulped down after his meal, swilling them into his gullet with brandy, kept him afloat in a cherry-red cheery cloud of gentle warmth and happiness.

His son was dead and vanished. His bitch-wife would soon have jolted herself into the grave. There was a pretty little doll with the longest legs waiting in the guardhouse.

And his prodigal brother would soon be ragged flesh and gnawed bones.

"Life is so good," he said to himself. The bell chimed once, and he gave the signal for the hunting party to move out.

"So good, good, good, good," he chanted.

"TIME," SAID THE SEC OFFICER, looking toward the distant bell tower.

"Yeah," Ryan said, leading the others off among the trees.

Chapter Thirty

RYAN CAWDOR FELT fiercely exultant. There was going to be some chilling done, and that was something he was good at. Maybe the thing he was best at. He had three people he could trust with his life, running free in a country that he knew well. And there was a stout blade sheathed in his belt.

He'd read in an old book once—or it might have been in a crumbling vid: If you're goin' down, take some of the bastards with yer.

Ryan was a realist, and he knew that long before sundown they would probably all be mangled corpses, dragged behind horses, ready to be shown to the people of the ville.

"So die all traitors." Something like that.

But right now they were sprinting along a narrow trail, beeches and sycamores on either side, the sound of their feet softened by the carpet of dead leaves. Ryan led the way, followed by Krysty, flaming hair tied back to avoid its catching on branches. Jak came third, his white mane similarly clutched in a length of twine. J.B. jogged easily at the rear. Despite his slight build and age, the Armorer kept himself honed to a critical edge of fitness.

They'd only had a few minutes for a council of war. There had been two simple possibilities: split up or stay together. They had all agreed that their only, razor-slim hope was to keep together.

Ryan remembered the area called the Oxbow Loop. The river was known locally as the Sorrow, on account of the number of times it flooded and took away livestock and homes. And folks.

It was true that nobody could hope to try to get across the Sorrow. She ran at this time of year like a ravaging animal, her course studded with jagged granite boulders that turned the brown flood to scudding foam. With a long, fixed rope from bank to bank, it might be worth the gamble. Set against dying it might be worth it. But without a rope it was a fine way of chilling yourself.

Across the neck of the Oxbow was a strip of trail less than a quarter mile long, with an expanse of stunted bushes and low scrub. With mounted men keeping watch there it would be death to try to cross it.

Krysty had suggested they could hide until dark and then break out. Ryan had shaken his head. They could escape the dogs by going for the trees, but they'd get trapped, and the men would follow the barking of the hounds and pick them off.

"Easier'n fish in a can," he said.

"What looking for?" Jak panted after they'd gone a half mile into the dense, prickling woods.

"Place to fight and kill us some hounds. Mebbe bring in a sec man or two. Then get us a couple of blasters. Then...?" Ryan hesitated a moment. "Then we'll see what happens."

They heard the pack arrive with Baron Harvey Cawdor a little after two hours past noon.

There was a moment of silence, with only cicadas and a few mosquitoes. Then, the second the pack caught the trail of the runaways, there was the spine-freezing sound of hunting dogs in full cry: a belling, endless wailing that rose and fell but never ceased.

"Best draw the blades," J.B. suggested quietly. "Be needing 'em soon."

"Guts or throat with hunting dog," Jak said.

"Take out a hamstring," Ryan added.

"Any place we could make a stand?" Krysty asked.

"Places I knew as a kid. No good for this. There's a small redoubt where some of the ville's gas is stored. Always double-locked. In any case, you get inside it and they got you."

The sound of the dogs was already beginning to close in on them with frightening speed.

"Water fuck 'em," Jak said, looking to their left where there was a narrow stream meandering gently between low, muddied banks.

"Not these bastards. Mutie bred. Take the scent out of the air as well as the ground."

"When hounds are on a trail, you can distract them with blood. Any blood'll turn them," J.B. suggested.

Ryan nodded, gripping the hilt of his knife. "Yeah. That's my thinking."

The Oxbow Loop was a wilderness of tall trees and stunted bushes with patches of deep swamp and tangling willows. There were a few clearings where the sun lanced through with a startling brightness that made you blink at it—and acres of leprous earth where only spear grass grew. Streams divided and subdivided the land. No birds ever seemed to fly above the Oxbow Loop, and no creatures scurried there. Even as a child, Ryan had known it as an eerie place, tainted with death. Renegades had been driven there to die for several generations, and there were handed-down tales of runaway slaves being hunted to their lonely and fearful deaths in the Oxbow Loop during the Civil War.

Ryan led the others at a fast pace, moving to where he'd once had a hiding place, a den where he would come when the bullying of Harvey became too much to bear. Nobody ever found it. Nobody ever tracked him into the wilderness by the Sorrow. He knew that the wind and the rain would have torn down his woven brushwood secret, but the place was good for a stand.

The dogs would split up into smaller hunting units, and the terrain would make it impossible for them to maintain close contact. The biggest and strongest animals would be in the lead, the rest strung out behind them.

Not far from the gas store, where a smaller stream looped in a near-circle, was a steep bank with several stately live oaks nearby, places a man with a knife could turn and dodge and protect his back against a charging dog.

They were nearly there. The howling was very close, so close that they could distinguish the echoing sound of individual animals. One, in particular, was racing ahead, seeming less than a hundred paces from them.

Jak looked at Ryan. "Can hear horse. Sec man?"

"Could be. Wanna go for him?"

The albino boy, face streaked with gray mud, hair plaited with dirt, nodded. "Get blaster. Be help. You take dogs."

Ryan patted him on the shoulder, watching the lad as he vanished into the undergrowth, wriggling through invisible gaps. Raised in the bayous of Louisiana, this was like home to Jak.

"I'll take the first one. J.B., you gut the second. Krysty, pick up what's left. Make it quick and ugly. Put 'em down and put 'em out."

They stood in a loose semicircle, backs against the earth bank, tall trees on either side to give some measure of protection on their flanks.

"Fireblast!" Ryan exclaimed as the pack leader burst over a rotting stump of a decayed walnut tree.

The fragmented sunlight dappled the animal's sleek coat like scattered gold. The crossbreed frothed at the muzzle, teeth bared. Its eyes glowed like embers and it howled as it sighted its prey, far louder than the baying sound as it had tracked them down.

"Mine," Ryan said, taking a half step forward. He didn't have time to say more.

The dog was enormous, its sides streaked with innumerable old scars. Its muzzle was long and narrow, the jaws wide. The top of its lean head came higher than a man's waist, and its weight must have been close to 120 pounds.

Dogs like that were trained to go either for the throat or for the genitals. Ryan had seen sec dogs bred to take an intruder's arm and hold him. Not the Cawdor pack. They were trained only to hunt and to kill.

It went for his groin.

Ryan half turned, protecting his testicles from the foaming teeth. He used the dagger almost like a hammer, ramming it with all his power at the side of the animal's muscular neck.

In the last fraction of a torn second, the hound tried to avoid the blow, but it was too far committed to its attack. The knife opened up its throat, blood jetting sideways, soaking the dry earth fifteen feet away. The howl died, and the animal jerked and kicked, hooked on the blade like a gaffed salmon. Ryan used the impetus of the rush to push it away, withdrawing the knife, feeling hot blood spurting over his wrist. His thrust had been so deadly that it had penetrated into the chest cavity, and as the dog fell there was blood and air frothing from the cut.

The black beast stumbled forward, muzzle striking the dirt, its hind legs scrabbling to give it purchase to turn and go again at the man. But Ryan was quicker.

He stooped and hamstrung the dog, crippling it, leaving it a whining, helpless thing. It snapped feebly at him as he moved back, but it was no longer a threat.

Even as he straightened, Ryan saw the second, third and fourth hounds come leaping into the small clearing.

J.B. stood straight and calm, waiting until the last second before ducking and turning, hand faster than the eye could follow. He opened up the dog's belly, spilling its guts in bloody loops, stepping away from the crazed animal as it bit and tore at its own stomach.

Krysty faced a smaller, leaner dog, a sinewy bitch that jumped incredibly high, going for the woman's exposed throat. Krysty's reflexes were breathtaking. She stooped, knife held point up, and stabbed the dog through the center of the breastbone, ripping its heart in rags of pumping muscle. The creature tried to twist in the air, teeth meeting with an audible click, but it was dying even before it hit the earth.

Three of the four were down and done in less time than it took to draw a deep breath.

The last of the dogs was a grizzled veteran, seamed along the flanks, one eye staring blankly ahead of it. It hesitated between the three potential victims for its slavering teeth. Krysty was off-balance, and Ryan saw the dog turn to her. He shouted, trying to distract it, drawing its attention to where he stood above the corpse of the chilled pack leader.

It came in on a crabbing, sidling attack, keeping its belly low to the earth, head to one side, watching Ryan through its good eye. In the brief pause Ryan could hear more dogs coming toward them. And the clatter of hooves. Someone was shouting in an enraged, hoarse voice.

"Watch it!" J.B. called out.

The warning wasn't necessary. This animal wasn't like those in the first trio. This was a wily campaigner that saw three of its pack dead or dying and a man with a long silver tooth in its hand. It came in, feinting to spring, then snapped at Ryan's knee. He only just dropped his guard low enough, cutting the dog along its shoulder.

But it was lightning fast, biting at Ryan's knife hand despite its own wound. The teeth missed, but the muzzle rapped him across the knuckles.

Making him drop the blade.

"Gaia!" Krysty yelled, quickly reversing her own knife to throw it at the dog, but the animal was too close to Ryan to take the risk.

The dog jumped for the throat, jaws gaping, its foul breath making Ryan gag. Its sightless eye rolled skyward, the other fixed on the man's face with a demonic intent. There wasn't time to dodge.

As it jumped, he braced himself for the charge, grabbing at the raking front paws, gripping one in his right hand and one in his left. A Tex-Mex puma hunter from down south, near Lubbock, had told him this trick during one long night of drinking.

Ryan had never had the chance to try it before now.

And he was only going to get one chance to try it. Or the crossbred black dog would rip his face off.

With all of his power, Ryan wrenched the animal's forelegs apart. There was a ghastly sound like splitting a hickory log with a long-handled ax. The hound's rib cage was burst apart by the savagery of the man's attack, rupturing its heart and lungs in a single devastating moment. Its head snapped back, and its good eye glazed. The body shuddered as life departed, and Ryan was able to drop the lifeless corpse into the dirt at his feet.

"Nice," J.B. said admiringly. "Very nice."

"Thanks, friend." He stooped to pick up the fallen dagger and grip it ready for the next wave of attacking dogs.

"Getting real close," Krysty said, stooping to clean her own blade in the dry earth by her boots. "If they all come together, we'll go down."

It was undeniably true.

Over the years Ryan had seen a few vids from before the long winters and read some books as well. One or two were adventure stories, where the hero always seemed to have a plan. Right at that moment, Ryan didn't have any real plan at all.

Kill as many of the dogs as possible. Even take a few sec men along to the chilling. Live for an hour or so before buying the farm yourself.

Wasn't much of a plan.

Half a dozen of the pack appeared, muzzles foaming, red-eyed, on the edge of the clearing. They were hesitating, cautious, as they scented and then saw the dead dogs. Ryan, Krysty and the Armorer faced them, knives blood-slick and ready, knowing it wouldn't be easy to hold off so many of the killer animals at once.

"Back-to-back," Ryan said. "Don't let 'em get in behind us." He paused a moment. "For as long as we bastard can."

The dogs sniffed uncertainly at the trampled ground, edging closer to their prey. The open space reeked with spilled blood, and it quietened the animals, their howling sinking to low growls. In the woods beyond them, the noise of horsemen and shouting came nearer.

Ryan licked his lips, tasting his own sweat. It wasn't going to be long now. He was conscious, not for the first time in the past few hours, that he had fled the ville of Front Royal to save his life. Now, within a day or so of his return, after twenty years, he was going to lose it.

A whip cracked, and it seemed to trigger the cross-breeds. Like greyhounds loosed from the slips, they charged simultaneously. Ryan braced himself for the shock of the attack.

The burst of automatic gunfire scattered the dogs in a heap of kicking, biting, mewing flesh. Ryan's keen ear heard about a dozen rounds, continuous fire. Only one animal escaped the burst, and it turned tail and ran back toward the huntsmen.

"Thanks, Jak," J.B. shouted, grinning at Ryan and the woman. "One of the M-16s. Once you've heard it, you never forget."

The fourteen-year-old albino boy appeared like a ghost from the thick brush. He held the smoking rifle in his right hand, and his lips were parted in a broad smile.

"Found this in hand of dead sec man. Didn't want no more."

"Thanks, Jak," Ryan said. "Now they know we've got a blaster, it's a different game. They'll hold the dogs back and press us in toward the river. Trap us there. Spare ammo?"

"No. Bitch, ain't it?"

Krysty pulled at Ryan's sleeve. "I can hear them, lover. You're right. Calling the hounds in. I can hear your brother screaming for sec men to come in after us. No takers. Not with half a mag left in the blaster."

"Without the dogs, we could..." Ryan checked himself. "No. They'd... Fireblast! Best we got. Follow me."

"Where?" J.B. asked.

"Gas store," he threw back over his shoulder as he ran toward the northeast, farther into the Oxbow Loop.

"KILLED HOW MANY?"

"A dozen of the bravest dogs, Baron Cawdor. Some with knives, others with Trooper Rogers's stolen blaster."

"And he's chilled by the twisting, turning, whoreson Ryan?"

"Throat opened, my lord," the sergeant said. He'd known things were going wrong ever since that mumbling dotard had turned up and broken off his rotting tooth. Then the embarrassment of the puppy being splashed all over the main hall of the ville. Now it was going from bad to much, much worse. A dozen hounds butchered. The best of the pack. And signs that the baron was about to slip over the edge into one of his trank-fueled rages.

"They can't get through to the ville?"

"No, my lord. Every yard across the neck of the land is patrolled. Not even a water rattler could slip by. No, my lord, your brother and his friends are still in the Loop."

"His traitor friends, Sergeant," Harvey said, smiling his crooked smile. Sweat was pouring off his lardy face in rivulets, drenching the ornate cloak.

"Traitors, indeed, Baron," the sec officer agreed. "We got the dogs leashed. Only place they can be is near the gas store, close by the Sorrow's banks."

"What if they get in there?"

"Then they never get out. We'll have 'em like flies in a bottle. Shall we all lead on after the dogs, my lord?"

"Lead on, bleed on, read on, weed on, bleed on and on."

The sergeant turned away, face schooled to impassivity from years of working for Baron Harvey Cawdor.

THE GAS STORE was a squat, ugly building isolated at the end of a narrow trail that cut off the main road away from the ville. It dated from before the holocaust, but nobody had ever known what its use had been. An old woman once told Ryan that she'd heard from her gran that it had been used for taking and storing ice from the Sorrow, before the turbulent river had been called by that name and before the nuking had upset some of the shifting rocks underpinning the Shens, making the Sorrow the untamed terror it now was.

Trees grew thickly around the store, which measured around thirty feet square. The walls were of stone, held together by crumbling mortar. There was a window at the rear that had been filled in a century before. The door was of iron, secured by a massive padlock, now rusting. Knowing what the price of failure would be, nobody from the ville or the country around would have dared to try to break into the baron's own store of gasoline. The liquid was stored in metal drums, placed along the inner walls of the building.

One of the greatest necessities in all of Deathlands was gas—for the wags and for powering generators that were generally the sole source of power in most villes. Occasionally a cache would be found hidden in redoubts from before the winters. But this was of superior quality and greatly valued. Most gas came from near the Gulf of Mexico and from places in the high plains country, where it was crudely refined by small, highly armed communities. Front Royal got most of her gas from a ville close to what had once been the border with Canada.

The store held several thousand gallons.

Ryan led them there.

Chapter Thirty-One

THE DOOR WAS a little way open, the inside of the gray building—its walls splashed with a sickly lichen—in almost total darkness. The dogs had brought the hunt straight to it, past the mangled corpses of the other hounds. The sergeant had ordered them held back on long leashes, keeping anyone from going near the store until the baron himself arrived to give them his orders.

Any conversation was difficult against the thunderous roar of the Sorrow, pounding its crazed route toward the distant sea.

The sec officer refused anyone the chance of going closer, keeping them back in a skirmishing line at the edge of the clearing. A couple of men held the horses while the rest of the party dismounted and waited, carbines at the ready, for further orders. Eventually Baron Harvey Cawdor came up, swaying in the high-pommeled saddle, humming a tuneless song to himself. With the help of a half-dozen sec troopers he battled his way to the ground, immediately deciding that he wanted to be back on his horse.

"To be able to see better, Sergeant," he explained in ringing tones.

"Yeah, my lord." It took several minutes before the grossly fat man was once more in the saddle of the shire stallion.

"We've got 'em caught, eh?" Harvey bellowed, though the sergeant stood patiently waiting right at his stirrup. "Caught?"

"In the gas store. Looks like they shot off the old lock. Or, likely, smashed it with a stone or the butt of the carbine."

"They're in there?"

"Must be. Dogs covered both ways and they don't come out. There's only the Sorrow behind. Must be in there. If'n you look close, my lord, you see the patch of blue from the ville's clothes they wore."

Harvey giggled, rubbing his pudgy hands together, the array of gold rings jingling and clashing. "The end, brother dearest. At last, after so many years and years and years and years and... Get the men to close in."

"Still got a few rounds left in the blaster, my lord."

"Can't kill you all. I'll wait there." He pointed behind him to where the screen of trees would protect him from a stray bullet.

The sergeant still didn't quite understand. "Just move in, all together, my lord?"

"Do it. Dogs an' all. What's that smell in the air?"

"Gas, my lord."

"Leaking?"

"Store always smells."

Harvey wrinkled his scarred nose. "Why not burn them out?"

The sec officer shook his head. "No! No, my lord. There's enough gas in there to blow away half the Shens. We can..." A thought struck him. "Would you not rather have them taken alive, for the sporting, my lord?"

Harvey began to kick his heels into the ribs of his gigantic horse. "Yes. Good. Have them alive, Sergeant. Alive."

Nobody was in any hurry to be the first to push open the door of the store, knowing that there were four renegade traitors waiting inside, one of them with a loaded M-16. It was like being first man up a siege ladder.

Most men, given the choice, might prefer that someone else got to be the dead hero.

The sergeant chivvied them on. The dogs were subdued, hanging back, having to be whipped on. The stench of gasoline, combined with the rich scent of blood from the dead animals, was enough to put them off their hunting desire.

There had been no sign of life inside the store. As the sun came and went from behind tattered banks of high-altitude purple chem clouds, the advancing sec men could glimpse the sleeve of a jerkin just visible in the gloom. The baron's men closed in, ringing the front of the building, glancing nervously at one another, the noise of the Sorrow pounding in their ears like the drumming of the gods. The nearest of them was less than fifteen paces from the door.

Ten paces.

Still no shot. No sign of resistance. The sec men looked back at their sergeant, who waved them on with the barrel of his own carbine. He'd given them the orders to take the four alive, warning them to watch for the knives.

Five paces, and the line held, motionless, nobody eager to take the next few steps.

Ryan cradled the stock of the M-16 against his shoulder, just touching the side of his cheek. At such close range there wasn't any point in using the adjustable rear sight. The selector on the left was pointing straight down between Safe and Auto. It was on Semi, which meant single-shot. Ryan's finger was on the tapered trigger, hand

DEATHLANDS

cradling the pistol grip, his eye lining up the front and back sight, ready. His breathing was slow and regular.

The noise of the Sorrow seemed to fill the inside of his skull.

The sergeant looked back over his shoulder. The afternoon was oppressively warm and humid, and he could feel sweat soaking through his uniform at the armpits, across his stomach and the small of his back. Baron Harvey was barely visible, head sticking up above an earth bank, the absurd feathered hat nodding like a child's toy.

"Why not send the dogs in, Sarge?" one of the troopers asked.

"Because the baron wants to see it happen right in front of his eyes. That's bastard why, Trooper. Course, you can go and tell him you want to do it your way, if you want? No? Then let's get to it." He was shouting at the top of his voice in order to be heard above the river.

The inside of the store was still silent, the rich smell of refined gasoline filling the nostrils. It vaguely crossed the sergeant's mind that the scent was stronger than usual.

"In!" he yelled, straining his lungs, suddenly finding himself in the lead, nearest the half-open metal door.

Ryan had watched the hesitant advance of the overwhelming force of sec men. Apart from a skeleton guard left behind to protect the ville, this was virtually the entire strength of the Front Royal garrison.

He whistled soundlessly between his teeth. A stupid little kids' song came to him, sticking in his mind. It was something Doc had taught Lori a week or so ago, and the girl had kept singing it, laughing to herself at its absurdity.

"Wop bop a loobop, a wop bam boom," was all it was, repeated over and over again. Now it clogged Ryan's brain. His finger was still taut on the trigger of the M-16.

"Wop bop a loobop . . ."

Baron Harvey Cawdor's skull was awash with tranks so that he drifted in and out of reality. Now he was a teenager, chasing his little brother, Ryan, hunting him through the wilderness of the Oxbow Loop. When he caught him he'd kill him, tell their father it had been an accident. Harvey knew that to kill Ryan was to end his troubles. He smiled to himself, craning his neck to peer over the slope at the gray gas store, now with its entrance packed with dozens of his loyal, steadfast and true followers. Perhaps they would give three rousing cheers for Baron Harvey as they conquered.

"Hurrah, hurrah," he said to himself.

The sergeant was first in, carbine at his hip, blinking in the darkness. Sec troopers crowded behind him, jostling and pushing.

"A wop bam boom," Ryan hummed, the Sorrow overpowering his own voice.

The sergeant's feet felt deathly cold. Wet and cold. He tried to look down to see what was wrong, but the crush around him was too great, men and dogs all tangled together in the opening to the small building. The smell was overwhelming.

His eyes swiftly accustomed to the poor light, the sergeant could see the interior of the building. He didn't believe what he saw. There was a blue jerkin draped over an opened can of gasoline, placed so that it would be just visible to men outside. A dozen of the metal drums had been opened and overturned, the liquid spilled onto the floor. Many of the other large cans had their tops unscrewed and dropped in the dirt.

Apart from that the place was empty. The fugitives weren't there.

The sec officer opened his mouth to scream out a warning for everyone to get away from the lethal trap.

Thirty yards away, hugging the steep bank of the Sorrow, hidden by its lip, Ryan Cawdor squeezed the trigger of the captured M-16, aiming the round so that it would ricochet and spark off the metal door of the gas store.

His lips moved. "Wop bop a loobop, a wop bam...*boom*!"

Chapter Thirty-Two

IT WAS ONE of the biggest explosions since the world had suffered the megachill of January 2001.

The spark of the 5.56 mm bullet was enough to ignite the massive store of gasoline in the small stone building. The strength of the walls compounded the horror, containing the force of the explosion for a vital fraction of a second, giving it the chance to build to a dreadful proportion.

Ryan flattened his face against the steep bank of the Sorrow, eye closed, hands over his ears, mouth open, taking the classic precautions against an intense blast. Despite everything, he wasn't prepared for the huge concussion as the store exploded. He was nearly plucked from his perch and dashed into the murderous current of the wide river. Krysty was lower down, as was Jak and J.B., and they were better protected.

None of them witnessed the result of their plan. They didn't need to see it to know that it had worked.

Worked better than any expectation.

For Baron Harvey, it was like witnessing the hammer of the gods.

His pretty cap with its nodding feather was whisked from his head and disappeared forever in the maelstrom of torn air. Heat seared his face, scorching the straggling hair, blistering his scalp. A giant's fist punched at the baron, striving to knock him from his saddle. But like his enemies he was protected by the bank of earth. Dirt and pebbles scoured at him, tearing the elegant robe across his shoulders. The horse whinnied its terror and whirled about. Fortunately it didn't rear, for the screaming shards of masonry would have ripped its lord and master to tatters of flesh. With Harvey hanging over its neck, his fingers tangled in its flowing mane, the huge horse began to gallop back along the narrow trail toward the ville.

The sergeant had had his mouth open, ready to bellow his warning. He heard the pinging sound of the bullet hitting the door behind him and out of the corner of his eye he noticed the trail of sparks from the contact. But his brain didn't have time to make the connection, and he died ignorant of his own chilling. The ignition of the gasoline fumes and then the spilled liquid took a lightning moment. And a quarter heartbeat later the opened drums went up, taking everything and everybody with it.

The sec officer's skull literally exploded, the fumes gushing into his mouth, tearing apart his sinuses, flaming through eyes, ears and nose. His brain boiled instantly, and the bones of his head simply disintegrated under the force.

All but a half-dozen men and a couple of the dogs died instantly.

And they were blinded, naked, hideously burned, their bodies thrown forty yards away in every direction.

Ryan, clinging to the living rock for his own life, felt the shock wave pass over him like the beating of the wings of the angel of doom, the heat taking his breath for a moment. The noise drowned out the roaring of the Sorrow, deafening him. The thunder rolled on, diminishing, and then things began to fall around them.

A few large chunks of stone dropped to the ground— edges charred and blackened by the explosion—and several of the twisted drums that had held the gasoline. Ryan looked up, seeing the sky was filled, blotting out the sun. He pointed upward, trying to warn the other three, then shielded his head as best he could. Fortunately the force of the blast carried most of the heavier chunks of granite and metal toward the north loop of the Sorrow.

But smaller lumps of stone, some the size of a baseball, began to thud on the turf and patter in the river. One big as a hen's egg hit Ryan on the left shoulder, bringing a sharp dart of pain.

A piece of gray metal he recognized as an old flash suppressor from an M-16 landed in the mud of the bank near his left hand. A jagged butt stock off another blaster dug out a gouge in the grass a yard in front of him.

Then came the meat.

You could hardly describe it as being any functioning part of human bodies, or animal. They fell all over them, covering them in a slick coating of sticky crimson dew, with globs of flesh and glittering white bone. Strings of tendon and fragments of dark blue cloth floated in the gentle breeze like falling leaves. An eye bounced just to the left of Jak, but it wasn't possible to tell if it was human or canine. A right hand, missing the thumb, hit Krysty on the back of her thigh, lying there like a bleeding hairless spider. A whole leg, still attached to part of the hip, thudded heavily into the bank by J.B.'s feet, slithering the last few inches and being instantly whirled away by the scything current of the Sorrow.

Eventually even the bloody mist ceased and a momentary quiet descended. Then a dog began to howl, thin and high like a woman in childbirth. Ryan, ears ringing, squinted over the lip of the bank, wiping blood from his face. He saw the animal, smashed against the trunk of one of the tall trees, one of the trees that had been tall seconds earlier. Now the top fifty feet were gone, torn away, the branches shredded and white from the impact of the gas explosion. The dog, hardly recognizable, was a broken husk of the proud hunting animal that had padded out of the ville. It was blind and broken and close to death. The howling quickly stopped.

Only one of the sec men was still conscious. He had been at the back of the press, saved from instant slaughter by the bodies of his fellows. Now Ryan could see him lying, like a discarded puppet, thrown into the smoldering undergrowth near the trail.

"That's it," Ryan said, standing up. He tried to brush himself clean, but found that his hands were covered in blood.

Krysty climbed the steep bank, dusting off her clothes. "Gaia! The smell of gas!" she exclaimed. "The world's filled with it."

J.B. was next up. He'd taken the precaution of tucking his fedora into the front of his jerkin, and he pulled it out and beat it on his knee, placing it carefully back on his head. "Worked well," he said. "Where's your brother?"

Jak answered him. The boy wore only a thin shirt, having sacrificed his own jacket to help fool the sec men. "Seen fat Harvey. On horse there." He pointed toward the high earth bank, near where the dying man lay and moaned to himself. "Gone now. Hill would protect him an' horse."

Ryan nodded. He, too, had seen his brother's grotesque hat bobbing above the top of the slope just before he'd squeezed the trigger on the M-16. "Probably halfway back to the ville by now."

"Where we should be," the Armorer said, looking down at his hands and clothes. "Be good to wash up some on the way."

Ryan looked around the stinking shambles. The land was littered with pieces of stone and fragments of twisted metal. And the bushes and torn trees around were draped with what looked like the contents of several butchers' stores, draggled and dripping.

In all his years with the Trader, which had encompassed much chilling, Ryan had never seen such a totally appalling slaughterhouse.

Jak wandered around, picking his way between the puddles of watery mud and blood. He called out that one or two of the sec men still retained a kind of life. But only the man flung against the bushes was still conscious.

"Lost arm an' leg!" Jak shouted. "One eye gone. Other leg broke an' bits o'bone showing."

Ryan joined the boy and looked down at the remnants of his brother's soldier. The moaning was low, bubbling through the crimson froth that dribbled from the slack jaws.

"Mum, Mum, want . . . to bed. Stop, Mum . . ."

Ryan gently inserted the tip of the M-16's muzzle between the jagged, chipped teeth. The man closed his lips on it like a babe at the bottle, the moaning stopping. Ryan squeezed the trigger once, feeling the gun buck against his wrist. The impact bounced the sec trooper's head hard against the earth. The leg kicked and then the body was still.

Ryan straightened. "Nothing to keep us here."

"We going back to the big house?" Krysty asked.

"That's where Doc an' Lori are." He paused. "And that's where my brother is. Come this far to settle up the account. Might as well walk the last mile to finish it."

A quarter mile away from the scene of the explosion they found a pool of pure, still water, unsullied by gas or by blood. In turn they knelt and washed away as much of the human detritus as they could. Jak rinsed out his mouth, spitting away the taste of death.

J.B. was stooped on the ground, hands cupped, the others around him, when Krysty suddenly snatched at Ryan's arm.

"Listen!"

"What?" he asked, swinging around to probe the forest with the carbine.

"Someone there." Krysty pointed into the deepest part of the undergrowth where Ryan could just make out a dark silhouette. The figure stood, watching them.

Before he could challenge the stranger, the branches of the witch hazel parted and out walked Nathan Freeman, holding his Smith & Wesson.

"The goodest of afternoons, Uncle Ryan," he said, half bowing. "Would that great explosion be something to do with you?"

The Virginian told them about Doc Tanner and Lori Quint's abortive attempt to infiltrate the ville, how it had gone wrong and how the word was they were held prisoners in the cells of the guardhouse. Nate also outlined what he had done, waiting for news of Ryan and the others. Hearing of the death hunt, he had followed the killer dogs and sec men.

"I'd decided that I'd try for the baron with this," he informed them, flourishing the blaster, "if he'd had you all chilled. Then the sky opened yonder." The young man laughed. "Heard me some chem storms over the Shens. Never nothing like that. Thought the nukes were back again. Then I glimpsed the baron, face like a madman, double-stupe, galloping toward the ville. Streaked with blood and dirt. Thought I'd come see what had been going down with you."

"They all died," Ryan said.

"What?" Nathan shook his head. "That can't be, Uncle."

"You keep calling me 'Uncle' and I'll start calling you 'Nephew.' Understand, Nate?"

"Sure, Ryan, but...all of 'em? That's nine tenths of the sec men from the ville."

"Guess that's 'bout right."

"And Harvey's driven clear-crazed. That means that anything could be happening back at Front Royal right now."

Ryan nodded his agreement. "That's right. Which is why we're heading there. Back to the ville." Under his breath, so that only Krysty heard him he added, "Homeward bound."

Chapter Thirty-Three

SEC TROOPER BAKER was in charge of the main gateway into the ville, with young Sec Trooper Lesser as his companion. They were two of the dozen or so guards left behind when Baron Cawdor had ridden out to hunt an hour past noon. They'd watched him go, each man rigidly at attention, carbines at port arms.

The ville was quiet. Word had quickly gotten around the small settlements that surrounded the main house—word that the long-lost Lord Ryan had returned and been captured; word that during the day, he and his companions would become the victims of the hunting pack of crossbred hounds.

It was something over an hour later—neither man was sufficiently high in the rankings of the sec men to merit his own chron—and they were talking quietly about the merits of a two-edged knife against a single blade.

Then the explosion came with a shock wave that fluttered dried leaves on the cobbles leading to the drawbridge, rippling the surface of the filthy moat.

The noise was like a hundred distant peals of thunder collected into one great booming crash.

Baker jumped, nearly dropping his M-16. "May Blessed Ryan save us!" he exclaimed, the words out before he could stop them. But his companion was too startled himself to notice the treasonable utterance bursting from Trooper Baker.

A cloud of smoke gushed straight up. It was dark and oily, and Lesser's sharp sight picked out black shapes that rose within it and then fell again into the trees. The light breeze tugged at the toppling crown of the smoke, tearing it into ragged streaks of gray. Within a couple of minutes the wind brought the faint smell of gasoline to the two men, overlaid with another scent, oddly familiar, yet elusive. It reminded Lesser of something in the kitchens, but he couldn't say what.

Neither man knew quite what he should do. The explosion certainly had come from the direction of the Oxbow Loop, where the hunting always took place, and it had been a truly awesome explosion. But what it portended . . . ? That was the question.

Neither man even knew who was supposed to be in charge of the ville. The baron was gone, and he'd taken virtually everyone with him, including the senior sec officer. Lesser wondered, nervously, if one of them ought to go and tell Lady Rachel about the explosion. But that meant going all the way to her suite of rooms and risking her anger if she was sleeping. Or "busy." And both men knew what "busy" might mean to the Baron's wife.

So they did nothing.

About half an hour later Baker heard a horse coming toward them at a fast canter from the general direction of the Oxbow Loop Road. And they could hear shouting—a man roaring in a hoarse voice.

With barely a dozen men in the whole ville, there was no question of turning out the guard. All they could do was move cautiously back inside the main gateway, readying their M-16s for whatever might be approaching them.

"It's the baron," Lesser said.

"Lost his hat."

"Cloak's torn."

"Gone stark crazy," Baker suggested, "shouting like that."

The horse was lathered, rolling from side to side with utter exhaustion, stumbling as it reached the far end of the drawbridge, nearly tipping Harvey Cawdor in to join his son. He hung along the neck, eyes wide and shot with blood, mouth open. It was difficult to make out any words in the harsh raging.

"Nevermore...all...all fucked. My brother comes and—"

Once inside the courtyard, Baron Harvey Cawdor slithered from the saddle and fell to the cold stones, lying on his face, weeping. The two sec men were joined by two more from the guardhouse.

"Bastard smell of gasoline," one said.

"And he's drenched in blood," Lesser observed.

"Where's the others, my lord?" Trooper Baker asked. "They coming, my lord?"

Harvey turned, and they all took an involuntary step backward. The face they saw was scarcely human. The eyes were frozen, the pupils like the pricks of a needle. The color had gone completely, and there were deep furrows etched around mouth, nose and eyes. Hundreds of tiny specks of crusted blood dotted his cheeks, matting the scorched hair. His whole body trembled.

"Coming? Who? Brother Ryan? Nevermore. Never ever more more."

"Where's the rest of the men and the dogs, my lord?" Baker asked, showing amazing courage to press the madman. Or incredible foolishness.

Lesser went back on the drawbridge, shading his eyes with his hand. The wind had freshened, veering to the east, with the promise of colder weather and some rain within the next day or so. The roads all around the ville were deserted. "Nobody coming," he called. "Not a sight of 'em."

"The rest?" Baker repeated.

Harvey Cawdor rose to his feet, drawing the remnants of his tattered dignity around him. "The rest, my good fellow, is gone. Are gone. Chilled. Blown to a better place or world or whatever. Each dog and each horse and each man are here, in my face." He rubbed at the congealed blood. "Each spot a life. And all chilled by my brother. I think he will be here shortly. So keep good watch." He clapped Baker on the shoulder and then kissed him on the cheek, turning on his heel and waddling crookedly away into the main body of the great ville.

Baker gathered together the remaining sec men, talking in whispers of what had happened. Their lord was utterly insane. His wife a jolt junkie and his son disappeared in a bloody mist. All of their fellows were slain in some gigantic explosion, and the ville was surrounded by hundreds of villagers, all waiting for the moment to rise against Front Royal and take their vengeance for the years of bloody oppression. And that vengeance would also spill against the sec men who'd helped the Cawdors keep their hold on that part of the Shens.

"And Lord Ryan will come..." Lesser said. "And he will hold us for..." The sentence trailed away into the late afternoon sunshine.

It took only four or five minutes for the dozen sec men to reach their decision. Within fifteen minutes they had gone and changed into civilian clothes, out of the ville's hated uniforms, making their way by ones and twos into the surrounding woods.

Most were recognized and murdered before they'd gone five miles.

RACHEL CAWDOR MET her husband in one of the maze of corridors that wound through the upper floors of the rambling house. She had woken from her drug-frozen sleep, calling for her servants, finding the ville was inexplicably deserted. The air carried the taint of roasted meat and gasoline. In the silence she began to wonder whether the jolt had finally scrambled her brains and transported her to some different world, familiar, yet oddly altered in detail.

Then she met Harvey, and the feeling of alienation intensified. His eyes stared at her, bloodshot and blank. There were spots of mud all over him, and his hair and eyebrows were grizzled to stubble. His clothes were torn and stained, hanging from his limping body like an ill-fitting and ornate shroud.

"Where's everyone? What's happened? Tell me, damn you!"

"Dead, my dearest dove," he said in the hushed tones you might associate with some great church.

"Dead? Ryan and the others? All the prisoners dead?"

He smiled with a surpassing gentleness, frightening Rachel more than any rage might. "No, my pearl of the Orient. I think they all live. It is us who are chilled. Chilled forever more, nevermore."

She shook her head, feeling a band of icy steel tightening around her temples. "If Ryan and the others live, then who is dead? And where are...?"

Harvey nodded to her, still smiling. "He is clever, my little brother. Led us on and in and then... Boom!" He clapped his chubby hands together. "Boom. They all died at once. It was wonderful. Fire and noise, and they were gone. More witchery, like Jabez."

"All dead!" she screamed, voice like a saw cutting across sheet glass. "Then we are lost? Everyone's gone off and left us to die! It's your fucking brother. Why didn't you give him to me to kill? You fool..."

Her hand went to the dagger at her belt, wanting nothing more than to slit the flabby throat of her husband and then run and run.

From the basement, they could both hear the hideous cacophony of the wild boars, upset by the scent of death that filled the Shens.

"At least the old man and the yellowhead still live," she screeched. "I can butcher them. Then we must go."

"Go? Where? Here's home. I'm home now, my sweet child. Ally, ally oxen free. Home and safe. I shall soon... The yellowhead girl? I had forgot her. Before I... I shall go and..."

The knife was out, flashing through the air. With a deceptive speed, Harvey batted it away from his neck. Bunching his ringed fist, he smashed it into his wife's face with a casual ferocity that sent her spilling to the stone flags, blood seeping from her mouth, a livid bruise springing to her cheek.

"The yellowhead," he said, turning away from his unconscious wife as though he'd already forgotten her.

DOC TANNER SLEPT CONTENTEDLY on the bunk, lying flat on his back, hands folded on his chest like a crusader resting in a cathedral vault. The explosion had hardly ruffled him. Lori had called out to ask him what it had been, and he had mumbled some reassurance before sliding again into a dreamless sleep.

Lori was also lying on her bunk, wishing that she was in bed with Doc, wanting him to cuddle her and do the nice, gentle things that made her feel all squirmy inside.

"Wop bop a loobop, a wop bam boom," she hummed to herself, repeating the nonsense verse over and over, like a mantra, lulling herself with it. The girl wondered how long it would be before they were released. It was getting really boring in the little stone room with the barred window. She stood up and looked out, seeing that the afternoon was wearing on. "Wop bop..."

She turned at the sound of the cell door grating open.

"Hi, there, yellowhead. Having a nice day?" Baron Harvey Cawdor asked.

"LOOKS DESERTED," J.B. said, squinting through the screen of trees at the ocher walls of the ville. There was nobody in sight, not a single guard on the ramparts or on the drawbridge.

"Trap?" Jak suggested.

Ryan turned to Krysty, raising an eyebrow in a silent question. She shook her head. "I can hear those bastard pigs he breeds. Nothing else. Feels empty to me, lover."

"Me, too," he agreed. "Nathan? You ever know it with no sec men showing?"

"No. Never. Baron doesn't sleep well o'nights. Fears death. If he came back here, he'd have the bridge up and blasters everywhere. I think..." He stopped, hesitating.

"What, Nate?" Ryan asked.

"If'n I didn't know better, I'd figure they've all done a runner on him. Heard of the massacre and fucked off. That's my guess."

"One way to find out," Ryan said. "I can't figure it for a trap. No reason. Let's go see."

DOC TANNER CLUNG to the bars, terrified that he might faint. His brain creaked with the effort of trying to do something. He knew the man was hopelessly mad, but he had to find the words that might save Lori.

Harvey stood against the door, his grotesque bulk blocking it. One of his pretty little pistols was in his right hand, pointing at Lori's stomach. The man was whistling tunelessly to himself, gesturing for her to hurry. His cloak hung open and he had unzipped his hunting breeches, revealing his tiny, budlike penis. Lori had taken off her top, showing her breasts, and she was now, slowly, stepping out of the skirt.

"She is my daughter, Baron Harvey. A child. Can you not spare her?"

"You croak on like some raven, old man. Mebbe I should close your beak," Harvey sneered, pointing his pistol at Doc's anxious face.

Lori was naked at last, hands by her sides, making no effort to cover herself from the baron's stare. His cock was struggling toward a partial erection, and there was a thread of spittle hanging from a corner of his mouth.

"I'll not..." Doc began, nearly weeping in his helpless frustration.

"Don't, Doc," she called out. "Don't hurting me. I'm used t'it. Don't watch it, Doc."

Lori was crying.

"Like tears and fears, child." The baron laughed. "Lie down and spread 'em."

"Beware of the teeth," Doc shouted, voice cracking with emotion.

"Keep her mouth shut. Mebbe fill it later, know what I'm meaning, huh?"

"Not the teeth in her mouth, my lord!"

"How's that?"

"Shames me to admit it to a great noble like yourself, and you ready to do her honor, but the girl's a mutie, my lord. Don't show much. Normal, apart from the teeth in…in her…you know, my lord. Can do fearsome harm to a double-stud in the coupling."

"Teeth…inside her…in her…teeth in…teeth for… You mean she could bite my cock off with…? You can't…"

"Try her, my lord," Doc babbled. "Times they only close a little. But they have razor-sharp points to 'em and…she can't help it, my lord. It's being a mutie."

Harvey drew back, reaching down to zip himself up again, the gun wavering. "Muties should be shot and killed," he muttered.

"She is a good girl, my lord."

"So many dead today," the baron said, letting himself out of the cell, leaving the key dangling in the lock. Without a backward look he left the guardhouse.

Doc let go of the bars, finding great weals across his palms.

Lori started getting dressed again, unconcerned by what had nearly happened. "Doc?" she asked.

Somehow there wasn't enough air in the cell for him to answer. So he cleared his throat and tried again. "What is it, child?"

"That about teeth in my…you know?"

"Yes, Lori?"

"Ain't true, is it?"

Doc laughed, feeling suddenly a great deal better than he had for some time. When he'd finished laughing, he pointed out the key to the blond girl.

RYAN LED THE WAY, now only a few paces from the end of the drawbridge. There was still no sign of any threat to them. The ville seemed utterly deserted. Jak was behind him, carrying the M-16. Then came Krysty, followed by

Nathan with his blaster in his hand and J.B. with his drawn knife.

The sky was darkening, and the air over the Shens seemed heavy and threatening. The wind rose and fell, driving a whirling column of dust ahead of Ryan's boots, which collapsed in on itself as it reached the water of the moat.

"See any guards?" Ryan asked. Nobody answered him.

Suddenly, with no warning, there was a figure in the main gateway to the huge house, under the spiked portcullis, a staggering person in burned clothes that shone and glittered. Ryan's first thought was that he was seeing some monstrously fat, drunk old gaudy whore. Then he saw the two matched Colts pointed at him.

And he realized.

"Harvey!" he shouted.

"Farewell, brother!" Baron Harvey Cawdor bellowed, opening up with both blasters.

Chapter Thirty-Four

A SMALL-CALIBER PISTOL—like Harvey Cawdor's pair of .22 Colts—wasn't the most accurate of weapons over any kind of distance. And it took a lot of skill and control to hit a target under any kind of pressure.

It didn't help much if you were stark mad, either.

Ryan dived to the cobbles, hearing the pettish snap of the blasters, bullets kicking off the stones around him. As far as he could tell, none of them went within three yards of him.

The others also took cover from the shooting. Before Nate Freeman or Jak could return the fire, Harvey had dropped one of his guns and darted back into the inner courtyard. He was pursued by Ryan, knife gleaming in his hand.

It was a bizarre chase from the present into the past.

Just inside the main gate, by the guardhouse, Ryan bumped into Doc Tanner and Lori, but there was no time for conversation. Harvey knew the ville like a rat knows its burrow, and Ryan knew he had to keep close if he wasn't to risk losing him. There was just time to throw a message over his shoulder, for the others to retrieve their own clothes and weapons as swiftly as they could. And to watch out for any ambush.

"Upstairs and downstairs and in my lady's chamber." That was the rhyme that one of the old servants of the ville used to sing to little Ryan to try to lull him into sleep. In his mind's eye he always saw it literally, imagining himself following the twisting passages and blind corners of the mansion, taking himself inside his own head into every room and staircase of Front Royal. It had been an exercise that had saved his life when he'd had to run for it the night Harvey had come to kill him. Now, all those long years later, the memories were still there, and he followed after his brother like a loping timber wolf after an elk.

His brother had a good head start, slipping through one of the entrance doors to the main body of the house and across the courtyard. Harvey had time to slam the door shut and slide across the bolt. But Ryan knew other ways. It struck him immediately that the ville was deserted. Not only the sec men had fled. Every single person who had served the Cawdors had left. The fires in the kitchens were dying, food prepared but uncooked. Bowls with eggs broken in them stood on scrubbed tables. Piles of washing dripped in the sinks. A cooling iron rested on its stand.

It helped Ryan. When he heard a distant slamming of a door, or feet pattering along a corridor a floor above him, he knew it could only be Harvey. It crossed his mind as he ran silently through his childhood home to wonder where Lady Rachel had gone, guessing she had either run with the pack or lay sleeping off her latest lines of jolt. Probably she had fled the doomed ville.

Once a fluffy white kitten came gamboling from an open doorway, fighting a large ball of yellow wool. Several times Ryan heard the unearthly noise of the wild boars in their cellar pens.

And all the time he drew closer to his brother.

"Closer, brother, closer."

Once he entered a long room, lined with dull paintings of muddy European rivers, just as Harvey was at its farther end. Ryan dodged back at the waspish snap of the small handgun, hearing the bullet whine into the wall some yards away. It wasn't likely that Harvey was carrying a spare magazine, and ammo must be running low.

He still had only the dagger to face his brother with. And that was how he wanted it. Face-to-face. Blood spurting hot against his hand. Looking into Harvey's piggy little eyes as they blanked in death. That would settle the debt.

He heard Krysty calling to him as he passed a third-story window, but he was sprinting toward a closing door and ignored her.

He was within a few paces of Harvey when he was distracted by a door that was gently shutting. He knew it was a dead end where his father had gone to check the accounts of the ville. It had no other exit, and he flattened himself against the wall, glancing around him. Over the entrance to the chamber he recognized the bust of an aristocratic man with a hooked nose. The name was carved into the marble plinth. Pallas. There was no sound from inside the room.

The door began to open, and Ryan tensed, fingers holding the blade low, ready for the classic knife fighter's upward thrust to the belly. But the door continued to open, and he felt the fresh breeze from the window. The room was dusty and empty.

Harvey climbed toward the top floor, then took the water-operated elevator toward the kitchens, hoping to fool his pursuer. Ryan heard the familiar creaking noise of the ropes, cables and gears and darted to a spinning staircase with narrow, worn treads. He was within two turns of the bottom when he heard the grille of the elevator slamming shut.

Now the noise of the boars was much louder.

"The night's come and the land's dark," an eldritch voice shrieked from somewhere ahead of Ryan, beyond the storage rooms that fed the kitchens. Harvey was going ever deeper, singing to himself in a wild, cracked voice.

There were other knives and axes in the kitchens, and Ryan considered getting a better weapon, electing in the end to stick with the hunting dagger that felt right to his hand.

Now Ryan knew where his brother was going. The passage was damp, the walls slick with moisture. A ramp led up to the right, slippery with wet mud and animal droppings. It went in a great winding bend to come out in the courtyard and was the way that the boars were brought in and out of the ville. The sound of the ravening creatures was stifling.

And Ryan remembered. On the occasions that his oldest brother Morgan had stood up for him against the bullying of Harvey, the middle brother had often gone cowering into the bowels of the ville, where he fled now.

Twice more he glimpsed the scurrying shape ahead of him, and once Harvey turned and fired the pistol at him. Ryan ducked back, bullets sparking off the walls. He listened until he heard the familiar click of a hammer falling on a spent cartridge.

"No more bullets, brother!" he shouted, feeling his whole body racing with tension and the anticipation of pleasure.

There was one more doorway.

It stood ajar and Ryan, ever-cautious, eased himself through it. His nostrils filled with the ammoniac stench of the pigs, his ears bombarded with their squealing.

Harvey had made changes down there since Ryan had lived in the ville. The boars were milling together in a circular pit, a barred door at the bottom showing how they were moved. The sides were of slimy granite, fifteen feet high. A balcony, six feet wide, ran around the top of the pit, with a low wall as its parapet: Harvey and any of his guests who wished to could come and admire the creatures from a position of safety. Apart from the entrance door where Ryan waited, accustoming his eye to the dim light, there was no other way out.

Except into the boar pit.

"You're dead, Ryan! Been dead for twenty years! Go back to the grave, Ryan!"

"Gonna kill you, brother," Ryan called out.

He could make out Harvey now, on the far side of the room, wrapped in the tattered cloak, holding the empty pistol. His face was in deep shadow, only the eyes gleaming like tiny chips of molten gold.

Ryan glanced down into the pit, seeing better than a dozen of the animals jostling one another, all of them looking up at him. They were at least five feet tall at the shoulder, weighing several hundred pounds. They all had ruby eyes, and curling ivory tusks that ended in needle points.

Now, in a way that sent a chill down his spine, they stopped their squealing, and the basement pit fell silent, except for the shuffling of their hooves in the wet straw.

"This is the end, brother," Ryan shouted, holding the dagger up as though it were a holy relic. "Gonna cut your throat with this."

"No, never, no, my dear little brother." Harvey's voice was calm and gentle. Ryan recognized the style. Harvey had used it when he was attempting to fool Ryan into something, or trying to con him. Or when he had some unsuspected trick up his sleeve.

"All these years, Harvey, and now it's you and me. Like I dreamed, hundreds o'nights. At last I can do it and get on with living."

Harvey moved from behind a pillar, aiming the handgun at Ryan. "Got a fresh mag for the blaster, brother. Never thought of that, did you?"

"Bluffing, Harvey."

The obese figure clambered clumsily onto the parapet, waving down to the watching, motionless boars. "See, my pets," he called. "I shall shoot this one-eyed renegade from the shadows and then you shall have his corpse for food."

Ryan stood where he was, watching Harvey's insane posturing. The knife was nicely balanced, and the range was short enough, but he wanted to feel his brother sweat as the blade sliced open the soft flesh and drew out his life.

Somewhere above them they both heard the sound of feet and a voice calling out. "My sec men, brother." Harvey Cawdor beamed.

"No. Fireblast! Can't you fucking see the truth, Harvey? It's done and finished. Your power's gone. The ville's empty. They've all gone. There's nothing left for you."

"Nothing left?"

"Nothing."

"Yes, there is, Ryan. There's *this!*"

The little gun flashed, and Ryan staggered back, feeling the fiery pain in his left shoulder. Even a small-caliber gun like the .22 packed enough of a punch to knock a man off-balance. Harvey laughed delightedly, seeing blood flowing on the jerkin.

"And again, brother," he said.

Ryan threw the hunting dagger underhand, seeing the lamplight catch the blade as it spun in the fetid air. Despite his own wound, Ryan's aim with the knife was deadly accurate.

It thunked home where Harvey's rippling chins melted down into the top of his chest, burying itself deep in the soft flesh. Harvey Cawdor squeaked in shock, dropping the Colt from numbed fingers, watching as it fell into the pit. He leaned forward, swaying, his vast bulk making it hard for him to keep his balance on the shallow wall.

"May you die of nuke rot," he said in a reasonable, conversational sort of voice.

Then, as though he'd given up on the struggle, he fell heavily into the pit, landing with the clear crack of breaking bones.

Ryan, holding his shoulder, feeling that it was only a minor wound, looked down into the semidarkness. His hands told him that the bullet had gone clear through without hitting the scapula or the collarbone. He felt dizzy for a moment, but knew he was going to be all right.

Below him the last rites were swift and deadly for Harvey Cawdor.

Both ankles broken by his fall, the gross man lay there on his back like some obscene insect, his rich cloak spread around him in the straw. His mouth opened and closed, but no sounds came from it. One hand touched the taped hilt of the knife where it protruded from his chest, but Harvey made no attempt to withdraw it. The great boars had eased away from the thing that had come crashing down into their pit, but now they were gathering courage, shuffling nearer, snouts lowered, jaws gaping.

Ryan watched, leaning on the wall, flexing the fingers of his left hand to make sure the bullet hadn't severed any ligaments or tendons on its way through. Apart from a dull ache, it didn't feel too bad.

One of the great brooding heads dipped, and the teeth closed on Harvey Cawdor's right leg between knee and ankle. There was the savage crunch of gnawed bone, and the man screamed, a terrified cry of gut-deep anguish.

"Brother . . . help me!"

The sudden noise disturbed the rest of the tusked monsters, and they all seemed to attack at once. The bloated body vanished under the bristled boars, and the last scream was muted and silenced, ending in a dreadful gagging, bubbling noise. Then there was only the grinding of teeth and the rending of meat.

Ryan straightened and heard the voice from behind him, a dull, flat voice that seemed bereft of any life.

"Now you can join your brother, Ryan. Jump in after him."

He turned and looked into the meltwater eyes of Lady Rachel Cawdor. She was holding the lethal dart gun that had once belonged to her son, and it was aimed at Ryan's stomach.

Chapter Thirty-Five

THE DART GUNS HAD originally been manufactured by an armament firm with government contacts operating out of a guarded sec complex east of Butte, Montana. Not many of them were still around. Ryan had only seen a dozen or so in his life, mostly out west in the deserts and lagoons of what had once been called California.

They used a tiny explosive charge and held a half-dozen or so darts, a half inch long, barbed and made from the finest surgical steel. They tumbled on impact, for maximum impact, and were lethally difficult to locate and remove.

Rachel had been bleeding, and there was blood crusted around her mouth. Her face also bore the clear imprint of a ringed fist. The eyes were venomous with hatred for Ryan. She wore a long black dress that dragged on the floor, hiding her dainty feet. The stiletto was sheathed at her belt. The bag that she normally carried was missing.

Her voice was quiet and gentle, difficult to hear above the crunching of bones from the pit below them, but loud enough for Ryan to hear every word.

"I offered you the chance, didn't I? Now see what you've done. Harvey dead. Jabez, sweet child, dead. The ville ruined and everyone gone. All by the return of a middle-aged, one-eyed double-poor hired killer. You, Ryan."

"Aw, it weren't nothing, lady," he replied, grinning wolfishly. "Anyone would have done the same if'n they'd had the chance."

"I'm going, as well. I have my jewels packed. My favorite mare is in the stables, saddled and ready. She can outrun anything in the Shens. By sundown I'll be forty miles south of here."

"I thought you could run from your past," he said, feeling warm blood easing itself stickily down the side of his chest. "I ran for twenty years. In the end, I find I'd run clear back to where I'd started. You can't run from what you've done."

"Watch me, Ryan." A ghost of a smile flitted at the corners of her bloodless lips.

"You won't even get out of the ville."

"You won't even know, Ryan. Because you'll be dead with a gutful of steel darts. And I shall look back and enjoy watching you kicking at my feet. I shall remember that . . ." she concluded, leveling the gun, finger tightening on the flat, broad trigger.

"Nevermore," Doc Tanner said, squeezing the trigger of his beloved antique Le Mat pistol.

The blast of the .63-caliber scattergun damned near blew Rachel Cawdor's head clear off her narrow shoulders.

Ryan ducked away from the devastating noise and power of the old handgun, but he was splashed with blood and brains. The noise stopped the boars at their feeding for a few seconds. Then they resumed dining on the ragged body of the baron of Front Royal.

Rachel's corpse slipped untidily to the stone floor of the balcony, the dart gun still held in her right hand. Powder smoke hung in the cool air of the pit, and the stench of cordite was heavy in the nostrils.

"Just before being trawled forward by Project Cerberus, I worked in a laboratory with an elderly English geneticist," Doc said, holstering his blaster. "At the end of each working shift he would fold away his coat and say, 'And that, gentlemen, concludes the entertainment for today.' I think, my dear Ryan, this concludes our entertainment for today."

"Thanks, Doc."

IT WAS RAINING HEAVILY.

Evening had come early to the Shens, borne in on the teeth of a rising wind and the threat of a severe chem storm sweeping from the blue-ridged mountains to the north and west of Front Royal. Ryan and his friends regained their own weapons and clothes, then found ample food in the empty kitchens. None of the local villagers came near the fortress that first night of freedom from the oppression of Baron Harvey Cawdor.

In the abandoned palace it was easy for Ryan and Krysty to find an empty bedroom for themselves for the night. There was some wine from a crusted green bottle that Doc found in one of the old cellars. Called Chateauneuf-du-Pape, it was a delicious soft red wine that lay like a silk ribbon on the palate. There were words on the dusty cobwebbed label that Krysty said she thought were French.

They made love with an infinitely gentle slowness, relishing each other's body, doing for each other the things they knew would give limitless delight. Afterward Ryan lay with his head cradled on Krysty's stomach, one hand stroking her breasts. The shoulder wound had been thoroughly cleansed and bandaged, and the pain had now abated to a steady throbbing. Nothing vital had been harmed by the .22, and he knew from previous experience that he would be as good as new within a week or so.

"Decision time, lover," she said.

"Stay or go, you mean?"

"You've done what you came for. Revenged your brother, Morgan, and cleared out the stables. Now you can take over."

"I know."

"Nobody'd say a word 'gainst it. I'd stay here. Mebbe Doc and Lori would stay on."

"Not J.B. or the kid?"

She shook her head. "Some men need to keep on moving. Can't stay still. Both of them."

Ryan sat up and pulled the sheets around him against the chill of night. "What 'bout me, Krysty? Can I stay here for the rest of my life? Do I want that? Step into Harvey's shoes? Live as baron of Front Royal?"

She reached out and laid her hand against his face. "If you want to, Ryan. That's the only reason. It's there for you. That's what we came for—to give you the peace of mind from knowing. Twenty years wondering. Now you know. Gaia, lover! Inside your head you must know what you want to do!"

Ryan knew she was right.

THE HEADS AND OLD MEN and women from all the hamlets within the control of Front Royal ville had been sent for and brought in. It took four days, by which time the place was back and running, with most of the servants returning to their old jobs. But there were no new sec men appointed. Ryan had made it clear he wouldn't agree to that.

He made a long speech—the first he'd ever undertaken—and told the listeners what was going to happen.

When he spoke of the ville existing for the good of all, there were scattered cheers.

But his announcement that he and his friends were moving on and leaving Nathan Freeman, now called Cawdor, as the baron of Front Royal was greeted with a stunned dismay.

"Why him, Lord Cawdor?" called out a toothless old crone in the front row, leaning on a blackthorn staff.

"Because he is the son of my oldest brother, Morgan Cawdor, murdered by Harvey. He is baron by right and by succession. I name Nathan Freeman as my own heir to Front Royal."

So Nathan, son of Morgan Cawdor and the mutie girl Guenema, was duly installed as the baron of Front Royal in Virginia, controlling the lands and woods for many miles around.

Chapter Thirty-Six

THE BATTERED WAG that had brought them so many miles south was brought in and refueled from one of the other gas stores that serviced the ville. The six friends were once more dressed in their own clothes and carrying their own weapons. Nathan had asked Ryan if he wished for something from his old home to carry with him.

"I've carried this place with me for twenty years, Nate. Now I'm finally free of it."

There had been no discussion between them as to where they should go. All of them wanted to take the long road north, back to the hidden gateway up on the Mohawk.

Jak engaged the gears, and the big wag lumbered off, its engine and exhaust fixed. It was a fine sunny day, and they had the ports and ob-slits open. Ryan hung on the main door, staring back as the ville disappeared behind them. He had one arm around Krysty, the other hugging his Heckler & Koch G-12 caseless blaster.

"Glad you came, lover?" she asked him. It was difficult to hear above the rumbling of the powerful wag, and she had to repeat the question. "Are you glad you came back, lover?"

"Yeah. Paid all the debts. Laid it all to rest. Now we can move on again."

They held each other tight as the wag moved steadily away north.

**A secret arms deal
with Iran ignites a powder keg,
and a most daring mission is
about to begin.**

THE BARRABAS STRIKE

JACK HILD

**Nile Barrabas and his soldiers undertake a
hazardous assignment when a powerful top-
secret weapon disappears and shows up in
Iran.**